I0645105

WAKAN MAN

FREDRICK W. BOLING

Copyright © 2001 by Fredrick W. Boling

ISBN 0-9722808-0-4 (Previously ISBN 1-59146-043-3)

Published by:

BIGHORN PUBLISHING
35 La Canada Way
Hot Springs Village, AR 71909

Printed in the United States of America

For all of those
who have encouraged me,
especially, Wilma.

Chapter 1

It was June, the Lakota Moon of Fat Horses, in 1866. The day was tepid and filled with anticipation as two black and white piebald ponies trotted over the crest of a grassy knoll. The bronzed hand of Oglala Warrior Chief Red Cloud reined back his pony. His eyes narrowed and jaw muscles rippled as he scanned the valley below. Scattered across the basin surrounding Fort Laramie were scores of tents and campfires. Two hundred wagons with USA stenciled in black across their weathered canvas tops were parked in neat rows. Beyond the wagons, hundreds of horses, mules and beef cattle were grazing on the lush bluestem growing along the banks of the Laramie River.

Red Cloud was impressed but not surprised by the city of tents. He and Lakota Medicine Man, Yellow Elk, sat their ponies and fixed their eyes on the awesome spectacle of power. Winds, gusting from the southwest, flitted eagle feathers tied to Warrior Chief Red Cloud's staff while he pondered the intentions of the washichun*'s* call for peace talks. The vast assemblage of troops meant one thing, treaty or no treaty, the washichun bluecoats intended to build their forts on Oglala Lakota land.

Yellow Elk signed with his hands as he spoke to Red Cloud. "Washichun bluecoats will come. Lakota must prepare for war."

Red Cloud nodded. "The washichun bluecoats are wolves—show us many teeth."

Yellow Elk scanned the valley once more, clucked his

tongue and pointed at a large white tent in the fort's quadrangle. "We must turn back. The washichun wait to steal the fat from Lakota land."

"No, Spotted Tail and Standing Elk are old women. The chiefs of the Brulé Lakota will not stand with the Oglala Lakota. They will sign the talking-paper and let the washichun build their forts."

Yellow Elk nodded and rippled his pony's flanks with the heels of his moccasins. He and Red Cloud rode toward the fort that had its beginning in early June of 1834. They were determined to show Oglala Lakota teeth to Treaty Commissioner E. B. Taylor and his bluecoat soldiers.

While riding toward the conference tent, Red Cloud pondered how fickle the washichun treaty-makers had been. His eyes darkened and anger pulsed in his temples as he remembered another treaty. The one made here at Fort Laramie during September, the Moon of Drying Grass, in 1851. He was a young warrior, a veteran of wars with the Crow, Kiowa, Arapaho and Pawnee. He was very angry when he stood up to confront the washichun treaty-makers. "You want to split Lakota land and I don't like it," he had said, and then turned to address the Lakota chiefs. "These lands once belonged to the pony-thieving Crow. We took many coup on their warriers and sent them in defeat across the Yellowstone. We bought this land with Lakota blood."

He had wasted his words. For a mountain of trinkets and the promise of an annual payment of $50,000 worth of goods for fifty years, the talking-paper had been eagerly signed. Chiefs of the Lakota, Cheyenne, Arapaho, Crow, Gros Ventres, Assiniboine, Arikara and Shoshone tribes agreed to dwell forever within territories laid out in the treaty for each tribe. The washichun would protect the boundaries of each tribe's territory. They would live in peace with the washichun from that day forward.

The washichun did not honor much of the talking-paper's promises. Congress terminated the annual payments after fifteen years. Fraudulent agreements had been entered into with Indians who did not have the authority to be signers. Of such were the Laramie Loafers, those Brulé Lakota who loitered in the shade of tipis outside the fort. The Oglala considered them to be no more than camp dogs begging for handouts. They had been used by the washichun less than a year before when they agreed to permit the gold-seekers to travel Bozeman's trail across Lakota lands. For this the Laramie Loafers received more trinkets and more empty promises. Now another round of talks was to be held. The U. S. Army wanted to build three forts along the Bozeman Trail. This time the Laramie Loafers would not sign for the Oglala Lakota.

As they jumped off their ponies, Red Cloud and Yellow Elk were determined—no more concessions would be made. There would be no forts built on Lakota land north of Crazy Woman Creek. Bozeman's road would be closed to all washichuns traveling to their gold mines in Montana.

The scent of campfires, sweating men, horses and smoke from E. B. Taylor's cigar wafted through the conference tent. Fort Laramie commandant Colonel Henry Maynadier, Commissioner Taylor and commandant of the Army's Mountain District, Colonel Henry B. Carrington, pleaded with the Lakota to let the Army build their forts. They assured the Lakota that three forts were necessary to prevent whites from violating Lakota hunting grounds. After Taylor asked for the Lakota's response, Red Cloud stood up, faced Taylor and proceeded to give the commission a scathing lecture.

"Red Cloud speaks for the Oglala people." He then aimed his antler-handled quirt like a coup lance at the silver eagles on Colonel Carrington's shoulders. *"White-Eagle* comes with many bluecoats. You prepare to build your forts while you say let us have peace. You ask us to trust your God and the Great Father in Washington. Your God is a stranger to us. Our medicine men tell us that our God, *Wakan-Tanka*, says you lie."

"Hetchetu Aloh!" agreed Yellow Elk.

"Your tongues spit lies," Red Cloud said, glaring at Commissioner Taylor. "You write lies on the talking-paper and ask us to swear with you that they are true words of the Great Father in Washington. We do what you want—your bluecoats kill us anyway. Your promises are empty like Lakota bellies after you kill our *Pte,* the one you call 'buffalo.' You think we are blind, do not see the things of this world. Great Spirit *Wakan-Tanka* has opened our eyes. We *see* your bad medicine.

Commissioner Taylor raised his hand to interrupt Red Cloud. "We speak true words."

"Your words lie. You call them true, but bad spirits wag your tongue. I tell you what is true. Listen to my words. The white men have crowded the Lakota back, year by year, until we are forced to live in a small country north of the Platte. Now our last hunting ground, the home of the Lakota, is to be taken from us. Lakota women and children will starve, but for my part I prefer to die fighting rather than by starvation. The Great Father sends us presents and wants this road, but *White-Eagle* comes with soldiers to steal the road before we say yes or no. If *White-Eagle* leads the bluecoats beyond the creek you call 'Crazy Woman', you will all die; your women, your children—none will escape the rifle, the lance, the arrow of *Wakan-Tanka's* Oglala Lakota." Red Cloud aimed his quirt at Taylor. "We will sign no treaty."

Yellow Elk leaped to his feet. "Hetchetu Aloh!"

"Hear my words and you will live. Close your ears and it is war."

Red Cloud and Yellow Elk stalked from the meeting. Taylor pointed at Sinte-Galeshka, which means Spotted Tail in the Lakota language, the chief of the Brulé Lakota. "Chief Red Cloud has spoken. Does Spotted Tail speak like him?"

Spotted Tail, sitting cross-legged on the ground, raised his stone-headed war club. "Red Cloud is not a principal chief. I, Sinte-Galeshka, am the principal chief of the Brulé Lakota. Red Cloud is a war chief, a 'Shirt-Wearer' of our brothers the Oglala Lakota."

"What do you say about our treaty, Chief Spotted Tail?"

Spotted Tail stood up. "If you hear the words of Sinte-Galeshka, he will hear yours."

"Speak as you will."

"The Brulé are at peace with the washichun. We will not raise the club in anger against the Great Father if you leave us alone on our land along the rivers and across the plains of sweet sage and Indian grass. Build your log-walled dens, but you must promise to stay on your road crossing Brulé hunting grounds—do not kill the *Pte*. I promised Ahho-Appa, my daughter, I would fight the washichun bluecoats no more. This promise I will keep if the Great Father writes true words on the talking-paper."

Fleet Foot, called Ahho-Appa by the Brulé, had fallen in love with Captain James Rhinehart garrisoned at Fort Laramie. Their brief affair ended when he was killed during an expedition sent to quell a warring band of Brulé Lakota. She was inconsolable and had pleaded with her father to never fight the bluecoated washichun again. He agreed to her wishes and moved the Brulé away from the Platte River to an encampment near the Powder River east of the Bighorn Mountains.

There Fleet Foot, afflicted by the "coughing sickness", grew very ill. Spotted Tail, discouraged by the failure of Brulé medicine men to cure his daughter, headed back to Fort Laramie. Maybe Major Joshua Leslie, the garrison surgeon, could cure the coughing sickness. Several miles from the fort, Fleet Foot ceased her coughing. Spotted Tail knelt beside her travois, wept and chanted the death song.

According to Brulé custom, women accompanying the expedition wrapped Fleet Foot in a deerskin creosoted by pine smoke. The following day she was hoisted onto a burial scaffold in the fort cemetery. Out of respect for Spotted Tail, Colonel Maynadier assembled the entire garrison for the burial ceremony. Sleet and snow began to fall from a bleak overcast as an honor guard fired three volleys. Fleet Foot was at rest next to the grave of her lover, Captain James Rhinehart

Taylor and Colonel Carrington whispered together as Spotted Tail stood erect, stiff and unflinching, his eyes boring at them like a falcon ready to attack. Taylor nodded at Carrington and then stood up. "Chief Spotted Tail, we agree to your words. My secretary will prepare the treaty and we will sign it with you in the morning."

With Spotted Tail's agreement, Taylor boasted of success in negotiating a treaty with the Lakota and so informed Washington—failing to acknowledge Red Cloud's belligerence.

* * *

Seven hundred soldiers of the 18th Infantry, commanded by Colonel Henry B. Carrington, went about preparing for their journey into Lakota country. Carrington was a graduate of Yale and had served during the Civil War as Ohio's Adjutant General. He had no combat experience but had built a formidable reputation for getting a job done. He did this by building several prisoner-of-war camps in Indiana. And then at the behest of President Lincoln, he had captured Copperhead traitors in the Northwest Conspiracy. The U. S. Army was confident that Carrington was the man to build their forts along the Bozeman Trail.

Mountain man Jim Bridger, recently hired by Colonel Carrington to guide the expedition, believed the Lakota land was no place for women, children or any other nonessential civilians. This conviction prompted his calling on Colonel Carrington.

"All I need is one more goddamn scalp hangin' from the lance of one of Red Cloud's warriors," Bridger bellowed, slamming his floppy-brimmed hat on the floor.

Colonel Carrington winced at Bridger's outburst. He was intolerant of such behavior by soldier, guide or scout, but respected the opinions of this tough old mountain man. In spending more than forty years in the Rocky Mountains, Bridger had become as much a part of the wild frontier as the Grand Tetons or Colter's steaming geysers. Having lived, traded and fought with Cheyenne, Shoshone, Arapaho, Bannock, Crow and Lakota weighed heavily in favor of his opinions.

In 1822 William H. Ashley had run an ad in the St. Louis Gazette beckoning enterprising young men to ascend the Missouri River to its source to be employed as trappers for one, two or three years. Young Jim Bridger, longing to see the wild frontier, responded to the ad. He spent seventeen years in the wilderness, married an Arapaho woman and traded with most of the Indian tribes in the Rocky Mountain region. He became a successful fur trader and then built a trading post on the Oregon Trail near the Green River in southwestern Wyoming. He became one of the most knowledgeable frontiersmen of his time. This factor made his services as a scout and guide greatly prized by the Army.

"Mister Bridger, I have no fear of the Lakota. I have over seven-hundred men in the 18th Infantry."

"Hell, Colonel, most o' them boys is green for the Army, greener about fighin' Injuns."

"Over three-hundred of them are battle-seasoned."

"Yeah! Fightin' Confederate Rebels ain't nothin' like fightin' the Lakota. That ain't botherin' me as much as the prissy women folk and their snot-nosed paps traipsing along. Now this goddamned preacher you're wantin' me to take along."

"The Reverend Joel Leslie is going to the Montana gold fields as a missionary. His brother, Major Leslie, has apprised him of the dangers involved."

"What the hell does Doc Leslie know? Nothin' about Red Cloud's Lakota."

Colonel Carrington nodded and chewed his unlit cigar. "Maybe he doesn't. That is not important. Reverend Leslie is going to accompany the expedition. I hope that is clear, Mister Bridger."

"Well, him and all the rest would keep their hair if we just stayed out of huntin' grounds claimed by Red Cloud."

Carrington struck a match, held it to his cigar and spoke between puffs. "I know how you feel... Mister Bridger... but I've got my orders... and they don't say anything about changing our route."

Bridger, biting hard on his chaw of tobacco, refrained from his usual profanity. He pointed at the map hanging behind Carrington's desk. "Colonel, just look where that road laid out by Bozeman runs. It goes right through Red Cloud's grounds. Now over west of the Bighorn Mountains, I can show you a way to Montana that's as safe as a baby's crib."

"I know, but General Sherman has rejected your route."

Bridger picked up his hat and stomped out of Carrington's tent mumbling his resentment. "Damned paper-collared dandies. They *intend* to provoke the Lakota."

Bridger crossed the post quadrangle, stepping aside for the color guard hoisting the flag. Notes from the bugler's horn echoed across the arid plain as Bridger shoved open the infirmary door.

"Major Leslie!" Bridger called, his voice sharp as a chisel.

Major Leslie did not look up from his task, the examination of a man lying on an infirmary cot. Bridger removed his hat and fingered its brim. "Mister Bridger, ye may wish t'wait on the porch," Leslie said, his attention riveted on the sweating patient. "This is a very sick man."

"What's he got, Doc?"

"Cholera."

"The hell, you say," Bridger said, stepping backward.

Joshua Leslie nodded at the motionless form lying beneath a sheet on the next cot. "So did that fellow. He died within an hour after becoming ill."

"Who are these men?"

"Colonel Carrington's woodcutters."

Bridger leaned over Joshua Leslie's shoulder and peered at the sick man's ashen features, shrunken and covered with clammy sweat. The fellow moaned. "Am... I... dyin', Doc?"

Joshua glanced at Bridger and slipped his fingers around the man's wrist. He found only a feeble and flickering pulse. He shook his head. His vigil soon ended as the man's chest sank, jaw relaxed, lips parted and eyelids opened as sightless eyes stared at nothing. Joshua closed each eyelid and pulled up the sheet, covering those eyes that would see no more suns rising over virgin prairies or setting beyond lofty mountain peaks.

Bridger frowned, pondering the situation. "How many are goin' under from this cholera?"

"I'm not knowin'. A quarantine we must enforce on the woodcutters Colonel Carrington hired at Fort Kearney."

Building forts on the western frontier required a lot of wood for stockades, bastions, battlements and buildings. Carrington's expedition included two sawmills to prepare the needed lumber. Woodcutters were required to supply and operate the sawmills. To fulfill this need, additional men experienced in lumbering—all civilians heading west—were hired at Fort Kearney, Nebraska.

"The Colonel ain't goin' for no quarantine. He wants to

move out tomorrow for the Bighorn country."

"He will leave the woodcutters and their families behind if he does."

"Hell, he's got to have them woodcutters. He's got three forts to build before snow flies."

"An epidemic of cholera among the soldiers will make any fort useless. If he wants to take the civilians along, Colonel Carrington will not be leavin' tomorrow."

Bridger pulled at his wiry, gray beard. "When then?"

"At best, two weeks."

"At worst?"

"I'm not knowin'."

"Does this include all civilians?"

"Nay, only the woodcutters and their families."

"What about your twin brother, the reverend preacher?"

Joshua Leslie stood up, rolled down his sleeves and fastened each cuff while he and Bridger looked at each other.

Leslie's piercing eyes, called blue as the bonny sky by his mother, searched Bridger's face. Both men were tall, lean as two poplar trees. Bridger, now past sixty, searched the younger man's face with his dark eyes, which were set deeply within wrinkled and bronzed features. He saw a squared jaw, shaved clean and set in determination. A lock of wavy black hair slipped across a broad forehead beaded with sweat. He saw a man trained in medicine at Edinburgh University, now seasoned by war. Blue eyes reflected the horrors seen at Gettysburg, the Wilderness, Cold Harbor and days and nights spent amputating mutilated limbs. The experiences of closing lifeless eyes, the nauseating stench of gangrene and faces blanched white by hemorrhaging wounds had aged his features beyond their thirty-three years.

Bridger prided himself on being a good judge of men. *Now there's a man. I like these Scots that sputter their "Rs" and count each penny. This feller's preacher brother might be all right in a tight spot. And we're goin' to have them between here and the Bighorns.* "Reckon he'll be comin'?"

"Aye, Mister Bridger, that he will."

Chapter 2

The Reverend Joel Leslie walked from the Brown Hotel, a single storied log structure adjacent to Fort Laramie. It was a frontier inn. A respite for travelers crossing Dakota Territory to Virginia City, capital of the Montana gold fields.

Joel was no stranger to death, having been a chaplain in the Union Army. While his twin brother Joshua had opted to study medicine, he had committed himself to the ministry, and then to being a Presbyterian missionary to America. He and Joshua had served together in the Army of the Potomac. After emigrating from Scotland in 1861, both had volunteered to serve their adopted country. Following the surrender of Lee's Army at Appomattox, Joel resigned his commission and resumed his calling to serve as a missionary to the pioneers in the West. Except for his clerical attire: a black frock coat, white double-winged collar and black hat, his appearance was identical to his twin brother.

He had just arrived at Fort Laramie in the company of Carrington's 18th Infantry. The fort had its beginning in 1834 when fur traders constructed a trading post near the junction of the Laramie and North Platte rivers. It became known as Fort Laramie where mountain men and Indians bartered their furs. The demand for beaver pelts declined and had almost disappeared by the latter part of the 1830s. During this time westward migration began to multiply as pioneers headed for the fertile lands in Oregon and California. Fort Laramie's importance grew with the ever-increasing traffic of wagons rumbling along the Oregon Trail. Consequently, the fort became a caravansary, a place of respite where worn and broken wagon wheels were repaired and diminished larders replenished. As the people moved westward, the Army was not far behind. The Indians' resistance to white migration brought swift action by Congress. Following its purchase by the government, the U. S. Army garrisoned Fort Laramie on June 16, 1849. From that time on, the fort became a dominant government influence in the western frontier.

Now death was marching through the quarantined civilian encampment outside Fort Laramie. Ministering to the sick and dying and burying the dead left little time for anything else.

Joel walked past the abandoned encampment of several bands of Brulé Lakota. Their tipis were gone. Only charred fire pits remained. They had gone to the Powder River Basin east of the Bighorns to join Chief Spotted Tail and the main body of Brulé. They wanted no more of the White man's sicknesses.

Joel followed the pathway to the cemetery, soft underfoot from mourners' shoes treading it into dust. The path grew steeper, winding its way around the face of an eroded, rocky hill. Reaching its crest, he paused to ponder what the knoll represented. *Golgotha, the hill of death, that's what this place has become.*

He straightened the wings of his clerical collar and rested from the steep climb as he looked down on the white buildings of Fort Laramie gleaming in the warm spring sunshine. From his vantage point, he watched Joshua hurrying along the pathway below.

"Joel," Joshua called, "wait, I have something for ye."

"Aye, I'll wait."

Upon reaching Joel, Joshua withdrew a small doll made of cornhusks from his tunic. "This doll belongs to the wee lass you're buryin' this mornin'."

"Aye, I remember her clutchin' it when she died."

"It's the only thing she had to comfort her after ye buried her parents last week."

"I'll open her coffin."

Joshua slipped his hand around Joel's elbow and they walked together toward the cemetery gate. Smoke from fires boiling drinking water hung over the fort and its growing cemetery as they walked past Fleet Foot's burial scaffold toward an open grave into which four woodcutters were lowering a little pine coffin. "Wait!" Joel called, holding up the doll. "Do not let her down—not just yet."

One of the woodcutters pried open the coffin. Joshua

slipped the doll beneath the child's hands. Joel completed the burial rites and walked with Joshua back toward the fort.

The deaths of so many children and young parents were overwhelming. Some children were orphaned. A number of parents became childless and a few were widowed as well. Sadness burdened them, reminding Joshua and Joel of their home, of how much they missed Scotland and their family.

Dakota Territory and northeastern Scotland are both harsh lands. Dakota, high and naked, is crowned with craggy, granite peaks rising above bristling forests and arid sage-covered plains. The lords of its vast expanse are the Lakota, Northern Cheyenne, Crow, Arapaho, and Shoshone red men. Cold winds and tempestuous tides often batter northeast Scotland, whose green highlands descend toward the rocky shoreline of the North Sea. Here the clans of Scotland have made their home for centuries, not all that much different from the Indian nations and tribes.

The Leslies and Condiffs, once separate clans, were joined when Angus Leslie married Neilli Condiff in 1831. Twin sons, Joshua and Joel, were born to them on June 15, 1833 in a farm cottage near the town of Turriff and the river Deveron in the northeast of Scotland. The Leslies were highlanders, the descendants of the Gaelic family of Mac an Fhleisdeir. Their ancestral name had been changed many years before to Leslie, which was taken from the Lands of Leslie in Aberdeenshire. Angus Leslie was a stockbreeder and an exporter of Aberdeen-Angus cattle. Neilli, a beautiful highlander, was a gifted woman who loved to cook, weave and sew for her husband and twin sons. She spent hours weaving the green and black Leslie tartan from which she made fine kilts for her three men.

"This mornin', I long t'see Scotland," Joel said, looking across the hills surrounding Fort Laramie. "This land holds so much misery, so many findin' death while searchin' for... I wonder what?"

"Aye, remember how we used to play on the old brig o' Castleton across the river Deveron?"

Joel winced at the memory. "Aye, scary it was too."

"Poor Colie, how he feared the troll, the one we believed

lived under the bridge."

Their cousin Colin Condiff was also born in Turriff, the son of their mother's brother, Major Forfar Condiff, and Sarah Dawson. Colin, Joshua and Joel were frequent companions as they went on afternoon rambles in the countryside around Turriff. Colin attended Elgin Academy in Edinburgh, and afterward worked as a journalist in Edinburgh and London. In 1864 he left London bound for Chicago and a position with the Chicago Times.

Joel nodded. "Mother wrote that Colie is writin' for a Chicago newspaper."

"Aye, I read her letter too."

"Of course."

They walked on, silent, longing to see their mother's blue eyes, feel her touch and kiss her cheek.

"Ah, the North Sea breakin' o'er the shore at Banff," Joshua said, "would we could see that torrent just once more."

"Aye, and Colie."

"Maybe some day," Joshua replied with a tinge of nostalgia in his voice, "we'll see him again."

"Major Leslie!" Jim Bridger called. The fringes of his buckskins danced like willow leaves in the wind as long strides carried his hunched torso along the pathway from the fort.

Joel sheltered his eyes from the morning sun with his hand. "I wonder what Mister Bridger wants?"

"We shall soon know," Joshua said, and then called to Bridger. "What is it, Mister Bridger?"

"Colonel Maynadier wants to see you."

"He must know that I have patients to attend."

"A courier just rode in from Fort Reno. Colonel Carrington is waitin' there for me to bring the woodcutters."

"The woodcutters? I can't raise the quarantine yet."

"You'll have to tell that to Colonel Maynadier. He says they will leave for Fort Reno in the morning; at least the ones ain't sick by then."

"That is insane."

"Maybe so, but the Colonel thinks the cholera will have burned itself out by the time they get to Reno."

"God help us if it hasn't. Cholera could kill more of Carrington's soldiers than Red Cloud's Lakota."

Bridger nodded and looked squarely at Joel. "Ain't no never mind. If'n the reverend preacher's goin' to Montana, we'll be leavin' at first light in the mornin'."

* * *

Fort Laramie lay far behind Joel—the fort, the crowded cemetery and his twin brother who had welcomed him to this raw, naked western frontier. The woodcutter's wagon train had forded the North Platte River after leaving the rutted Oregon Trail. No longer could they see Register Cliff covered with carved messages, nor even the snow-crowned Laramie Mountains. The land had changed. Grassy hills covered with rocky outcroppings and scrub conifers that were bent and twisted by prevailing winds had given way to basins surrounded by cliffs of gray stone. Beyond these basins, they had followed the ascending trail of John Bozeman across high plateaus toward the Bighorn Mountains and the hunting grounds of the Lakota.

Their wagons had crossed Willow, Brown's Spring, Sand and Antelope creeks, all dry with stone and gravel beds, winding like serpents around sandy hills covered by a scattering of smooth stones. Groves of cottonwood, willow and box elder, whose leafy limbs moaned in the wake of ever-present winds, sheltered their banks.

The taste of this new frontier lingered in Joel's mind like heather honey. He gazed at the blue sky broken with clouds puffed like cotton spilling from open bolls. He watched racing herds of pronghorn antelope, their white rumps flashing in the bright sunlight. He savored the tangy scent of sage and the mellow aroma of sweating mules and horses. He watched bald and gold eagles circling high in the sky and listened to the clatter of steel-rimmed wheels grinding along rocky ruts. These had lulled his senses and buried his fear. The ever-present fear, planted by Red Cloud, seemed far away like the snowcapped Bighorn peaks lying jagged along the western horizon.

Joel glanced at the leather-clad figure of Jim Bridger slouched in his saddle. Beneath the floppy brim of Bridger's hat, hawkish eyes searched and keen ears listened for danger, reminding Joel of Joshua's words the morning the wagon train left Fort Laramie. "Trust Mister Bridger," Joshua had said, "he thinks like the red man and knows their habits and how to survive in their land."

Aye, Mister Bridger and Almighty God, Joel thought.

Far away, barely audible above clopping hooves and creaking wagon wheels, came the winsome strains of a melody being played on a harmonica.

Bridger glared back at the wagon train. "Who's playin' that confound harp?"

"A frightened woodcutter, I imagine."

"Reckon so. Feared of cholera and Injuns most likely."

"Aye, most likely."

"Well, ain't in Lakota country yet, but we will be soon enough."

"How much farther is it to Fort Reno?"

Bridger pointed back at the flat crowns of several towering buttes they had passed during the morning. "Them's Pun'kin Buttes. We got five, maybe six more miles afore we reach Reno."

"That is comfortin'."

"I reckon," Bridger said, "but after we leave Reno and cross Crazy Woman Crick is when that feelin' will fly away like pissin' in the wind."

* * *

Yellow Elk stood in front of his bed of sweet sage, facing east, chanting his morning prayer toward the sun rising above gleaming white pinnacles. A cold wind tumbling over the Bighorn peaks rushed through the valley of Yellow Elk's vision-vigil. The medicine man's copper features glistened in the bright morning sunshine. Sunbeams filtering through the grove of quaking aspen played dancing patterns across his face and naked chest. Aspen leaves humming in the wind provided nature's harmony to Yellow Elk's prayer-song. The rhythmic Lakota rendition spilled across his tongue, ascending like a bird to the ears of *Wakan-Tanka*, The Great Spirit. "Hey-a-a-hey! Hey-a-a-hey! Hey-a-a-hey! *Wakan-Tanka*, Maker Of Everything Above, hear me. My offering of sweet cedar sends smoke from my morning fire. Smoke from the sacred pipe has risen to the Heavens, across our Mother Earth and to the Medicine Fathers riding on the four winds. Open your ears, hear my prayer. Many washichun in blue coats with long guns are leaving the bluecoat's log-walled den on the river of Powder. Soon, they will cross the creek called Crazy Woman into our hunting grounds. Yellow Elk and Red Cloud wait for your words. Washichun, the fat takers, come to steal from our land, our buffalo and our wapiti. They tell us much lies. They are crazy for the yellow metal in our ground and the ground of our brothers, the Flatheads, the Piegan, the Bloods and the Cheyenne. The talk of war is in our lodges. Send me a vision, *Wakan-Tanka*, on the wings of my Medicine Father, Great Eagle. Show me. I will stay here in this place where you have filled my eyes with truth many times. Show me, Great Spirit. I will not eat until you send the *Wakanpi*, the spirits of power over everything on earth, to me. Hear my prayer, Great Spirit Above, Maker of Everything. Aho! Aho!"

Yellow Elk stripped away his breechcloth, leggings and moccasins. He walked to the edge of a pool fed by springs and plunged into its icy waters, an act of purification for his spirit within. His cleansing complete, Yellow Elk climbed from the pool. With his teeth chattering, he faced the rising sun and sang a song to the Medicine Father riding on the north wind. "Aho! Aho!" he said, then dressed and sat down on his bed of sage and patiently waited for the vision.

When the sun sank beyond the Bighorn peaks, Yellow Elk stood up and gathered wood for his evening fire. He sprinkled bits of sweet cedar into the flames and sang his prayer song. "Hey-a-a-hey! Hey-a-a-hey! Hey-a-a-hey! Smoke of sweet cedar carry my prayer to my Medicine Father, The Great Eagle. Tell him I wait; I will sit here all night not sleeping until the sun comes again. Then I will build my morning fire, smoke the sacred pipe and say my morning prayer. I wait for you, Great Eagle. Aho! Aho!"

Night brought a chilling wind, and then it died. Frigid air settled like quicksilver into the valley from high mountain snowfields. Flames from Yellow Elk's evening fire died. He shivered. His hands ached, feet cramped and arms stiffened from the cold that was seeping into the marrow of his bones. Yet Yellow Elk sat motionless and waited for his vision. None came that night. The sun rose, crossed the sky and sank below the western pinnacles the following three days. Each morning, Yellow Elk welcomed the sun, repeated the vision-seeking ritual, abstained from food and drank little water. Still, the awaited vision did not come.

On the morning of the fifth day as dawn bleached the eastern sky, Yellow Elk heard the north wind rushing through the aspen grove. High above, the shrill shriek of a bald eagle echoed across the valley. Yellow Elk stood up, peered into the vast blue and searched for the bird soaring on outstretched wings. "My Medicine Father rides the north wind. *Wakan-Tanka*, show The Great Eagle to Yellow Elk," he prayed.

He did not see the smoky bird, his white head, neck and tail glistening in the morning sunshine, until it landed on a dwarfed pine growing from the sheer face of a granite cliff. Yellow Elk stood, motionless, staring at the eagle perched on the pine swaying in the wind. The eagle and the Lakota *wicasa wakan* stared at each other. Yellow Elk felt giddy, staggered, grasped an aspen sapling only to fall, dazed and shaken. He reached for his medicine bundle, a deerskin bag containing his sacred fetishes. Great pleasure swept through him as he clutched his medicine bundle. Rising up, he scanned the cliff. The eagle was still there, motionless. It gave out its shrieking call one more time and then fell silent.

Raising his hands above his head, Yellow Elk waited. The vision came. "I see you Great Eagle, messenger from *Wakan-Tanka*," Yellow Elk called to the bird.

"I bring you power of the *Wakanpi*," the eagle cried, his voice thundering through the valley. "His name is White Wapiti with Flaming Eyes. Tell Red Cloud that I will show him the *Wakanpi*, the spirits of power over everything on earth, after the washichun cross the creek of Crazy Woman. That is when power will come to the Lakota. *Wakan-Tanka* will give you victory over the washichun, but you will find with them a washichun *wakan* man. You may capture him. He must not walk in the hereafter. His hair must not hang from a Lakota warrior's lance. Tell Red Cloud my words."

The vision faded. Yellow Elk stood facing the granite cliff. The eagle was gone. "Hetchetu Aloh!" Yellow Elk cried, lowering his arms.

Chapter 3

Smoke from the woodcutters' campfires had drifted down the sage-covered hillside and settled like a shroud over Fort Reno. Chattering magpies had awakened Jim Bridger as dawn unveiled Carrington's 18th Infantry camped on the west bank of the Powder River. On a knoll south of the fort, the woodcutters' tents encircled by canvas-covered wagons, languished in silence as surgeon D. D. Vanderhoerst watched over two sick woodcutters. Bridger walked into the camp, his .45-90 side-hammer Sharps slung across his shoulder. Doctor Vanderhoerst held up his hand. "Better not come any closer, Mister Bridger. I've quarantined the camp."

"Cholera?"

Vanderhoerst nodded. "Two mild cases."

"Doc Leslie said we was headin' out o' Laramie too damned soon. Any gone under?"

"No, these men will live."

"Carrington is leadin' the 18th north this mornin'. I can't stay behind."

Vanderhoerst frowned. "Who's going to guide these folks?"

"Reckon Carrington will leave a detachment behind for that," Bridger said. "I'll see to it, Doc."

The next morning, Captain Joseph L. Porter, the commanding officer of Fort Reno, and Joel Leslie watched from the fort's northwest bastion as the 18th's long, blue line disappeared beyond the northern horizon. A rising cloud of dust finally drifted from view as the land of the Lakota swallowed Bridger, Carrington and his force of 536 men. Soon, they would cross Crazy Woman Creek, Red Cloud's line in the sand.

A week later on the twentieth of July, there being no more cases of cholera, Doctor Vanderhoerst lifted the quarantine. At first light *The General*, blown by the garrison bugler, called for packing up, striking tents and loading wagons. Mounted infantrymen straddled their McClellan saddles as *Boots and*

Saddles echoed across the Powder River. Other infantrymen, serving as muleteers, snapped whips over the rumps of army mule teams drawing the woodcutters' wagons.

These soldiers detached from Company G, 2nd Battalion of the 18th Infantry led by 1st Lt. George M. Templeton, escorted the wagons onto the Bozeman Trail. Their destination, the new fort being built by Carrington in the middle of Red Cloud's domain on Piney Creek near the Bighorns.

Dust rising from hooves and wheels engulfed the wagon train. Joel urged his mount out of the powdery haze to ride beside Lt. Templeton's black gelding. Templeton nodded a silent greeting. Joel said, "I'm hopin' ye don't mind my ridin' with ye."

Templeton scanned the changing terrain ahead of them. "You're welcome, Reverend, You can help me keep a lookout for Indian sign."

Joel nodded and looked to the northwest where the mountains were much higher. Their eastern slopes, greened by forests, extended beyond the northern horizon. "There's a lot of country out there for the Lakota to hide in."

"Yeah, mountains, dry coulees, hills covered by scrub pine and a million other places. There's one thing for certain, Red Cloud knows all of it and he'll choose where to attack us."

"Aye, no doubt that is true."

Lt. Templeton studied Joel, his curiosity searching for answers. "If you don't mind my asking, Reverend Leslie, just why are you traveling across this hostile country?"

A reflective mood descended upon Joel as he considered Templeton's question. Joshua, Bridger and he had attended the Laramie peace conference at the invitation of Colonel Maynadier. Haunting words spoken at that meeting by Red Cloud once again came to mind, causing him to ponder, to question their meaning.

"My callin' is to establish a mission." Joel said, gazing at the distant horizon. "Now... I'm not so certain... these Indians...."

"What about the Indians?"

"Ye heard Red Cloud say our God was a stranger and

that their God *Wakan-Tanka* says we lie."

Templeton nodded. "Yes, but you must remember that the Indians are murdering savages. They torture, kill, mutilate their enemies and worship animals, birds, rocks, just about anything they take a mind to."

"Maybe that's because God is a stranger to them."

"What about Father de Smet? He's lived with the Flatheads up in the Bitterroot Valley for years."

"Aye, we need more de Smets."

"I reckon so," Templeton said and reined his horse about. "Sergeant Peck!" he called to a trooper whose sleeves were filled with blue chevrons.

"Yes, sir!"

"Sergeant, ride ahead until you get to Crazy Woman crossing."

"Yes, sir."

"Be alert, if you see any Indian sign, get back quick as you can."

"Yes, sir."

"Take one of your men with you."

"I will ride with ye," Joel said, stroking the withers of his horse. "This geldin' is fast and solid. I wager he's faster than any o' Red Cloud's ponies."

"Didn't know you were a betting man, Reverend," Templeton said.

Joel grinned. "Aye, now and then a wee wager I'll make, like any good Scotsman."

"What about it, Sergeant? You want a preacher riding with you?"

The sergeant's eyes grew somber. He scanned Joel, his buckskin gelding, and the .44 Henry repeating rifle tucked inside a saddle scabbard. "You say you can ride, Preacher. How about killin'? I mean Injuns with that Henry."

The question welded Joel's stare at the sergeant. "If need be, y'can count on me."

"Well, sir, let's ride."

* * *

It was hot. The noonday July sun bearing down upon

the Bighorn country baked the mountains, plains, the Lakota and their enemies, the washichun soldiers. Red Cloud, wearing his warrior shirt bearing tassels of hair contributed by many members of his Oglala clan, sat cross-legged in a circle of Lakota war chiefs. Their council was atop a ridge overlooking Porcupine Creek near a circle of stones called the Medicine Wheel. This was a holy ground to the Lakota, Crow and Cheyenne tribes.

In the circle of warriors with Red Cloud sat Man-Afraid-Of-His-Horses, who was the principal chief of the Lakota, as well as High Hump Back, Fool Bull, Medicine Hawk, Yellow Elk and his son, Lone Wolf. Red Cloud dipped his fingers into a bowl filled with red dye. His forefinger traced sacred symbols across his face, thighs and legs. Bowls of white, black and yellow hues provided additional designs, each a message of 'coup' won in battle. The bowls of dye were passed from one chief to another until all were painted.

Yellow Elk stood up after all of the chiefs had taken their turn with the sacred pipe, offering smoke to the North, East, South, West, Earth and Sky. "My Medicine Father, The Great Eagle, has given me a sacred promise. He came to me on the fifth day of my vision quest during the Moon of Fat Horses promising a *Wakanpi*. White Wapiti with Flaming Eyes will come to us before our first battle with the blue-coated washichun. The *Wakanpi* will give us victory. We will gain many 'coup' against them. We will not spare any who cross the creek called Crazy Woman, except one, a washichun *wakan* man."

The chiefs murmured to one another their wonder at Yellow Elk's words. Fool Bull spoke. "One will be spared—a washichun *wakan* man? Yellow Elk, how is it that a *wakan* man rides with the soldiers? Does he bring their Great Spirit to do battle?"

Man-Afraid lifted his war club above his head. "A-haa-eee, their Great Spirit walks behind them like a helper, not in front like *Wakan-Tanka*. We will close his ears with our war cries. He will not hear the washichun calling for help."

"Hetchetu Aloh!" agreed Yellow Elk, "but the Medicine

Father says the blood of their *wakan* man must not sink into the land of the Lakota. His hair must not hang from a Lakota lance.”

"Washichun bluecoats are all alike, no difference, no painted faces, no 'coup' sign on horses. How will we know this *wakan* man?" one of the chiefs, Man Of Arrows, asked as he made sign with his hands.

"Their *wakan* man has two faces," Yellow Elk replied. "One wears black robe. They call him 'father'. Other wears white collar split like wings of the white goose under chin. He is called 'preacher'."

Red Cloud stood up, folded his arms across his chest and walked to the center of the medicine wheel. "You have heard the medicine of Yellow Elk. We will gain many 'coup' against the bluecoats. *Wakan-Tanka* will go with us into battle. Many scalps will hang before our lodges. Now we go to the great mountain in the clouds that wears the bonnet of snow above the creek called Clear Waters. We will wait there for White Wapiti With Flaming Eyes. Then we will ride to do battle with the washichun."

"Hetchetu Aloh!" chorused the council of chiefs as they stood up and held their rifles, bows and war clubs high above their feathered war bonnets.

* * *

Winds blowing from the mountains swept the tall, bluestem grass blanketing the Bighorn foothills into swells like a rolling sea. Yellow-bellied larks fluttered overhead, songless, their voices muted by the noonday heat. The hot arid air was sharp, charged by sage and sweating mules. Joel perceived no danger, only majestic beauty, silent and peaceful. He and Sgt. Peck felt alone, as if they were the first explorers to see, smell and feel this strange new land.

The nearer they rode to Crazy Woman crossing, the more tortuous the trail became. Its rutted course carved by wagon wheels skirted every deep coulee. *How easily red savages hidin' in these washes could attack without warnin'*, he thought, peering into the depths of one.

They rode onto a ridge overlooking a vast basin. Peck scanned through binoculars and saw cottonwood and willow trees on the banks of a creek that looped back and forth toward the northeast. "That's Crazy Woman Creek," Peck said. "Reckon we'd better wait down there at the crossing."

Joel berated himself for feeling uneasy. No charging Indians had ridden out of the gullies. No hissing arrows, whining bullets, signals of smoke or flashing mirrors had been heard or seen.

After the horses drank their fill from the Crazy Woman, Joel and Peck tied them to cottonwood trees. Joel sat down in the shade and cradled the Henry in his lap. Sgt. Peck sat near him and stuffed tobacco into his old, briar pipe and lit it with a match swiped to life across his britches. Smoke rolled from his nostrils as he took several deep drafts.

"Goddamn, but it's hot," he said, as he wiped his brow and then continued as Joel wagged his head, "excuse my profanity, Reverend."

"'Tis hot, indeed. Instead of profanin' God, you should thank Him for the shade beneath these trees. It truly is a godsend."

Sgt. Peck nodded. "Better get used to my cussin', Reverend, you got to cuss to live in this Army."

Joel didn't reply. He was aware of the sergeant's meaning.

Peck sat down, leaned against a cottonwood trunk and puffed on his pipe. Joel tossed his hat on the ground. The horses swished their tails driving away pesky deerflies. "Have ye ever killed an Indian?" Joel asked.

"Yeah, but more Yankees durin' the war, I reckon."

"Y'were a Rebel?"

"Stuart's 1st Virginia Cavalry," Peck said, sitting up a little straighter."

"What are y'doin' in the U. S. Army?"

"I got unhorsed and captured by Custer's Wolverines east of Gettysburg. Three months spent in Fort Delaware Prison on Pea Island was enough for me. They galvanized me into a Yankee by makin' me swear allegiance. That's when I got sent west to fight Injuns."

"I was at Gettysburg."

"A Yankee, I reckon?"

"Aye, a chaplain."

"Reckon you know some about killing and weeping and burying."

"Enough to hate war."

"You aren't done with war yet, Reverend, that is if Red Cloud has his way."

Sgt. Peck's mount, sensing danger, flared his nostrils and whinnied long and loud. "Whoa, boy," Peck said, reaching for the skittish horse's reins.

Joel pointed toward a nearly naked warrior silhouetted against the sky beyond Crazy Woman crossing. His copper legs bore jagged yellow thunder-stripes. Several eagle feathers tied into his long, black hair fluttered in the wind. His torso, painted white and covered with red battle symbols, glistened in the afternoon sunshine as he sat a piebald pinto. The young warrior's pony, covered with 'coup' symbols of red, yellow and white, neighed and pranced. Peck reached for his carbine. "Yeah, I see 'im. Got that Henry loaded?"

Joel eased back the Henry's hammer. "Aye."

"We'd better stay low 'til we see how many o' those red heathens there are," Peck said, motioning for Joel to follow and crawled behind the trunk of a fallen cottonwood tree.

Peck peered through binoculars. "He's Lakota. Them sonsabitches has taken all this country away from the Crow Injuns. Now they act like it's their goddamn native land."

"Is he goin' to attack us?"

"Not likely 'less we shoot at him first."

"Then, what is he about?"

Peck lowered the binoculars. "No damn good. You can bet that Henry he's letting us know if we cross the creek there'll be hell to pay."

"What about the wagon train?"

"They're okay until they ford this crossin'."

"What makes you so certain?"

Peck knocked the dollop of ashes from his pipe. "I know these Lakota. They're proud o' their word. You can bet your all-together on them never reneging on a promise. Red

Cloud said you go beyond this here creek and you're dead meat. Yes sir, that's what he said. That's what that painted warrior is tellin' us. That's for certain."

The Lakota warrior lifted his feathered lance and shook it above his head. "Y-a-h! H-e-e! Y-a-h!" he yelled. The pony leapt into a gallop carrying the warrior toward the creek, his 'coup'-feathered tail sweeping behind him like an unfurled guidon. "Don't shoot," Peck yelled, "he's just struttin' his courage."

With hindquarters dragging the ground, the pinto slid to a stop. The warrior, his features animated with excitement, plunged the lance into the ground. The pinto stood motionless while the warrior signed with his hands, delivering Red Cloud's warning.

"Do y'know what he's sayin'?" Joel asked Peck.

"Yeah, he says that white men crossin' this creek into the land of the Lakota will have no hair in the hereafter."

The painted pony carrying Red Cloud's messenger galloped away, back over the ridge and out of sight, but not out of mind.

"Reckon I got my orders," Peck said. "I have to report this to Lt. Templeton."

Joel eased down the hammer of his rifle. "I'm wonderin' about the fate of Col. Carrington and his men,"

"Don't know, but there's one thing for certain. Red Cloud intends to kill 'em all, and that includes us after we cross this goddamned creek."

Chapter 4

Red Cloud could see for miles and miles in every direction, except west toward the saw-toothed tops of the Bighorns. His vantage point, a sheer ledge of granite high up the eastern face of Cloud Peak was shared with Yellow Elk. Being so high up, it was cold on the first morning of their vigil. Morning clouds floated beneath them, carpeting the Powder River Basin with a blanket of fog. During the first hour after midday the blanket rose, its only remnant left was a shroud of clouds covering the pinnacle of Cloud Peak.

Yellow Elk pulled his blanket around painted shoulders and rubbed life back into hands stinging from the bite of frigid winds racing across snowfields high above the timberline.

Red Cloud stood on the ledge overlooking the mountain's principal game trail. Below were forests of conifers interspersed with groves of quaking aspen, and beyond them were grassy plateaus descending into the drainage basin of the Powder River. Down in the basin, heat waves from the late summer Moon of Ripe Cherries sun blurred their view with scintillating currents, rising higher and higher before blossoming into puffy, cumulus clouds.

Red Cloud and Yellow Elk continued to wait for the return of Lone Wolf and the promised *Wakanpi*. One, two, three hours passed while they gazed down the steep mountain incline. Finally, they saw a rider astride a painted pinto climbing the game trail just above the timberline of Cloud Peak. Red Cloud's bronzed hand slipped from beneath his blanket and pointed at the rider. "Lone Wolf, the son of Yellow Elk, returns."

Yellow Elk, standing beside Red Cloud, nodded his head and chuckled. Red Cloud stretched his arms skyward. "The Great Eagle rides the north wind this day. We shall soon hear the words of Lone Wolf."

"We must smoke," Yellow Elk said, lighting his sacred pipe packed with kinnikinnick. Smoke from the mixture of tobacco, dried sumac leaves and inner bark of the red willow, bit their tongues as they each puffed the pipe. Then they raised their hands toward the east. "Hear us, *Wakan-Tanka*," Yellow Elk intoned. "We wait for the *Wakanpi*. The Lakota are ready to do battle with the washichun, the fat takers that steal from our land. You have returned Lone Wolf, son of Yellow Elk and Otter Woman, to us, riding the wind of The Great Eagle. Make his medicine our medicine. Give us victory. Aho! Aho!"

Red Cloud clasped his hands, pointed them toward Crazy Woman Creek and began to chant. "Heh-a-a-heh! Heh-a-a-heh! Heh-a-a-heh! *Wakan-Tanka,* Maker Of Everything, hear your children, the Lakota. When we see White Wapiti With Flaming Eyes, we will ride to do battle with the washichun. Aho!"

Yellow Elk lowered his arms. "Hetchetu Aloh!"

Lone Wolf, bending low behind the flying mane of his pinto, urged the agile pony up the stony trail. The gallant little horse, straining against the steep slope, leapt and lunged, sucking great drafts of air. Foaming sweat streaked with red and yellow dye from melting 'coup' designs trickled down his withers.

When he reached their lookout, Lone Wolf leaped to the ground and called to Red Cloud and Yellow Elk. "The feathers on my war lance dance in the wind at the creek called Crazy Woman."

"This is good, Son of Yellow Elk," Red Cloud called back. "You have made the Lakota proud."

"Hetchetu Aloh!" agreed Yellow Elk. "Climb up and wait with us for the *Wakanpi*. The bluecoat washichun building their log-walled den on the river called Piney will soon be marching without hair in the hereafter."

"Hetchetu Aloh!" chorused Lone Wolf and Red Cloud.

The three Lakota warriors sat on the high precipice, their vigil becoming more painful as the sun disappeared beyond Cloud Peak. The great mountain, whose shadow spawned frigid winds, cast them over the fields of snow covering her crest. Down the mountain's steep slope, the winds raced toward the warmer plateau below. The three *seekers* waited, shivering within their world of suffering.

Their bellies cried out for food and water. Their muscles

cramped, ears throbbed, eyes watered and hands and feet ached from the cold. Twilight enfolded them as they waited for the promised *Wakanpi*.

The night is swallowing the day—Wakan-Tanka must give us light, Lone Wolf thought, and then spoke. "When will the moon walk above us?"

"Before the sun comes again, the moon will bring us light," Yellow Elk signed with his hands.

The three warriors waited, their vigil carrying them into stark misery. Finally, stars scattered above the eastern horizon grew dim and the purple sky paled. Far below, a great horned owl hooted his welcome to the rising moon. Yellow Elk whispered, "Our feathered brother sings for us."

As darkness fled before the rising moon, the mountain, its snowy crest and granite cliffs above the timberline took on an eerie, silver-green glow. Red Cloud raised his arms. His numbed fingers trembled. Grimacing from pain, he faced the rising moon. "*Wakan-Tanka* sends us light. Now we can see White Wapiti With Flaming Eyes."

"Hetchetu Aloh!" Yellow Elk agreed, rubbing his aching hands together.

"Red Cloud! Yellow Elk!" Lone Wolf cried, jumping up and pointing his war club at a shadowy figure trotting out of the timberline on the game trail ascending the mountain. The three warriors stood at the cliff's precipice, peering down the steep slope. At first, the approaching figure lacked form. Then the animal's towering rack of antlers took shape as he lunged up the steep slope. His coat was white as the mountain snowfield above them. The elk with eyes as red as the blood flowing through them stopped and stood motionless below the granite ledge. "The *Wakanpi*!" Red Cloud said. "He stands there, all white, his eyes burning like the dancing fire."

Lone Wolf raised high his stone-headed war club. "Death to the washichun bluecoats! Victory to the Lakota!"

"It is a good day to die," chorused Red Cloud, Yellow Elk and Lone Wolf.

* * *

Woodcutters, with their wives and children, hid

themselves beneath canvas tops stretched over ribs of hickory covering each of the wagons. Crazy Woman Creek lay behind them. It was a tortuous stream whose looping course was laid out like a new rope of braided sinew drying in the sun. At the Bozeman crossing, eyes filled with fear had looked away while passing by the feathered sentry plunged into the earth by Lone Wolf.

Puffing infantrymen, with rifles at the ready, trudged beside the wagons, their eyes ever scanning for painted ponies carrying bronzed warriors.

"That preacher's collar you're wearing sure isn't white any more," Lt. Templeton said to Joel.

Joel swept a handkerchief across his shoulders. "Nay, 'tis covered with grit."

"Yes! The wagons and mules are stirring up a lot of it."

Sergeant Peck, riding out of the cloud of dust covering the train of wagons, called to Lt. Templeton, "Red Cloud sure won't have any trouble findin' us."

Lt. Templeton glanced up at the dirty haze billowing above them. "True enough, Sergeant, but he'll not surprise us, not with our scouts riding fore, flanks and rear."

Sgt. Peck eyed the young lieutenant. "Foolishness, he muttered. How could we be surprised? Red Cloud's words were certain. So was the message delivered by that painted warrior. When? That's the goddamned question."

The sun and the trail were climbing higher toward the mountains. It was hot and growing hotter. Cloud Peak, whose white-tipped spire rose higher than any of her sisters, loomed like a great cathedral in the west. Muleteers snapped their whips and cursed their mules already weary from the ever-ascending frontier roadway. The woodcutters and their wives and children were tormented trying to ride the wagons bouncing over rocks, potholes and sage. Disassembled sawmills strained at their lashings as the eroded trail heaved against the wagons. Yet woodcutters, wives, children and soldiers hardly noticed the dust, heat and jarring terrain. Not even the towering beauty of the Bighorn range of mountains could divert them from wondering what danger lay ahead, behind, to the east or west.

When would the red-hoard come over one of the ridges, shriek their war cries and send swishing arrows into mules and human beings alike?

Lulled by the rocking gait of his buckskin and the shimmering heat rising from the land being baked by the noonday sun, Joel turned inward.

Here I am, called by God, of that and that alone am I certain. Why am I here? Oh, aye, I was sent on this journey by the Presbytery of Northern Scotland to the American wilderness. I'm to build a mission for the miners high in the mountains of western Montana Territory. Aye, 'tis needed, but ... I wonder. Am I like the priest on his way to do a good thing, when as he, I walk by a man in need lyin' in a ditch. I can see his wounds, his glazed eyes and hear him crying for my help. Can I walk on, my mission consumin' me? Red Cloud cried out—nay, he pleaded, sayin' that the white man's God is a stranger to the Lakota. Is he like the Macedonian callin' for help in St. Paul's vision?

"I could use your Henry, Reverend."

Joel reached for his rifle. "Of course."

Sgt. Peck shook his head. "No, I mean I'd like for you to ride with me."

"Where?"

"To relieve the scouts riding point."

Joel nudged his heels against the buckskin's flanks. "Let's go!"

As they rode along the trail, Joel was through with pondering. The past and the future held little interest now that they were ahead of the slow-moving wagons, the cussing muleteers, the dust and the luxury of daydreaming. Danger, imminent and oppressive, weighed heavily upon him. Like the others, he could smell, taste and hear it in the wind as he and Sgt. Peck rode out of sight of the detachment of soldiers, the mule teams, wagons and their human cargo.

"Keep a sharp eye," Peck said, "we'll be catchin' up with Stith and Wiggins anytime now."

Corporal Waylon Stith, Private Jeb Wiggins and Sergeant Peck, all galvanized Yankees, had been garrisoned at Fort Conner, later named Fort Reno, since August 14, 1865. It was they, troops of the Powder River Expedition commanded by General Patrick Connor, who built the post. It was a crude affair made of a rough, cottonwood-log stockade surrounding a warehouse and stables. The officers and men were quartered in unprotected buildings outside the stockade.   To their good fortune these quarters, better described as sheds with earth-covered roofs and dirt floors, had never come under attack. But it was home, the only one that Peck, Stith and Wiggins had known since coming to Dakota Territory. They had reenlisted for another term after their unit, Company C of the 5th U. S. Volunteers, had been mustered out and replaced by Company G of the 18th Infantry. The garrison, with the exception of Stith, Wiggins and Peck, had departed for home without a single regret. The remaining trio, with little incentive to return to their homes in a South undergoing harsh reconstruction, had opted to stay. They would continue to be "Army" serving at Fort Reno on this raw, unforgiving and hostile frontier.

"I see nothing yet," Joel said, sitting his buckskin straighter than usual. "How far ahead were Stith and Wiggins supposed to ride?"

Peck did not answer, his stare was held fast on vultures circling high in the distance. These scavengers of the sky, always foreboding since their only sustenance was carrion, could be searching for any dead animal. Their senses were adept, often detecting death before the stricken one had succumbed. Joel's eyes followed the finger of Sgt. Peck pointing at the birds spiraling downward on outstretched wings. "What does this mean?" Joel asked, already knowing the answer.

"Goddamned buzzards, they're gettin' ready for dinner. It could be an elk, a deer, a buffalo or... a human bein', I reckon."

"That is disturbin', with gruesome possibilities."

"You got that right. We need to find out, but we got to be careful. Don't want no buzzard sayin' grace over us."

The congregation of vultures, a dozen or perhaps more, alighted in a box elder, its dead limbs barren for several seasons. A lesser number, squatting on a rocky ledge nearby, flapped restless wings and hopped about jostling for an advantage. The goal of their avian ritual was to become the first scavenger to perch atop a carcass—to become king or queen for a moment, tearing choice morsels with its powerful beak, but the time had to be right. Only the vultures' senses could determine when that time had arrived. The time had not arrived, not yet. Their chosen carrion, a gray gelding, his McClellan saddle and ribs pierced with arrows, lay in the shaded bottom of a dry coulee.

Sgt. Peck jumped off his horse and pointed into the wash. "That's Wiggins's gray."

A hoarse murmur rose from the coulee as the great birds took flight, their wings carrying them out of the wash. All of them, except two old, feathered crones circling high above, waited for the intruders to leave. The persistent duo swooped back into the coulee, landing in the box elder. They refused to give up their advantage, even when Joel and Peck slid and jumped their way down into the coulee. "He's still warm," Peck said, stroking the gray's neck.

Joel walked around the dead horse. The ground was crusted and dry and covered by a scattering of gravel. "I don't see any boot tracks."

"Naw, Wiggins didn't ride this gray down here, that's for sure. Let's leave those buzzards to their dinner."

Backtracking the dead gray's flight from pursuing arrows brought them to a cluster of sage. Behind the bushes, they found tracks made by unshod ponies. Peck stepped out of his stirrup and walked around studying the tracks. "These are Injun-pony tracks, Lakota most likely." He continued to search the ground for *Army* tracks, those made by steel-shod horses. There were none.

"Let's ride back to the coulee," Joel said. "Corporal Stith probably picked Mr. Wiggins up close to where his horse fell over the embankment."

Near the coulee, they found hoofprints made by an army horse, and boot tracks made by Jeb Wiggins where he mounted Stith's horse. The horse had galloped northwest toward the mountains. Peck motioned for Joel to follow. "They couldn't get back to the train," Peck said, looking at the maze of unshod tracks. "This is where the Lakotas cut 'em off."

Uneasy silence surrounded them. Joel strained to listen, could hear nothing, no gunfire, no shrieking warriors, nothing. The shod trail they followed was often obscured by the unshod tracks of pursuing Indian ponies. Their search carried them farther and farther from the column of canvas-covered wagons and their escorting detachment of soldiers. They were alone, on their own, relying only on themselves, their weapons and luck, which could turn bad as well as good.

Up the ascending terrain they rode, seeking Stith and Wiggins. The sun, now standing just above the white top of Cloud Peak, cast long shadows across the high plateau. The strength and stamina of Stith's mount seemed unbelievable, carrying two men for such a distance while outrunning the smaller Indian ponies.

They crossed a high rim overlooking a basin, which surrounded a creek flowing from the mountains. Here they sat their horses to let them blow for a few minutes. "I reckon that's Clear Creek," Peck said. "We can water there."

With their horses rested and watered, they left Clear Creek behind. They approached a phalanx of pine, spruce and fir trees growing along a hog-backed ridge. Joel's buckskin perked his ears and sauntered into a sideways gait. Joel's eyes caught color, black and white, color that was out of place. He reined back his buckskin. Through the swaying tall grass next to the grove, he could see the feathered butts of three arrows pointing skyward.

Peck dismounted, walked his horse toward the arrows, stopped, knelt down and pulled a kerchief from around his neck. "Them bastards kilt ol' Jeb... scalped him too." He covered Wiggins' bloody head with the kerchief and slammed his kepi on the ground. "Them heathen savages!" He grasped an arrow protruding from Wiggins' back. It held fast. He yanked on another one. It did not budge. Equal failure was met with the third arrow. "My god, Reverend, I can't get 'em out."

Joel broke the shaft of each arrow and tossed them aside. "Now we can bury him proper, facin' the Lord on resurrection morning."

Peck stood up and shook his head. His gaze swept the

plain and the ascending slopes toward the mountains. He offered his bayonet to Joel. "We got here too late to help Jeb. If you will bury him, I'll keep following Stith's tracks."

"Nay, we can bury Mr. Wiggins later."

"No, we can't. The wolves or those stinking buzzards will eat him."

Joel laid his hand on Peck's shoulder. "Your friend is deceased and at peace, Corporal Stith may be also. Night is near. The chances of finding him are slim but improved if we go on together."

Peck pulled a piece of paper from his blouse and began penciling a message. "Reckon you're right. Lieutenant Templeton will be sending help."

"Can we be certain of that?"

"He knows we're in trouble since Wiggins and Stith didn't report back."

"Maybe we should wait for them."

Peck thrust his bayonet through the paper and jammed it into the trunk of a tree near Wiggins' corpse. "We still have a couple hours o' daylight. Let's go find Stith."

Chapter 5

Corporal Stith, riding low and hatless with hair flying, whipped his horse again and again. Yelping Lakota warriors were getting closer, close enough to make their arrows lethal. The tiring gelding, almost used up, strained and lunged beneath Stith's saddle.

Stith clutched his revolver and spoke to his horse. "Got two rounds left in this Colt, one for you, the other for me."

He spurred the sweating sorrel up a steep incline. At the mountain's base, Stith yanked on the reins, leaped to the ground, slammed the Colt's muzzle behind the gelding's ear and pulled the trigger. He dropped behind the dead horse and yanked his Spencer carbine from its scabbard. There he waited, watching the pursuing warriors sit their ponies at the foot of the hill. One of them, his chest painted white and adorned with red symbols, signed with his hands. Four of them leapt to the ground, crouched low and scrambled up a ridge.

Stith looked up the steep incline behind him. Its ascent was almost perpendicular for nearly a hundred yards before taking a less severe rise toward the forest covering the mountain. He looked back at the scrambling warriors and spoke to his dead horse. *Those bastards are tryin' to get above us.*

He swung the carbine toward the leading scrambler. The Spencer roared. The Lakota tumbled from the ridge—the three that remained scurried out of sight.

Stith's attention returned to the white-chested warrior and four others sitting their ponies beyond the range of his carbine. They made no effort to move. "What are they up to?"

Once more, he scanned the steep mountain incline. Near the forest, he could make out a field of boulders. "Reckon they intend to get me with a rock slide."

S-w-w-i-s-s-h! An arrow arced out of the sky and slammed into the ground several yards in front of his dead horse. Another arrow slashed closer and another thumped into the horse's belly. "Who's shootin' all them arrows?"

Stith saw a Lakota rise up, his bow held above the ridge while drawing an arrow from his quiver. He notched the arrow and aimed it toward Stith. "That's got to be the Injun I shot at—don't see how I could have missed."

He watched the arrow take flight, ascend on a high arc and turn downward toward him. He hunkered down closer to the horse's back and listened to the singing arrow until it plummeted into the dead horse. Another, and then another followed, all of them plunging into his shield of horseflesh.

The bombardment of arrows seemed continuous. Stith raised his head—a hissing arrow forced him back down. And then the reason for the Lakota bombardment of arrows became evident. From above him, a rumble, its roar like a cascading Niagara, shook the mountain. Scooting backward, he shoved himself against the cliff hoping to escape the cascading onslaught.

"Aaarrhh." Pain with a hundred barbs slashed through his left shoulder as a serrated arrowhead tore into muscle and bone, lodging itself within the muscles of his back. The pain stopped his ears. No longer could he hear the avalanche of rock as it tumbled down the mountain. The first boulder smashed into his horse, followed by a rock-storm of earth, uprooted pines and boulders of all sizes. He lurched backward, flattening his back against the cliff. "God help me... goddamn you savages."

Dirt, stones and limbs torn from pine trees continued to slam over him. Before the pummeling finally ceased, it seemed to Stith that an eternity had passed. Then silence, dark and stifling, engulfed him. Pine needles clawed at his face. He recoiled, gasping for air.

* * *

Lone Wolf raised his war club and yelped as Stith disappeared beneath the slide. The other warriors raced after him as his pinto charged toward the dust-cloud rising from the torn mountain. "H-e-y-y-a-h!" he yelled. "The *Wakanpi* fights beside us."

The Lakota war party swarmed over the mound of torn earth, stone and trees. Lone Wolf thrust his lance into the mound. "We will kill all washichun coming into the land of the

Lakota."

"Hetchetu Aloh!" cried the others.

"Hetchetu Aloh!" Lone Wolf yelled and leaped astride his pony. "Now we attack the washichun wagons. Hoka Hey!"

* * *

Searing pain aroused Stith. Lone Wolf's lance had pierced his belly. He grasped the lance and tried to pull it free but could not. His head throbbed—lungs cried for air. He gasped, sucking dirt and pine needles into his mouth and throat. His hand searched and found his holster. He pulled the Colt free, thumbed back the hammer and pressed the cold muzzle against his temple. No one heard the Colt's muffled report as his finger squeezed the trigger.

* * *

Evening shadows stretched across the broken foothills along Rock Creek, a tributary from the mountains draining into Clear Creek. The heat of the day was replaced by the chill of evening, filling the dry, mountain air with a hint of juniper. Time had nearly run out like an hourglass with only a few grains of sand remaining in its upper bulb. It was becoming impossible for Joel and Peck to see the tracks made by Stith and his pursuers along the creek's rocky bank. They were riding farther and farther into Lakota lands, hostile and deadly places. Each phalanx of trees, solitary granite boulders and crevices deeply eroded into the hills could cover warriors waiting to end their lives. Peck held up his hand. "Reckon we've about run out o' luck. It's gettin' too dark to go any farther. We got to decide where to spend the night."

Joel shivered, reached for his coat lashed behind the cantle of his saddle, slipped it on and pulled up the collar. "Aye, Lt. Templeton isn't coming to help us, I fear."

Peck spat, wiped his chin and wagged his head. "He's got his own troubles or he would have. Let's water the horses and then hide in those pines up there on the slope."

A fire couldn't be built. It was too risky. Peck handed Joel a strip of buffalo jerky. "That's supper, chew it slow and it'll calm your belly."

Joel savored the dried meat, its peppery sweetness heady

on his tongue. "Ah, 'tis good, where did y'get this?"

"From the Brule' Injuns. Their squaws dry strips of meat from every buffler they kill. It doesn't spoil, so you can carry it with you anywhere and it's still good."

The night crept by like a waddling terrapin, sleepless and cold for Joel. He watched shadows dancing and likened them to highland maidens, their outlines sculpted by the moonlight through the trees. He listened to the forest, full of sounds, echoing the cries of night critters. Wolves howling out on the plain, owls hooting among the trees, a bull elk bugling in the distance, all of them joined into a symphony of sounds. The warmth of the blanket wrapped around him augmented the odor of horse sweat rising from the pillow he'd made from his saddle blanket.

He shoveled his hip into a bed of pine needles and stared through the trees at the star-splattered darkness above the mountains. Unable to sleep, his pondering skipped from thought to thought like a bee buzzing from one flower to another. These musings seemed to multiply, filling his mind with questions. *Just how many galaxies are out there? How, who, when and what created them? I wonder if the Indians have considered these questions? Why do they worship animals and blow smoke toward the winds?*

His reflections were abruptly interrupted by a cracking sound. *What was that?* He sat up, listened and peered through the shadows. Peck continued to snore, undisturbed by the noise. The horses strained at their halter ropes, snorted and stamped the ground. "Sergeant," Joel whispered, "are y'awake?"

Peck continued to snore. "Sergeant—wake up,"

Peck's snoring ceased. "What is it?"

"Did y'hear that noise?"

"No," Peck said, crawling out of his blanket. "What kind of noise?"

"I'm not sure, a crackin' sound."

Joel and Peck crouched together, their eyes searching for the unseen danger, their ears straining, but they did not hear the warriors' moccasin-clad feet creeping through the trees. Like a charging cougar, silent and swift, the Lakota attacked. Peck's

Colt roared. A young Lakota, barely fourteen, collapsed, blood oozing from his pierced chest. Joel reached for his Henry, but an attacker's fingers already grasping the rifle slung it aside and reached for Joel's neck. Peck's Colt roared again. Another young warrior fell. Joel strained, his hands pulling at the fingers imbedded about his neck. His vision, already blurred, failed to see Peck collapse beneath descending war clubs. He felt himself slipping into a dark abyss, and then there was nothing.

Lone Wolf lunged at the warrior strangling the life from Joel. "A-a-a-e-e-h-h!" he screamed and clawed at the strangling fingers. "*Wakan* man! *Wakan* man! He wears the goose-wing collar! He must live!"

Joel fell to the ground, his eyes sightless, bloody saliva flowing from his mouth. "A-a-a-e-e-h-h!" Lone Wolf cried and knelt down. "If *Wakan* man's spirit flies, *Wakan-Tanka* will take away power of the *Wakanpi*."

Old Soldier, the one whose hands had encircled Joel's throat, dropped to his knees, raised his hands upward and began to chant. "Hey-a-a-hey! Hey-a-a-hey! Hey-a-a-hey!" His Lakota prayer to *Wakan-Tanka* rose through the pines, seeking mercy for the washichun *wakan* man to survive, for the power of *Wakanpi*.

* * *

Sticks punched into Joel's ribs by chattering children aroused him from the world of nowhere that he had experienced since the attack. The children's laughter taunted him as he tried to open eyelids swollen and stuck together. His head, spinning within a dark domain, ached and throbbed. He tried several times to swallow the sticky mess holding his tongue to the roof of his mouth but could not. Beneath his tormented body, a travois being dragged behind Lone Wolf's pinto bounced over stones. Bantering voices of Lakota squaws, trotting beside the travois, added to Joel's discomfort. Breathing required a great effort, his throat rasping with each gasp for air. His mind began to clear. Concern and fear tempered his thoughts as he pondered the situation, which seemed dire and foreboding.

Joel recognized the strident voice of Red Cloud speaking with Yellow Elk, but could not understand their Lakota language. He was certain they were talking about him, his fate and what their plans for him might be. Yellow Elk seemed to agree with Red Cloud's comments by emitting frequent chuckles followed by "Hetchetu Aloh."

Overwhelming thirst began to torment him as he lay on buffalo robes in the shade of a tipi. After groaning several times, he heard footsteps shuffling toward his bed. A hand slipped beneath his head and another sponged cold water across his eyes. The cold bath cleared his muddled brain. He managed to open his swollen eyelids just enough to see the face of a woman. It was an ageless kind of face with tawny features, full and round with brown eyes peeping between slightly slanted lids. She nodded and asked a question in pigeon English. "Washichun pain big?"

She gently lifted his head and held a ladle carved from a buffalo horn close to his lips. "Otter Woman made willow tea. Make pain run like wapiti."

Joel sipped from the ladle and gagged on the bitter concoction. A Lakota warrior jerked the ladle away, poured the medicine on the ground and berated Otter Woman in harsh Lakota words. She responded with severe signing by her hands, refilled the ladle from a pot and poured more willow tea between Joel's lips. "Good," she said, easing his head back down. "Pain go quick—washichun sleep."

Several days and nights passed with Otter Woman ministering to his needs with water, brewed herbs, greasy soups, cool compresses on his bruised neck and words of encouragement. He could sense her growing friendliness and dedication to seeing him through his injuries.

On the evening of the third day of his captivity, Joel decided to ask Otter Woman about the fate of Sgt. Peck. "The soldier that was with me, do y'know what happened to him?"

She looked away for a moment and then faced him. "Washichun bluecoat walks in hereafter."

"He is dead?"

"Gone under."

Joel cringed at the thought of mutilation and scalping. "Did Lone Wolf scalp the soldier?"

Otter Woman pointed at a tipi across the grounds. Atop a pole in front of it was a scalp with gray-streaked blond hair twisting in the wind.

* * *

High in the Bighorns where the Lakota lived, water sweet and clear from melting snowfields flowed down steep inclines, spilled over granite ledges, wed waters from cold mountain springs, found streams whose graveled floors wound downward seeking the plateaus below where this gathering of waters tumbled into the Tongue, a river flowing deep and cold.

Scattered along this river was the Lakota's summer encampment. Their tipis, which were covered with buffalo hides bleached by the sun, overlooked the river and mountain meadows that were grazed by deer, elk and Lakota ponies. Bushes laden with clusters of wild chokecherries grew along the river. Soon they would ripen into sweet and meaty treats. The encampment was a place of peace filled with happy days, but the talk of war with the washichun was making the Lakota wary.

On the morning of the fifth day of his captivity, barking camp dogs awakened Joel. The sun was rising, its flaming orb rimming the eastern horizon. Man Of Lakota, the camp crier, walked through the encampment blowing on a whistle made from the bone of an eagle's wing. He stopped, stood still and lowered the whistle from his lips. "Arise! Arise!" he called. "Lakota men, *Wakan-Tanka* brings us the sun. Go take a plunge in the river. Quickly, to the river for purification and prayer."

One by one, the men who followed the spiritual road, the *Wakan* path, left their lodges and walked down toward the blue-green waters of the Tongue. They stripped and dove into its frigid depths. From their teeth-chattering experience, they crawled out of the river, stood facing the morning sun and chanted their prayers.

Smoke from the squaws' cooking fires drifted across the grounds. Its pungent scent a reminder of soon to be eaten meat and fish. Before food was to be taken by the medicine men and chiefs, a decision had to be made. Red Cloud called them together for a council, not to make war, but to decide what to do about their captured washichun holy man. They sat down cross-legged in a circle in front of Red Cloud's tipi. Yellow Elk filled a sacred pipe with kinnikinnick. Each one blew smoke to the winds, earth and sky, and then Red Cloud spoke. "The washichun bluecoats are encamped near the river they call Piney. They have many tipis. Their axes and saws of iron make a log-walled den for many warriors. They bring guns, sicknesses, women and children. They did not hear the words of Red Cloud. They are like the big cat roaming the Snowy Mountains, creeping across Lakota grounds, seeking to kill us and steal the fat from our land."

The others voiced their agreement, "Hetchetu Aloh."

"*Wakan-Tanka* sent a Medicine Father, The Great Eagle, to Yellow Elk. The Great Eagle foretold our capture of the washichun *wakan* man that wears the goose-wing collar. The ears of his God are closed and do not hear his cries for help. *Wakan-Tanka* says we cannot kill this one. Men of Lakota, you must say whether the washichun *wakan* man will be a brother or a slave. What do you say?"

The circle of men did not utter a whisper or a grunt—only the sounds of the encampment were heard. Joel strained to listen as they began to speak. He couldn't understand their language, but sought answers to his fears from the speakers' signed gestures and facial expressions.

Lone Wolf stood up, stepped outside the circle and turned to speak. "Lone Wolf walks from the council to speak to his brothers." He pointed a finger at Joel lying on his bed next to Yellow Elk's tipi. "The washichun *wakan* man does not walk in the hereafter. Old Soldier, who was trying to save our people, captured him. I say this washichun is a dog. Let him beg squaws for bones, sleep with dogs, eat with dogs."

Several grunted agreement, "Hau," as Lone Wolf returned to his place in the council.

Yellow Elk began to speak and make sign without standing. "Lone Wolf is angry. Yellow Elk is angry. The Lakota are angry. The washichun *wakan* man has no *Wakanpi*. The sun of *Wakan-Tanka* has withered his medicine. His power is no more. He is not worthy to be a brother of the Lakota."

"Yellow Elk speaks strong words," Man Of Arrows said,

his fingers signing *power*. "I have seen the power of the washichun bluecoats in their encampment at the river called Piney. They have many long guns, many long knives, many warriors that walk together and many warriors that ride the four-leg sky dog. They have the gun on wheels that roars twice like the great humpbacked bear. Yellow Elk says the washichun *wakan* man has no power. Man Of Arrows says how do we know this?"

Grey Bull shook his head, grunted, "Hau," and leaned toward Red Cloud. "Man Of Arrows speaks straight words. I say the washichun *wakan* man will bring his medicine against the Lakota. We must take away his black cloak, his goose-wing collar and his black book. I say dress him in skins of dogs. Cut his eyes. Cut his tongue. Then the washichun Great Spirit will not understand his words."

Slowly, with great effort, a wizened old man struggled to stand. He leaned on a long, hooked staff made from willow stripped clean of its inner bark. His voice, weak and thin from age, quieted the mumbling council. "Medicine Hawk, a Sun Dance Chief of the Lakota speaks. All things are the work of *Wakan-Tanka*. He is inside everything, the sweet cedar, sweet grasses and flowing waters. He roams through the great Snowy Mountains where the Ancient Ones walked this land we call our home. He lives inside the feathered people, all the four-legs, in everything. I say this is true—we must respect all *wakan* men, even a washichun *wakan* man. *Wakan-Tanka* will take the power of the *Wakanpi* from the Lakota if we do as Grey Bull speaks."

Medicine Hawk sat down. "Medicine Hawk speaks wise words," Red Cloud said. "We wait for the words of Man Afraid."

Man Afraid raised his hand, acknowledging Red Cloud. "The washichun bluecoats are here, more will come. Now is the time for the power of the *Wakanpi* to war against the washichun. The words of Grey Bull are my words, but we must listen to the counsel of Medicine Hawk. Man Afraid says kill all the washichun at the log-walled den, and then Lakota can do the words of Grey Bull."

The council remained silent, their eyes staring at the ground while contemplating Joel's fate. Across the grounds, a mangy camp dog trotted toward Joel. He sniffed and licked Joel's hand. Lone Wolf pointed at the dog. "There is our answer. The dog knows the washichun. He is a dog."

All of the men, except Medicine Hawk, nodded their agreement, grunted, "Hau," and stood up. Red Cloud spoke. "He is a dog. *Wakan-Tanka* has spoken."

Lone Wolf taunted Joel, "*Wakan* Dog! *Wakan* Dog! Your name is *Wakan* Dog. Now you live with the dogs."

Medicine Hawk walked toward Joel, stopped beside his bed, leaned on a willow staff and shook his head. He spoke in clear English. "*Wakan-Tanka* spoke to the council. They did not hear. Their ears are closed. The council has decided that from this day your name will be *Wakan* Dog. The Lakota are very angry at the washichun, but *Wakan* Dog will find *Wakan-Tanka* in the lodge of Medicine Hawk."

Chapter 6

July and most of August had passed without any word from Carrington's expedition into the land of the Lakota. Joshua walked from the infirmary every day to Col. Maynadier's office, seeking any word about Joel. *Where is he? Had he gone on to the gold fields in Montana?* Always, there was no word, no couriers or messages from travelers returning from Fort Reno. Today, that changed. A young private whipped his sweating horse through the gate of Fort Laramie. Col. Maynadier, seated at his desk, opened the courier's pouch and read the dispatch from Col. Carrington:

15 August 1866

Colonel Henry Maynadier,

Commanding, Fort Laramie,

Dakota Territory

Please be informed, the 18th U. S. Infantry has raised the flag above the place I have selected for Fort Phil Kearny near the Bighorn Mountains on Piney Creek.

Our woodcutters are attacked daily by the Lakota, which requires close support from our troops.

The woodcutters' wagons, which were guarded by a detachment from Company G, were attacked near Crazy Woman Crossing on the Twentieth of July by Red Cloud and a sizeable force of Lakota warriors. I am pleased to report that minimal losses were encountered due to the prompt response of troops from this fort.

I regret to inform you of the loss of Sgt. Cabot T. Peck, Corporal Waylon Stith and Private Jeb Wiggins, all killed in separate actions near Clear Creek on the twentieth of July. Reverend Joel Leslie is missing and presumed dead due to the hostile actions surrounding his disappearance.

Please convey my sincere condolences to Major Leslie on the loss of his brother.

Henry B. Carrington

Colonel, 18th U.S. Infantry

Commanding, Mountain Dist.

Colonel Maynadier walked across the quadrangle toward the post infirmary to convey Carrington's dismal report to Joshua.

Joshua met him at the door. He knew from Maynadier's somber expression that the dispatch bore disturbing news. Joshua read the dispatch and handed it back to Maynadier. "I appreciate your bringing this to me, Colonel Maynadier."

"Yes, I just wish Colonel Carrington's dispatch had borne only a good report regarding Reverend Leslie. I'm sorry, Joshua."

"Thank you, sir."

At a loss for words, Maynadier nodded and walked away. Joshua opened his medicine cabinet, pulled out a bottle of brandy, poured a glassful, latched the infirmary door and slumped into his chair. *Why did we come to this wretched place?* he mused, gazing at his reflection in the glass door of his instrument cabinet. *God knows I did not want Joel to take such a risk. I tried to warn him. Now he's presumed dead just two months past thirty-three years.*

He sipped brandy and stared at the amber liquid in his glass. "What kind of God would allow this," he muttered. "The brutal slaying of a good man, a missionary... it cannot be... Joel must be alive."

Joshua downed all of the brandy while pondering what could be done. He felt anger toward Colonel Carrington for presuming that Joel was dead. His rage seethed, stoked by more brandy. He paced the infirmary floor, tossed down gulps of brandy, emptied the bottle and reached for another. Finally, emotion and alcohol overwhelmed him. He slumped into his chair and slammed the bottle of brandy into the fireplace. He wept, cursed Red Cloud and his warriors and made a vow through numbed lips. "I will find you, Joel. Presumed dead, hell, I'll presume no such thing."

Joshua staggered across the quadrangle determined to get a leave of absence from Maynadier. The hour was late, half-past eight in the evening. Colonel Maynadier had retired to his quarters where he was enjoying a cigar and a glass of bourbon.

Joshua slammed the door open. Maynadier jumped up. Angered by the intrusion, he called for his orderly, "Corporal Hart!"

Hart charged into the room. "Yes, sir."

Joshua stood unsteady, eyes blinking, staring at Maynadier. Maynadier nodded. "Major Leslie—come in."

"Aye, sir, I uh—will—uh—am. I am, sir."

"Please, Major, have a chair. I'd offer whiskey, but it had better be coffee."

"Aye, sir, whiskey I'm not needin'. It's a leave I'm wantin'."

"Corporal, get the major some coffee. Let's sit and talk."

Joshua slid his wobbling frame into a chair. "Aww... right."

Maynadier sat down, puffed on his cigar and gave Joshua some advice. "You're angry and drunk. You are in no condition to make any decisions tonight, wait until tomorrow. Heaven knows, I'd be drunker than you if I'd lost a brother."

"Lost, hell, what does that mean? If Joel is alive, I intend to find him."

"And if he isn't?"

"I'll kill 'im, the goddamn savage that murdered him."

Maynadier studied Joshua's eyes and saw the fires of determination and rage pushing reason from his mind. "Yes, I believe you would try."

"Try, hell... I will."

Corporal Hart offered Joshua a cup of steaming coffee. He shook his head, pushed the cup away and leaned toward Maynadier. "I intend to go in the mornin'. A leave of absence, I'm askin', sir."

"Go back to your quarters, sleep off the booze and we'll talk in the morning. Corporal Hart, help Major Leslie to his quarters."

Booze-stoked anger raised Joshua out of his chair. He stumbled and fell headlong, sprawling onto the floor. "God... damn... it... Colonel... I'm ridin' in the mornin' at first light," he said, trying to control his sluggard tongue.

Maynadier and Hart grabbed Joshua's arms, pulled him

to his feet and walked him to his quarters. "Turn me loose you sonsabitches," he yelled and collapsed on his cot.

Maynadier stood looking down at his disheveled surgeon. "I understand your rage, but I cannot grant you a leave. You are the only surgeon between here and Fort Kearney."

Early the following morning, Joshua awakened. His head throbbed, lips stuck together and eyes blinked back pain. He got up and staggered to the window. It was still dark. He rubbed his face, trying to clear his befuddled mind, and then poured water into a basin. "I got to go find Joel."

He splashed water on his face and gazed at his reflection in the mirror. "You're a sad sight. If you're goin', better get out of here afore daylight."

Joshua opened his footlocker and pulled out his bedroll, a pair of heavy mittens, brass binoculars, an Army Colt revolver and a parka. He stuffed a map of the Bighorns Bridger had given him into his saddlebags. He ran his fingers over the parka. Its rough woolen fabric reminded him of his mother, now past seventy, back home in Turriff, Scotland. She had made one for each of her twin sons and had given them to Joel and Joshua the morning they left home. He pushed the memory from his mind and peered through the window, but could see nobody in the dark quadrangle.

After filling a canteen with water, he picked up his gear, slipped out the infirmary door and walked toward the stables, keeping in the shadows until he reached the stable door. He turned the latch and grimaced as the cold metal hinges squeaked. He held his breath, stood still and listened. "Ah, all is quiet," he whispered.

The odor of horse sweat and leather hung heavy in the tack room where Joshua sorted through saddles, blankets and bridles. He picked up Colonel Maynadier's McClellan saddle, blue saddle blanket and carbine scabbard containing a new model 66 Winchester.

He avoided making any noise while saddling Maynadier's big gray gelding. After securing his bedroll and saddlebags, Joshua jumped on the gray and urged him out of the stables across the quadrangle. "Halt, who goes there?" a sentry at the gate called.

"Colonel Maynadier. Open the gate."

The young sentry eyed the gray and the blue saddle blanket with gold trim, but could not see Joshua's face clearly beneath the brim of his kepi. "That's the colonel's horse, but you don't sound like the colonel."

Joshua drew his Colt and aimed it at the sentry. "Drop that carbine and open the gate."

The sentry stared up the muzzle of the Colt, his eyes wide and white in the moonlight. "Yes, sir," he said, letting his carbine slide out of his hands.

"Good, open it now."

The sentry yelled, "Corporal of the Guard," as Joshua spurred the gray through the open gate.

The gray's pounding hooves, and the wind racing past Joshua's ears, blotted out the clamor arising inside Fort Laramie. He reined the gray away from the Laramie River and urged him westward along the North Platte River. He avoided the Oregon Trail and frequently glanced over his shoulder. If captured, he'd most likely be shot, a deserter during wartime. Red Cloud had declared war if and when the Army crossed the Crazy Woman. The Army had, and Red Cloud had been true to the threats he made at the Taylor Commission hearing.

Like Joshua's anger, the remaining days of August were hot as a cauldron. His eyes burned from the shadow beneath the brim of his kepi, searching, always on the move. They continuously scanned the panorama of dry coulees, scrub pines, greasy sage and rocky knolls covered with tall bluestem grass. He yearned to see copper-skinned savages with eagle feathers fluttering in their hair and war lances held high as they charged from cowardly ambushes.

He sat his gray gelding atop a ridge and peered through binoculars toward the southeastern horizon. The winding course of the Bozeman Trail over which he had just traveled was empty. There were no pursuing horsemen wearing blue army tunics— only the high plains, empty except for tall, bluestem grass swaying in the wind. He felt relieved. At least, today, he would not be arrested for desertion and returned to Fort Laramie for court-martial.

He took a deep breath and savored the arid mountain air laced with scents of spruce and juniper, and listened to clacking blue grouse perched in pines along the ridge. He scanned the steep incline beneath the ridge as it fell away toward a valley in whose bosom nestled a lake, its blue waters reflecting the cobalt sky, crisp and cloudless on this August day.

He turned the binoculars toward the northwest. The mountains and high plateaus spread before him bore no sign of Indian ponies straddled by painted warriors. He seemed to be alone. No other human, either Lakota or white soldier, could be seen. Yet, he knew it was not true. Red Cloud's vow to kill any and every white man entering their land had been as clear as the waters of Lake de Smet languishing in the valley below.

As he reined the gray along the boulder-strewn ridge above Lake de Smet, Joshua pulled Bridger's map from his saddlebags. He studied it and marveled at the stamina of Maynadier's horse, having crossed most of Wyoming in seven grueling days. He patted the gray's withers. "You're some horse, but now we've got to cross over these mountains."

He glanced to the southwest and up at Cloud Peak towering above the other Bighorn pinnacles. "Got to stay away from Carrington's fort."

He studied the map again and found where Bridger had written *Pass* below an X he'd penciled above the headwaters of Wolf Creek. "That's were we're headin'," he said, stuffing the map back into his saddlebags.

He pulled his heels across the gray's flanks and reined him to the northwest, up the rugged Bighorn inclines. He caressed the stock of Maynadier's Winchester. "A dozen of those red bastards I'll send to Hades if their *Wakan-Tanka* dare send them to me."

Chapter 7

Gusts of cold wind buffeted the tipis, swept dust high into the sky and swirled ashes from fire pits. Camp dogs howled, barked and whined. Joel stood up and gazed skyward, but his damaged sight was unable to perceive the black clouds towering above the Lakota encampment. However, he could see lightening flashes, each bolt an axe of fire splitting trees into smoldering splinters. Thunder, like dueling artillery, echoed up and down the mountains. He reached for a buffalo hide drying on a rack Otter Woman had made from green willow limbs. His fingers clawed for the hide but could not reach it. He strained against the rope tied about his neck that tethered him to Yellow Elk's medicine pole. The rope sank into his neck. He pushed against the pain and made a lunge for the hide. His hand gripped the hide and pulled it from the rack as he fell backward. Large rain drops pelted his naked back as he crawled beneath the hide.

He pulled the hide about his naked body. The storm became a raging torrent of frigid rain and wind that buffeted his shelter. His fingers clawed at the strangling rope. The noose loosened, but the memory of Lone Wolf's words kept him from untying it. *This Lone Wolf will do, my tomahawk will cut off Wakan Dog's fingers if he unties his leash.*

Joel knew Lone Wolf's threats were not empty ones. The memory of the night after the council had met was vivid. The taunting words, *"Wakan* Dog, *Wakan* Dog," were spat at him all evening by Lone Wolf and Grey Bull. Once again, he recalled hands awakening him in the night. They grabbed his arms, wrestled him helpless, stripped off his clothing and tied his wrists and ankles with strips of raw elkhide. Lone Wolf held a knife over Joel's face, its steel blade glowing red like iron pulled from a blacksmith's forge. Joel cringed and clinched his eyelids as the red-hot steel descended. The searing heat made him squirm and fight against the massive hands of Grey Bull. A lance of hot pain bored into his head as Lone Wolf branded each eye. Joel heard himself screaming, smelled burning flesh and then collapsed. In a senseless state, he was unaware of the knife as it excised the tip of his tongue. His attackers left him lying on the ground, naked, moaning, his wrists and ankles bound.

During that night, Joel heard moccasins shuffling toward him and the familiar sound of Medicine Hawk's voice. *"Wakan Dog, Medicine Hawk speaks for Wakan-Tanka. His anger rolls across the Snowy Mountains like great waves of thunder. The Lakota have done a bad thing this night."*

Joel felt the thongs binding his wrists and ankles loosen. The knife of Medicine Hawk had freed them. Before he walked back to his tipi, Medicine Hawk stroked Joel's forehead and spoke once more. "You must not try to escape this night. Grey Bull is a raging Lakota. He does not listen to *Wakan-Tanka.* He sits in front of his tipi waiting to make you walk in the hereafter."

The torrential rain stopped. The lightning and thunder no longer pummeled the mountain because the storm's fury had blown itself to the east over the Powder Basin. Joel lifted the buffalo hide and listened to Yellow Elk chanting his thanks to *Wakan-Tanka.*

Several days after the storm had passed, Otter Woman pushed a bone needle through tanned dog skin and tied the final knot in thread made from buffalo sinew. The shirt and leggings lying on her lap were finished. She held up the shirt, ran her fingers along the stitched seams, and nodded approval of her handiwork. She stepped from her tipi and tossed the garments at Joel. "Otter Woman make shirt, leggings for *Wakan* Dog."

Joel was naked except for a loincloth Otter Woman had fashioned from scraps of deerskin. His black hair fell long and matted down the sides of his face. He reeked from the stench of rancid bear grease Medicine Hawk had wiped over his sun-blistered skin. His filthy hands with grime embedded beneath fingernails, reached out and tried to find the garments. He strained to see but perceived only distorted images. He swiped his fingers across swollen eyelids encrusted with scabs. Then he reached farther, swept the ground with his fingers and found the shirt. He buried his face in the mangy hair, not minding that it still bore the stench of its donors.

After he dressed himself, Joel heard Otter Woman's taunting laughter, but could not see the smirk curling her lips, her brown eyes popping, her tawny features dancing. *"Wakan* Dog come with Otter Woman," she said, yanking on the rope of braided sinew tied around his neck.

Joel tried to speak, but his tongue was too swollen. He stood up to follow Otter Women and felt the sting of her switch across his back. *"Wakan* Dog walk like dog, not washichun man."

Joel dropped to his knees. The rope tugged at his neck. Like a dog he was supposed to be, he crawled after Otter Woman.

"Wakan Dog wait here," she said, tying the rope to the 'coup' pole in front of Lone Wolf's tipi.

Joel curled up, felt the warm rays of the sun and pondered what new tortures Lone Wolf intended. He was beginning to understand that the Lakota were convinced he was now a dog. A dog in human form somehow brought about by the power of their God.

Escape was impossible, because the Lakota were always vigilant in keeping him prisoner. Otter Woman kept him tied to the medicine pole in front of the tipi she shared with Yellow Elk. There, he felt the burning sun during the day and the warmth of camp dogs at night. Grey Bull's intent was clear. He intended to kill Joel, but most of the Lakota only wished to isolate him from the eyes and ears of his God. The acrid aroma of fear, which had been in his nostrils since his capture, united with revenge to become rage, rabid and consuming against the Lakota.

"Wakan Dog, come with Lone Wolf," Lone Wolf said and untied the rope from his 'coup' pole.

Joel crawled after Lone Wolf. The rope tightened around his neck. He couldn't keep pace. Gasping for air, he grasped the leash, yanked it away from Lone Wolf and clawed at the strangling noose. The foot of Lone Wolf slammed into his ribs, sending him tumbling down the hillside, over the river embankment and into the icy Tongue.

Joel sank. The frigid water shocked his muscles into

knots of agony. His arms and legs thrashed against the torrent as panic, stifling and consuming, gripped him. His head felt as if it would burst and his lungs screamed for a breath of air. In a vision, he saw himself in the river Deveron near his home in the north of Scotland when he was a lad fighting to keep from drowning. He felt the hand of his cousin, Colin Condiff, grasp his hair and swim toward the shore with him in tow.

The vision faded as another hand grasped his shirt and pulled him upward out of the darkness. He was unable to see the copper legs thrashing against the current, carrying him toward the surface. When his head broke from the water, he gulped air, warm and sweet, and heard Lone Wolf say, "*Wakan* Dog not walk in hereafter. Lone Wolf keep power of *Wakanpi* for Lakota."

The following day, Joel had recovered from his near drowning in the Tongue. Lone Wolf led him across a meadow where two days earlier a male grizzly bear had killed Lone Wolf's pinto, dragged the carcass into an aspen grove and buried it. "Humpback bear come back when four-leg sky dog stinks," Lone Wolf said. "Humpback like rotten meat."

Lone Wolf stopped beside a mound of earth, the place where the grizzly had buried the pony. He drove a sharpened willow shaft into the ground and tied Joel's tether to it. "*Wakan* Dog, when humpback comes, you bark big."

Joel was alone, unable to see beyond the trunk of an aspen tree standing beside him. *What sound does a grizzly make?* he wondered. He had never seen one, only a painting of one hanging in a Boston gallery. He cringed and slid down the aspen trunk as he recalled how the artist had depicted the huge animal. It was a towering beast, reared up, teeth bared with lips curled in a ferocious snarl. The bear's paws with long, black stiletto claws were stretched out, ready to slash the life from its victim. *Ursus horribilis*—the most ferocious carnivore in North America was engraved on a brass plate beneath the painting.

He crouched beside the tree trunk, listening for growls, roars, grunts and any sounds he could imagine that a grizzly might make. He heard the shriek of an eagle far above the Lakota encampment. In the grassy glen below, an anxious mare whinnied. Her venturesome foal squealed, snorted and squealed again. Although the Lakota encampment was a quarter of a mile away, the chatter of squaws preparing food seemed very near. Above, the singing wind transformed aspen leaves into an orchestra of woodwinds. The mountain air was light and warm with sounds, crisp as the crack of a whip. However, the day's tranquillity did not cause Joel to be less troubled. He waited, praying the grizzly would not return.

Like a sluggard snail, the day passed until twilight crept over the Bighorns. Joel shivered, chilled by fear and the darkness as evening ushered in the night.

"What's that?" Joel lisped. A cracking sound, maybe a dead tree limb being snapped, had come from somewhere beyond the aspen grove. He stood up, his crippled eyes peering into the darkness. His nostrils flared searching the air for the stench of a grizzly. Smoke rising from the squaws cooking fires and the musty dog skins he was wearing were all he could smell.

Joel's fingers clawed at the knot Otter Woman had tied into the leash about his neck. The rope of raw sinew had become hardened into a tenacious braid. The knot would not yield, having welded itself into the rope. His hands followed the leash and found the willow shaft. His fingers trembled and searched for the knot tied by Lone Wolf. He found it and again could not untie the hitches of sinew. He pulled and yanked and kicked at the shaft, but it remained steadfast. The sound of a limb breaking, now closer, stilled Joel. He crouched, unmoving, his hands grasping the slippery willow. He listened but only heard his own breathing, measured and tremulous.

His muscles, coiled from fear, suddenly sprang into action. He lunged upward. The earth released its hold on the willow shaft. He crouched down and thrust the sharpened shaft toward the sounds of approaching danger. The willow shaft that had made him Lone Wolf's prisoner had become a crude lance, his only weapon against the bear.

Joel stood poised for action. The sounds were now distinct, unquestionably ones being made by a very large beast. Dry pine needles crackled, twigs snapped, conifer limbs swished, yielding to the passing carnivore. He heard a low-pitched grunt with each breath exhaled by the bear. It could not be far away. Joel began to back away from the sounds. His mouth opened and tried to bark like the watchdog he was supposed to be. His crippled tongue, dry, sticking to the roof of his mouth struggled to cry out—but no sounds came.

Joel's hands grasping the willow shaft held it ready. He heard the bear, large even for a grizzly, ambling through the grove of aspen. The sounds stopped for a moment as it held its head high and flared its nostrils searching for the rotten pony. It wagged its great head. Saliva sprayed from its flapping lips. It arched its back and growled, deep-throated, resonating within its huge chest cavity.

Joel cringed, crouched lower and quickened his backward pace. Suddenly, without being able to see, he was aware of the bear as it reared up. It balanced itself on its hind legs, slashing the air with vicious swipes of its forepaws. The bear's chest heaved, emitting a roar that echoed over the mountain.

The swishing of an arrow zipped past Joel. The bear roared. Another swish was followed by a shrill, trumpeting roar. The bear charged, galloping like a horse. Joel fell beneath the beast. Its forelegs embraced him and jammed his face into its bristled chest. He struggled to free himself but could not. The bear snarled, its fetid breath blowing hot against Joel's neck. And then the bear's full weight pressed down upon Joel as its forelegs relaxed. The grizzly was dead.

"*Wakan* Dog! *Wakan* Dog!" Medicine Hawk cried, trying to push the bear off Joel.

Joel finally slid from beneath the grizzly only to meet terror once again. "The pitted-face sickness of the washichun*s* killed my wife and son many winters ago," Medicine Hawk said, pressing the cold blade of his knife against Joel's neck.

Medicine Hawk's riveting words terrified Joel. Had the old medicine man saved him from the bear so he could avenge his family for the white man's sickness? The blade of Medicine Hawk's knife answered the question as it slipped beneath the sinewy band tied around Joel's neck. "My days with the Lakota will be no more," Medicine Hawk said, slashing the noose free with his knife. "Now, we must hurry. My eyes will lead you over the mountain."

* * *

The Tongue River, the Lakota encampment and the dead grizzly were far behind Joel and Medicine Hawk as dawn drained color from the eastern sky. All night they had climbed along an ancient trail carved into the mountain by migrating herds of elk. The morning found them above the timberline where conifers and aspen had never grown. The mountain was barren, its naked slopes harsh and steep. The trail covered with jagged stones switched back and forth around granite boulders. As they struggled toward the pass between two peaks, their lungs ached, the air now thin as a spider's web.

The altitude and arduous trail continued to devour their stamina as they ascended the mountain. Medicine Hawk finally had to stop climbing. His aged legs were shaking and his chest was heaving like a spent racehorse. He untied a buffalo-bladder canteen from his belt and handed it to Joel. "Drink," he said, "then we must keep climbing. Grey Bull and Lone Wolf can't be far behind us."

Chapter 8

Near Porcupine Creek, high in the Bighorns, Jim Bridger sat astride an army mule he called Mule. He had spent nearly a week scouting the high country. His orders from Colonel Carrington were to seek out the Lakota encampment. Once found, he was to determine whether they were holding a white man hostage.

Warrior Chief Dull Knife and three other Cheyenne men had parleyed with Colonel Carrington the previous week at Fort Phil Kearny. The colonel had allowed them to enter the fort hoping to impress the Cheyenne with the fort's defenses and firepower. Dull Knife had said that the Lakota had a white man in their encampment, but he didn't know whether the white man was a captive or a squaw man living freely with the Lakota. No, he hadn't seen the man himself when Carrington asked how he knew about the white man. Carrington assumed the information to be suspect, a rumor perhaps, but one that needed investigation.

Bridger preferred mules over horses for traveling over mountainous country. Like most mules, Mule was surefooted, hardheaded and prone to kick at the most unexpected moments; however, Mule was unique for a mule. Mule's sense of smell was keen as a trail hound. Today, she proved this once more when she caught the scent of an Indian pony, perked her long ears, swished her tail and emitted several snorts through flared nostrils. Bridger's eyes scanned the terrain and saw an Indian mounted on a pinto among the pines on a ridge overlooking the creek. "I god Mule, you got a keen snout. I see him. He's likely one of Red Cloud's Injuns. If he is, maybe he'll parley instead of tryin' t'lift my hair."

Bridger reined Mule away from the creek, headed her through a thick growth of willows, pulled his side-hammer Sharps from its scabbard and urged Mule toward rocky outcroppings jutting from the mountain. He dismounted, leaned his Sharps against a boulder, gathered dry wood and then placed stones in a circle for a firepit. After starting a fire with flint and steel, he poured water from his canteen and ground-up coffee beans into a battered tin cup. "Got to make that Injun think I ain't seen 'im, Mule. Reckon curious will bring his red hide closer."

Bridger set the cup on a rock in the middle of the firepit and waited for the coffee to brew, and the Indian. He pulled his tobacco pouch from his 'possibles bag' and stuffed a generous chaw into his mouth. "Too bad mules don't like 'bacca, I'd give you some."

Bridger spat tobacco-laced spittle into the firepit and listened to crows cawing in the distance. He recalled the winter he had lived with the Lakota during the thirties while trapping beaver. They had accepted him and his partner, Jeremiah Hart, into their winter encampment because of the promises made to them. He and Hart would provide all of the steel traps they needed. They and the Lakota would pool their pelts to be traded the following spring at the fur trader's rendezvous on the Green River. Bridger and Hart would share the profits fifty-fifty with the Lakota. They and Lakota war chief, Man Of Arrows, smoked the sacred pipe to seal the deal. However, the deal soured when Man Of Arrows caught his wife, Running Waters, in Hart's tipi. Hart barely escaped with his hair when he wisely jumped on his horse and headed south at a gallop. Bridger stayed the winter and became a close friend of Man Of Arrows.

A half-hour passed, still the Indian did not come. "What's keepin' that Injun? Reckon I need more smoke."

He stripped green pine needles from a limb and tossed them into the fire. Sooty gray smoke billowed skyward through the pines. Mule raised her head, flared her nostrils and snorted. Bridger grabbed his Sharps, crouched down, cocked the side-hammer and waited. Mule reared back her head and began to bray, over and over, sending her convulsive trumpeting across the mountain. Bridger rubbed the back of his neck. "I god Mule, you tryin' to booger that Injun? Hell, he ain't scared o' you."

Bridger cupped his hands about his mouth and yelled, "This child ain't wantin' t'fight. Let's pow-wow."

As Bridger waited, the reedy wail of a harmonica caused

Mule to perk her ears. "Sounds like ol' LaRoche is tootin' his harp again," Bridger said, cupping a hand behind his ear.

While listening to the melody, he was barely able to make it out, but recognized it to be one that he had heard Lakota medicine man Medicine Hawk play on a Lakota flute. "Ol' LaRoche must be tryin' to warn me about that Injun," Bridger muttered to himself, then recalled the day south of Fort Reno when he and Joel heard a harp. That had been a warning by LaRoche, a half-breed scout for Red Cloud. He had crawled close to Bridger's tent outside Fort Reno and whispered that Red Cloud was getting ready to attack whenever they crossed the Crazy Woman.

LeRoche's harmonica had warned Bridger again. He listened but didn't hear the moccasins of the Indian creeping around a boulder behind him. With stealth, the Indian stepped toward Bridger and raised his stone-headed war club high above his head. Swift as an impala, he leapt through the air. Bridger spun around just as the copper-skinned warrior swung his war club. Bridger ducked. He felt the wind as it swished by his head. He embraced the charging warrior with the power of a grizzly. The Indian jammed the club's handle against Bridger's throat and pushed with both hands trying to crush Bridger's larynx. Bridger's knee accelerated upward. Again and again, it slammed into the Indian's crotch. "A-a-a-e-e-e," the Indian screamed.

Muscles and sinew coiled, heaved and uncoiled as the two wrestled. They fell into the firepit, sparks billowed and embers flew. They rolled out of the firepit. Bridger's embrace squeezed tighter. For the first time, he looked into the Indian's face. Brown eyes glared back at him. They rolled on the ground, face to face, staring into each other's eyes. "Man O' Arries!" Bridger yelled, loosening his vice-like embrace.

The Indian pulled away his war club. "Blanket Bridger!"

They lay on the ground, both spent from their struggle. Bridger laughed, then said, "I god, Man O' Arries, it's been several winters since these sore eyes laid on you."

"Many moons, Blanket Bridger," Man Of Arrows said,

got up and swept smoking embers from his leggings. "Why do you ride the long-ear-four-legs across the Snowy Mountains?"

Bridger stood up and signed while speaking. "This child wants to pow-wow with the Lakota."

"Blanket Bridger is a fool to ride into Lakota land. We are at war."

"We ain't at war, you and me, we're friends. Many times we have smoked the pipe together."

Man Of Arrows nodded and squatted next to the firepit. "We smoke again," he said, pulling his sacred pipe from a deerskin pouch. He filled the bowl with kinnikinnick, lit it with a brand from the fire and handed the pipe to Bridger. "Blanket Bridger, after we blow smoke to the Medicine Fathers, we will pow-wow."

After they smoked, Bridger said, "Did you hear that harp a wailin'?"

"I heard the harp singing the *Midnight Song Of All The Birds*."

"Yeah, I remember Medicine Hawk playin' that on his flute."

"It is sacred for healing the sick."

"Why the hell is somebody playin' that out here?"

Man Of Arrows knocked the dollop of ashes from his pipe and slipped it back into his deerskin pouch. He remained silent, gazing at the firepit.

"Y'ain't got an answer?" Bridger said and spat out his cud of tobacco.

Man Of Arrows turned to face Bridger. "Bird Face, the one you call LaRoche that scouts for Red Cloud. He played the harp to warn you about me. Some day I will kill that weasel."

"Chief Dull Knife says there's a white man livin' in the camp of Red Cloud. That true?"

"The washichun walks on the other side of the Snowy Mountains."

"Gone under?"

"No, Medicine Hawk leads the washichun without eyes away from Grey Bull."

"Who is this washichun?"

"Lone Wolf captured him. A *wakan* man."

Bridger signed while speaking. "Did he wear a white collar?"

"Like the wings of the white goose."

"Why does he have no eyes?"

"Grey Bull and Lone Wolf burned his eyes and cut his tongue. He unable to tell his Great Spirit how Lakota plan war."

Bridger, nodding, pulled his pouch of tobacco from his 'possibles bag' and offered it to Man Of Arrows. "Have some 'bacca and give some to Medicine Hawk."

Man Of Arrows took the pouch and shook his head. "No more will Medicine Hawk walk among the Lakota. He returns to his father's people, the Crow."

Bridger pondered Joel's fate after Man Of Arrows reined his pinto toward home. Colonel Carrington's orders had been explicit. Find the Lakota, determine who their white captive was and return to the fort. He had already been gone for nearly a week. Captain Kinney and two companies of infantry had been ordered by Carrington to proceed into Montana whenever Bridger returned. Bridger had selected a site near the Bighorn River for the third fort on the Bozeman Trail. It was early September—winter not far away. There was no choice, going after Joel would have to wait.

The next morning, Bridger headed Mule toward Fort Phil Kearny. He rode southeast, having been cautioned by Man Of Arrows to avoid the Tongue River and the Lakota encampment. Mule carried him around Shell Canyon, over Granite Pass and along the eastern slopes of the Bighorns. After two days of arduous travel, he reined Mule around thickets of willows growing along Wolf Creek.

The shade of evening was beginning to settle over the Bighorn's eastern slopes. Mule suddenly stopped and refused to move. Bridger pulled his heels into her flanks and slapped the reins against her neck, yet she continued to balk. He peered down the winding course of Wolf Creek and saw a slender column of smoke slithering above a grove of aspen. "I god Mule, must be Injun smoke. Army wouldn't be up here."

Bridger dismounted and tugged on Mule's reins. She

followed, reluctant, her muscles rippling with rebellion. He thumbed back the hammer of his Sharps and crept toward the aspen grove. His senses, honed by many years in the mountains, perceived the aroma of a blue grouse roasting. His mouth watered as the familiar scent tweaked his appetite. As he neared the scattering of aspen, he caught sight of a big gray, unsaddled, his forelegs hobbled. The horse was tall, well over fifteen-hands. He was grazing on a patch of grass, unaware that Bridger and Mule were near.

Bridger crouched down and looked the campsite over. Draped over the limb of a pine, he saw a blue saddle blanket, its edge bound with gold trim. "I god, Mule, that camper is Army, a paper-collared officer, unless that's a stole' hoss," Bridger whispered. He tied Mule to a sapling. "Stay here. Keep your bawlin' in your gut."

Bridger crept through the aspen grove. The gray stopped browsing, stared at Bridger, tossed his head about and neighed. Mule answered. Her harsh seesawing bray broadcast her nearness.

"Hello, the camp!" Bridger yelled, his presence revealed by the gray and Mule alike. He waited but heard no response. Again, he yelled, "This child is Bridger. Who you be?"

Joshua crouched in a thicket of willows well away from his campsite. When he heard Mule walking along the creek, he had grabbed his stolen Winchester, ran to the willows and hid. "Jim Bridger," he muttered, "what is he doing up here?"

"You in the camp," Bridger yelled, "this child ain't movin' till he lays eyes on your carcass."

Joshua thumbed the rifle's hammer and aimed it at Bridger about a hundred yards away. "I see you, Mister Bridger," he called. "This rifle is aimed between your eyes. Now where are the troops ye're guidin'?"

Bridger recognized the voice and tongue-rolling Scottish accent of Joshua. He hadn't known about Joshua's desertion until the morning Colonel Carrington had sent him to find the white man living with the Lakota. He and Lt. Templeton had just returned from several weeks scouting for a site to build the third fort. Bridger wondered what was bothering Carrington. He seemed disturbed and preoccupied while Bridger and Templeton made their report. And then understood as Carrington told them about Joshua taking Maynadier's horse, saddle and rifle and deserting Fort Laramie. If captured, Colonel Maynadier had ordered Joshua to be arrested and returned to Fort Laramie for trial.

Bridger had no desire to arrest Joshua and understood why he was compelled to find his brother no matter the cost. "Ain't guidin' nobody, Major Leslie," he said. "This child knows about your desertion, but that ain't no never mind. You're safe with me."

"Then ye are alone, Mister Bridger?"

"Just this child and ol' Mule."

Reluctant to trust Bridger, Joshua continued to aim the Winchester at the crouching mountain man. He pondered what to do. *Can I trust an Army scout bound by oath to follow orders?* A choice had to be made: squeeze the trigger or trust Bridger. The barrel began to waver as he gripped the fore-stock tighter and tried to steady his aim. He felt his heart quickening its pace, surging from the anxiety that had parched his tongue. He took a deep breath and slowly exhaled. Suddenly, he felt the rifle-butt slam against his shoulder. The barrel leaped upward, belching fire, smoke and a roar reverberating across the mountains. Bridger toppled over and lay still.

"My god, I've killed him," Joshua said, as he dropped the rifle, crawled from the thicket and walked toward Bridger. He stared at the quiet form clad in buckskin. He knelt down and reached for Bridger's wrist. Quick as a cobra, the mound of buckskin uncoiled, springing upward. Joshua fell backward. The rippling muscles of Bridger's arms embraced him. They writhed on the ground as Bridger's bear hug crushed the air from Joshua's lungs. Joshua strained to get free from the terrible suffocation coming over him. He opened his mouth and gasped for air but found none. He tried to strike out with his fists but could not. His arms were pinned tightly against his chest. He tried to scream but none came. His lungs were empty. He felt himself sinking into darkness.

Joshua awakened. Cold water was splattering across his

face. He blinked, sputtered and shook his head. Harsh strident sounds emitted from his throat as he struggled to breathe. Gradually, each breath came with less effort. "Well now, Doc," Bridger said, "reckon this child ain't kilt you, but I still might."

"I thought I'd killed ye."

"Naw, missed me by a foot. Playin' dead like ol' 'possum has saved this child's gizzard more'n once."

"I didn't intend—somehow the rifle went off."

"Gall will do that to a feller. Makes y'mean as a pack o' wolves."

"Gall?" Joshua said and struggled to sit up. "I don't understand."

"Ever taste gall?"

"Nay."

"Goddamned bitter."

"Aye—I see."

"Doubt if you do. Hate turns your innards into pure gall. It'll eat you up."

Joshua stood up, walked away several steps and looked down at his trembling hands. "I can't keep from hatin' the red heathens that killed Joel."

"Ain't no need. A Lakota war chief told me they didn't kill him. He clean got away."

Joshua turned around, his eyes wide and voice quivering. "Joel is alive? Escaped you say?"

"Yep," Bridger said, waving his hand toward the northwest. "Ol' Med'cine Hawk is takin' him over the mountains, away from the Lakota."

"Medicine Hawk?"

"Lakota med'cine man. Figger he's headed for Crow country seein' how he's half Crow Injun."

"Where is Crow country?"

"North o' the Yellowstone in Montana country."

"I find it difficult to believe one of Red Cloud's savages would help Joel."

"Known ol' Med'cine Hawk a lot o' winters. Ain't no savage."

"They are all savages, Mister Bridger."

"Just like white folks, some are, most ain't. I wintered with 'em back in twenty-nine trappin' beaver."

"Ye lived with those red heathens?"

"Well, they ain't heatherns. They got high principles."

Joshua shook his head in disbelief and motioned toward his camp. "Come, Mister Bridger, I have a fat grouse on a spit. While we eat I'd like for ya' to explain that to me."

Joshua carved the grouse as Bridger told his story about Medicine Hawk. "I spent lot o' evenin's in the lodge of Med'cine Hawk. We talked on a lot o' things, about how Injuns live and their ideas about religion and such."

"That is appallin'. Who do they worship? The devil?"

Bridger peeled bark from a fallen aspen and handed it to Joshua. "Just put my share o' that bird on this. They don't believe in no devil, 'cept maybe white Lucifers takin' over their land."

As they sat beside the campfire, Bridger finished telling Joshua who Medicine Hawk was; how he was born to Little Bird, a Lakota maiden captured by Crow Dancer during a Crow raid on the Oglala Lakota. She lived in the Crow encampment in the Wind River Mountains as the wife of Crow Dancer. Six years after the birth of Medicine Hawk, Crow Dancer was killed fighting the Piegan in Montana. Medicine Hawk's grandfather was Man Of Absarokee, a Crow medicine man and chief of the Sun Dance religion. Following Crow Dancer's death, Man Of Absarokee made Medicine Hawk heir to his sacred medicine bundle. In a secret rite, Medicine Hawk was dedicated to a life of being a medicine man.

Little Bird fell into deep depression after the death of Crow Dancer. She pleaded with Man Of Absarokee to allow her and Medicine Hawk to return to her home with the Lakota. After spending much time in prayer, many hours in the sweat lodge and days of fasting, Man Of Absarokee agreed to Little Bird's request. But only if the Lakota Sun Dance chief would honor Medicine Hawk's dedication to the Maker Of All Things Above, who the Crow call *Acba-dadea* and the Lakota call *Wakan-Tanka*.

Joshua pondered what Bridger had told him. Medicine

Hawk seemed like a decent fellow. Maybe he was not a savage, but the challenge remained unchanged. "I will leave at dawn," he said.

Bridger hesitated, spat on the ground and stood up. "Reckon afore we sleep, I need to tell you somethin' else."

Joshua's face fell somber, his eyes questioning. "What is that?"

"The Lakota hurt Joel."

"Hurt?"

"Cut his tongue… and… blinded 'im."

Joshua's face became livid. His fists sprang upward, defiant. "An eye for an eye, Mister Bridger—a tongue for a tongue."

Chapter 9

Joel sensed a change in the air. The day seemed intense and full of life. He listened. Cool northwesterly breezes whispered through the pine, fir and juniper. He lifted his face and felt the warm rays of the afternoon sun filtering through the trees. His sightless eyes could not see the cirrus clouds high above; those feathery wisps of ice crystals left in the wake of a lofty jet stream. But he could sense the changing season. The torpid days of summer had lapsed into shorter, more temperate ones. September, the Moon of Drying Grass, was settling over the high country.

Medicine Hawk and Joel struggled up an ancient trail, ascending ever higher toward the northwest. Before nightfall, they hoped to reach the Medicine Wheel, a great circle of rocks with cairns of stone at the base of each spoke. The ancient place of worship was on a high ridge above the headwaters of Porcupine Creek. Once there, Medicine Hawk was certain *Wakan-Tanka* would protect them from Lone Wolf and Grey Bull.

The trail was eroded and covered with loose stones that pummeled Joel's feet through the moccasins Otter Woman had fashioned from dog skins. Now worn smooth, their soles were slippery, often causing him to stumble. He gripped Medicine Hawk's elbow a bit tighter to keep from falling.

"What is the Medicine Wheel?" Joel asked.

"It is a sacred place where the Ancient Ones first smoked the pipe and prayed to *Wakan-Tanka* here in the Snowy Mountains."

"The Ancient Ones?"

"The grandfathers and grandmothers came out of our Mother-The-Earth many winters before the Medicine Fathers gave each tribe its name." Medicine Hawk paused, pointing a slender finger toward the craggy horizon to the northwest. "Your eyes cannot see. Not even the eagle can see the place. Beyond these mountains, beyond the land of the great white bear is where the Ancient Ones first walked. The Medicine Fathers showed them the path for their feet. It took many, many winters for them to come here."

Joel sensed the similarity of Medicine Hawk's story to man's beginnings in the Garden of Eden. "What did they look like? Were they red people like the Lakota?"

"Their skin was like the red cliffs, their hair like the raven, their eyes like our brother the buffalo. They stood tall, walked straight paths and were fed and clothed by the Medicine Fathers. Some day I will tell you more. Now we hurry on."

"Aye, I pray God will keep us safe."

Medicine Hawk frowned and wiped his fingers across Joel's eyes. "Your God does not hear, does not know that Lone Wolf and Grey Bull take away your sight. He is not here. He lives with the washichun, not here, not in the land of the Ancient Ones."

They continued their trek up the incline toward the Medicine Wheel. Medicine Hawk tried to hide his pain, tremulous legs and growing breathlessness. Advanced age and fatigue were taking their toll. More pauses were needed to rest. Joel could not see the grimacing twitches distorting the old Indian's face. He only heard labored breathing and felt quivering sinews in Medicine Hawk's arm. "Is it night yet?" Joel asked.

"It is near. We must find water."

"The bag is empty?"

"Empty, drained by our thirst."

"Is there any water up here?"

"Near the Medicine Wheel, there is a spring."

Joel fell silent as they continued to climb the rocky trail. The ancient medicine man walking beside him was an enigma, a perplexing mystery. He pondered the riddle. *Why was this Oglala Lakota sacrificing his home, all his possessions and his life as the Oglala Sun Dance chief to rescue him? He didn't have many years left in his life. Why didn't he just turn away and leave Joel's fate in the hands of Lone Wolf and Grey Bull?* The answers had to come from Medicine Hawk.

"Why are ye helping me?" Joel asked. "I'm just a dog in

the eyes of your people."

Medicine Hawk blinked, looked at Joel and searched the opaque corneas peering beneath scarred lids. "Do you not understand? Have the eyes of your spirit been blinded, also? Why do you ask such a question?"

"I must know."

"The Lakota have made you blind."

"Aye, but why are you helping me?"

"I am a medicine man, a Sun Dance chief."

"I know that, but why are you doing this?"

"You are a *wakan* man. Why do you not understand?"

"I don't know."

"*Wakan-Tanka* will give you the answer."

"I pray only to God, the great I Am."

"You must ask *Wakan-Tanka.*"

"No, why don't *ye* tell me?"

Medicine Hawk hesitated and wagged his head. "We must hurry and find the spring of clear waters."

* * *

As they walked on, Medicine Hawk sensed Joel's anger, his questioning and bewilderment. However, he was certain *Wakan* Dog would hear the Great Spirit. In due time *Wakan-Tanka* would speak to him.

"Lone Wolf must be close," Joel said.

"The Medicine Fathers will protect us once we are inside the Medicine Wheel."

"How can that be?"

"Ask *Wakan-Tanka.*"

Joel did not answer; instead, he turned and pointed back down the trail. "Listen," he said, "I heard something."

Medicine Hawk listened. "I hear nothing. What did it sound like?"

"I'm certain someone sneezed."

"Lone Wolf and Grey Bull!" Medicine Hawk said and grasped Joel's hand. "The medicine wheel is very near."

They ran at a faltering pace until reaching the crest of the ridge above Porcupine Creek. Medicine Hawk stopped, his chest heaving great wafts of air.

"Have we reached the medicine wheel?" Joel said.

"Yes, the Medicine Fathers have brought us to the wheel."

Atop the ridge was the great circle of stones. Medicine Hawk led Joel to the center of the wheel where he gathered dry wood and leaves for tinder. He sparked the tinder with flint and steel and an infant blaze began to dance as he fanned it with his eagle-wing fan. He removed pinches of sweet cedar from a pouch and sprinkled the aromatic dust into the fire. He began to chant his prayer to the medicine fathers in a sacred language. After he finished his initial prayer, he removed his sacred pipe from a deerskin pouch and packed the bowl full of kinnikinnick. He lit the pipe with a brand from the fire. The ritual was completed as he blew smoke to the four winds, earth and sky.

Lone Wolf, Grey Bull and five other Lakota warriors walked from the pines scattered along the ridge above the medicine wheel. As Medicine Hawk again began his sacred chant, Lone Wolf motioned for the others to remain on the ridge. He walked to the edge of the great circle of stones, but did not cross into the sacred arena. He waited for Medicine Hawk to finish his prayer.

With his prayer finished, Medicine Hawk stood erect as a totem with his medicine bundle held against his chest beneath folded arms. "Lone Wolf... Grey Bull... Little Eagle...Yellow Horse... Black Bear... Big Arrow... Old Soldier," he said with a loud voice, staring at each one as he called their names. "The Medicine Fathers are here, within the sacred hoop of the medicine wheel. You come to send *Wakan* Dog and Medicine Hawk into the hereafter. This you do against the words Yellow Elk revealed after his vision. You anger *Wakan-Tanka*. Unless you return to the camp of Red Cloud on the Tongue, The Great Spirit will take away the *Wakanpi,* the white wapiti with flaming eyes. Medicine Hawk has spoken."

The muscles of Lone Wolf's jaws rippled and his eyes flashed as he acknowledged Medicine Hawk's words with a nod. "We do not intend to harm *Wakan* Dog and Medicine Hawk. You must return to the camp of Red Cloud."

"Lone Wolf and Grey Bull have angered The Great

Spirit. You blinded *Wakan* Dog and cut his tongue. We will not return to the camp of Red Cloud."

Grey Bull stepped in front of Lone Wolf, waving his war club above his head. "Lone Wolf is an old woman if he listens to this old Crow *wicasa wakan*."

"No!" Lone Wolf said. "Medicine Hawk is Oglala *wicasa wakan*, a Lakota Sun Dance chief."

"He is Crow," Grey Bull chortled. "He is the son of Crow Dancer, a war chief of the Crow. He is the grandson of Man of Absarokee, a Crow Sun Dance chief."

"His mother is Oglala," Lone Wolf said. "Our people made him our brother. Medicine Hawk is not Crow."

Medicine Hawk remained silent while Lone Wolf debated Grey Bull. The other Lakota warriors wagged their heads and murmured their disagreement among themselves as Grey Bull berated Medicine Hawk.

Old Soldier stepped up to Grey Bull. Long gray braids dangled in front of his shoulders. His bronzed face, covered with deep scars left by smallpox, was accented with eyes deeply set beneath his brows. "The words of Grey Bull are like the words of the washichun," Old Soldier said. "You hide lies inside true words. Old Soldier will not raise his hand against Medicine Hawk."

Old Soldier abruptly turned around and walked away from the medicine wheel. He kept walking up the ridge. Lone Wolf motioned for the other Lakota to follow. Grey Bull refused; instead, he climbed atop a ledge overlooking the medicine wheel and called out to Medicine Hawk, "Crow medicine will not save Medicine Hawk and *Wakan* Dog from Grey Bull. You will walk in the hereafter when you leave the medicine wheel."

The darkness of night descended upon Medicine Hawk and Joel as they sat in the center of the medicine wheel. Beside the fire Medicine Hawk had built lay a meager pile of wood gathered by Medicine Hawk from within the boundary of the medicine wheel. Medicine Hawk opened the pouch in which he carried his food. It was nearly empty, only one cake of pemmican remained. He broke the cake in half and shared it with Joel. The peppery sweetness of the cake of dried venison, suet and dried chokecherries was a savory treat, but the thirst it provoked could not be appeased. The water bag was empty. A spring was nearby, but it might as well not exist since Grey Bull would kill them if they stepped outside the wheel.

The hazel eyes of Medicine Hawk looked skyward, searching for a nighthawk giving out its shrill cry as it darted after prey. He watched the slim winged bird disappear amongst the blue-white lights of a million stars.

From the forested Bighorn inclines below came the howling of wolves gathering together for their nocturnal stalk of some animal. "Do wolves attack people?" Joel said, listening to the eerie chorus.

"They will do us no harm. The wolf is very smart. They hunt in packs. One wolf cannot kill a large four-legs, an elk, a deer."

"They will attack an elk?"

"Only if it is lame, sick or very old."

Joel chuckled. "Maybe they will attack us. I am lame and you are very old."

"*Wakan* Dog speaks wise words," Medicine Hawk said, pointing at Grey Bull silhouetted against the orange brow of the rising moon. "Grey Bull is a crazy wolf that stalks. We are like the ancient bull elk that has lost his harem, having been defeated by a young bull. The old bull roams the mountains alone. He is very old and lame from many battles. The wolves will stalk and try to kill him."

Joel pondered Medicine Hawk's analogy. Indeed, they were the prey of Grey Bull's hatred for the washichun and the Crow. "How can the elk fight the wolf pack?"

"His antlers are like the lance, but he loses them each winter. If the pack is patient, waiting for the antlers to be shed, they will taste the elk's blood."

"We have no antlers."

"Medicine Hawk has the bow, many arrows," Medicine Hawk said, pulling an arrow from his quiver. He notched the arrow, but when he raised the bow Grey Bull was gone.

Out of the darkness came the taunting laughter of Grey

Bull. "The Crow *wicasa wakan* is a fool," Grey Bull jeered. "In the dark, he is blind like *Wakan* Dog. His eyes cannot see Grey Bull."

Medicine Hawk lowered the bow. "Grey Bull is cunning like the red fox. He will try to lure us from the sacred wheel."

"Lure us, how?"

"Water."

"Aye, we have none."

"We must not let him know that."

"When we do not drink from the bag, he will know."

"That is true; we will fool him."

"Fool him?"

Medicine Hawk untied the spout of the canteen. "Grey Bull will believe if Medicine Hawk and *Wakan* Dog drink from the bag.

"The bag is empty."

"Yes, but Grey Bull does not know this." Medicine Hawk placed the spout in his mouth, raised the bag and appeared to gulp several swallows. He handed the bag to Joel. "Now, *Wakan* Dog must make Grey Bull believe there is water in the bag."

* * *

With their charade for Grey Bull acted out, Medicine Hawk and Joel huddled together before the fire. The meager pile of wood was progressively consumed until Medicine Hawk placed the last stick in the flames. The fire flared for a while, then it began to subside as the burning wood slowly changed into a heap of smoldering ashes. Sleep came to Medicine Hawk, but not to Joel. He could only ponder their peril. *We have no water, no more food, the fire is dying and a crazy Indian intends to murder us. Dear God, what is there to do?"*

Joel listened to Medicine Hawk snore and the gurgling sounds of the spring just outside of the medicine wheel. His thirst soared at the sounds of the lively spring. If they were to get water, it would have to be between the setting of the moon and the first light of dawn. They had to have water if they were to endure the siege of Grey Bull. If they didn't visit the spring before dawn, they would have to do it during the day when Grey

Bull would have even a greater advantage. Joel decided to take the risk. He'd crawl to the spring before dawn.

Knowing that several hours must pass before the moon would set, Joel allowed himself to doze. Sleep came, fitfully at first then a more restful state settled upon him. Several hours passed before he was awakened by a scuffling sound. "What is that?" he whispered.

Medicine Hawk did not answer. "Medicine Hawk," Joel whispered, louder this time.

There was no answer. Joel reached out, swept his hands around where he lay, but felt only the cold ground of the medicine wheel. He realized that Medicine Hawk was gone, most likely crawling to the spring. He wanted to call out louder but refrained. Was Medicine Hawk going for water or was he stalking Grey Bull? Surely, the aged medicine man would not be so foolish as to do battle with the much younger Lakota warrior. Joel had no other option but to wait for Medicine Hawk's return.

He waited. Haunted by fear, he prayed for the safe return of Medicine Hawk. His patience waned like wax on a flaming candlestick as an hour or more came and went. *If he had gone for water, Medicine Hawk would be back by now. Where is he? He would not abandon me.*

Chapter 10

Joshua reined Mule through Granite Pass and headed northwest across the rugged terrain above Shell Canyon. Far behind, he had left Bridger astride Maynadier's gray gelding headed down country toward Fort Phil Kearny. If their ruse worked, Joshua would be declared dead by the Army and would no longer be a fugitive.

Bridger's spare buckskin shirt drooped heavily across Joshua's shoulders. It was patched, its fringes frayed, and the seams repaired with crude stitches of buffalo sinew. His Arapaho wife had fashioned the garment many years before during the winter of 1852. He hadn't worn it for a long time and only carried it in his bedroll as a remembrance of his wife now dead for fourteen winters.

Bridger had stuffed Joshua's blue tunic into his 'possibles bag,' intending to present it to Colonel Carrington. The tunic's tarnished gold oak leaves would be used by Bridger to support his story. He would claim it was near Red Cloud's encampment that an Oglala warrior wearing a major's blue tunic had attacked him. Mule had spooked, bucked Bridger off, and ran away. After killing the Lakota, Bridger caught the big gray gelding the Indian had been astride. When he found a USA brand burned into the gelding's shoulder, he was certain Major Leslie had been killed. The Indian had taken his tunic, saddle, and horse.

Joshua slipped on his woolen parka and pulled the collar high about his neck and chin. The day was brisk, chilled by a north wind. September, the Lakota Moon of Drying Grass, had ushered in a snow flurry of white flakes streaming from a dark overcast. The sudden change of weather, not unusual high in the mountains at this time of year, would bring in the colder nights and days of October, the Lakota Moon of Changing Times.

Green aspen leaves humming in the wind would soon yellow and turn the verdant mountain inclines into a green and citron patchwork. In the mountains, Indian Summer can be short, the high mountain passes filling with drifted snow during November, the Lakota Moon of Falling Leaves. Sensing urgency, Joshua clucked his tongue and jabbed Mule's flanks with his heels.

He knuckled his bristled chin, licked lips dried and fissured by the cold wind, and kneaded the aching muscles of his legs and back that were being pummeled by each jolting lunge Mule made up the steep trail. Pangs gnawing at his empty belly caused him to wish for another fat grouse like the one he had shared with Bridger. Mule had not fared much better. The sack of oats Bridger had brought along on his search for Joel was also empty.

All day Joshua urged Mule toward the crests of forested peaks making up the spiny ridge of the Big Horns. The game trail was becoming more arduous. Its course began to switch back and forth, ascending and descending the rugged slopes. With measured steps, Mule traversed the trail across a series of overhanging slabs of rock that projected out into space above a deep ravine. Joshua peered down the precipitous slope. His mouth turned dry. His hands gripped the saddle's pommel as he considered what would happen if Mule made a misstep, or if the ledge weakened by rotten rock should crumble and fall away beneath him and Mule. Their fall would traverse several hundred feet before smashing them against granite boulders at the bottom of the ravine.

The remaining trek to the floor of the ravine required an hour. The descending switchbacks were very steep and deeply cut into the mountainside by elk and deer during several centuries. Mule descended the trail at a determined, plodding gait. Joshua gripped the pommel, trusting in what Bridger had told him. "Let ol' Mule have her head in these mountains," he had said. "She's got the heart of an eagle and the legs of a mountain goat."

When they reached the floor of the ravine, the trail crossed a dry creek, the bed of which was filled with stones and boulders. Its banks were crowded by a matted grove of willow shoots. Mule hesitated to cross the dry stream, because the smooth stones and boulders were narrowly separated making for an easy entrapment of a hoof.

Joshua dug his heels into Mule's flanks. "Come on Mule. y'can jump over those rocks."

Mule balked, wagged her head and began to bray. Joshua raked his heels across her flanks again, and slapped the reins. "Get up you long-eared daughter of perdition."

Mule lowered her head, arched her back, and promptly unsaddled Joshua. He flew through the air, sprawling headlong into the willows. Before he could climb out of the thatched maze, Mule was retreating up the switchbacks.

"Whoa, Mule! Come back here!"

Mule continued her lunging strides up the mountainside, refusing to heed Joshua's pleas.

"Damn your stubborn carcass to hell!" He continued to watch the retreating mule until she disappeared over the ridge above the ravine. She was gone, no doubt bent upon returning to Fort Phil Kearny and the familiar hands of Jim Bridger. There was no hope that she could be caught in this rugged terrain.

Joshua was stranded. He didn't have a bedroll for the coming cold night or a rifle to kill game. The only items Mule had left him were the clothes he was wearing, his Bowie knife, binoculars, flint and steel, canteen, and the Army Colt strapped in his holster. And the only ammunition he had were the six percussion loads in the Colt.

Suddenly, he was aware of the cold. He glanced westward, up at the mountain peaks. Bands of orange sunlight streaming between the snow-capped summits were making the sun's farewell until tomorrow. If he were to see that sunrise in the morning, a shelter and a fire had to be built.

He cut willow shoots and evergreen boughs with his Bowie knife and built a crude wickiup with an opening that would face the fire he was going to build. He gathered and placed stones in a circle for a firepit, and then collected dead wood until darkness was near. He pondered the pile of mostly driftwood, hoping it would be enough to keep a fire going throughout the night.

He pared slivers for tinder from a piece of driftwood, placed them in the center of the firepit, and sparked them alive with flint and steel. The fire began to grow as he piled twigs and small branches onto the flaming tinder. Gnawing hunger and seething anger at Mule filled his thoughts as he built his fire. It was going to be a long night.

After crawling into his wickiup, he watched sparks like fireflies flit and dart into the night sky. A similar night came to mind. It was during the siege of Petersburg eight months before Lee's ragtag army would climb out of their trenches and retreat to Appomattox. Joel and he had built a campfire to chase away the chilling dampness of the night. They sat beside that fire, much like this one, watching sparks spiraling toward a starlit sky. It was one of those rare moments during the war that he and Joel found the time to be together. "I wonder when this war will be done with?" Joshua said, tossing a stick into the fire.

"God only knows," Joel replied.

"Aye, I suppose so," Joshua said, his voice tinged with a wistful tone. "When it is over, what do y'plan to do?"

Joel sighed and spat into the fire. "I'll be going to Montana to start a mission."

Joshua looked at Joel, his eyes reflecting the light from the fire. "That's Indian country. They're savages y'must know."

"Aye."

"A very dangerous mission."

"Aye, most likely."

"They are vicious and take pride in mutilating their enemies."

"So I'm told. Don't worry, God will protect me."

Those words spoken by Joel two years before echoed within Joshua's mind. "Where was God, brother Joel, when those savages put out your eyes?" Joshua mumbled while staring at the fire. "They still may take your life."

Joshua licked his dry lips, pulled the cork from his canteen and swallowed the last remaining mouthful of water. A fitful sleep finally came.

Shivering from the cold, Joshua awakened. The firepit seemed to be dead, its remnant only a blackened patch surrounded by a blanket of white. Large flakes of snow were streaming through the trees. He crawled from the wickiup and gouged a willow shoot into the firepit. Deep within the burned out pile of charred wood, the willow found several live coals. After rekindling the fire and piling on more wood, he crawled back into the wickiup and waited for sunrise.

It became increasingly difficult to keep the fire going, but Joshua knew it must be done. So, he frequently crawled from his shelter to stoke and replenish the firepit. Sometime before dawn, the snowing ceased. The sky cleared, revealing millions of stars and a moon whose face reflected only a sliver of light just above the western pinnacles.

Joshua sat beside the fire contemplating his situation. He hadn't eaten for two days, had no food, and had drunk the last swallow of water from his canteen. He knew that eating snow would devour his body's heat like a leech sucking blood.

He stripped away the woolen fabric covering his canteen, packed it full of snow and set it on glowing coals.

The inky eastern sky faded as first light ushered in the day. The rising sun peeked over the horizon, turning the mountains into a vast sculpture of snow-laden pines. Joshua pulled his kepi low to shelter his eyes from the blinding glare of whiteness.

With his thirst stayed, fearful thoughts crept into Joshua's mind. "What if the mountain passes become blocked with deep drifts?" he said aloud to himself. "I have no snowshoes."

While pondering, he shivered and held his hands over the fire. "If the temperature plummets, my parka isn't heavy enough to keep me from freezing."

He pulled out his Colt, spun the chamber, and counted the six loads. "What game can I kill with this thing?" He shoved the revolver back into his holster. "I'll probably starve if I don't freeze to death first."

His eyes scanned the blinding whiteness covering the trees and the steep mountain slopes. He spat into the fire, wagging his head in disappointment. After kicking snow into the firepit, Joshua abandoned camp and headed through the willows, hoping the dry creek would lead him out of the high country. If he were lucky, or if God so intended, he would find another blue grouse.

Getting through the entangling willow shoots proved to be impossible, so he abandoned that effort and retreated to the rocky creek-bed. There his boots slipped on stones slick from ice and moss, and his knees and elbows slammed against stones each time he fell. He frequently had to slither between lichen-encrusted boulders that blocked most of the creek-bed. All the time he listened for the call of a grouse or any other critter that he could shoot with his Colt.

By midday the high-riding sun began to melt the snow, which helped him replenished his canteen from puddles that collected between stones of the dry creek-bed.

It was nearing three o'clock in the afternoon when the shrill trumpeting call of a bull elk echoed across the mountains. Joshua stopped and listened, trying to determine from where the eerie sounds were coming. After the elk had bugled several times, he decided the animal was straight ahead. He pulled out his Colt, spun the chamber, and found all of the percussion caps to be dry.

He continued to follow the serpentine creek-bed until around four o'clock in the afternoon. When he rounded a bend, the heavy growth of willows abruptly ceased to populate the banks of the stream. Relieved that he no longer would have to stumble over slick stones, he climbed out of the creek-bed and walked toward a grove of aspen.

His feet ached and felt as if they were cramped inside boots that were two sizes too small. He found a fallen aspen log whose silver bark was pocked with buttons of gray fungi. He sat on the log and massaged his feet through his horsehide boots. He wiggled his toes and wanted to yank off the boots torturing his feet but dared not. Getting them back on would be almost impossible.

For the first time since leaving camp, he began to appreciate the mountain's beauty. The sunshine, filtering through nearly naked aspen branches, warmed his aching shoulders. A tepid breeze caressed his cheeks while he listened to the aspens whisper contentment. Slowly the feelings of frustration, anger and disappointment left him. Things began to seem all right. He would survive. It would get better. After all, he had heard an elk bugle and he still had six rounds in his Colt.

Amid the sounds nature was playing, he heard the gentle gurgle of running water like the bubbling fountain in his mother's garden. The thought of cool, clear water brought him to his feet. "There it is," he shouted, jubilant at the sight of water streaming down the mossy face of a boulder just beyond the grove of aspen. Oblivious of the torment in his boots, he ran toward the spring-fed pool at the base of the boulder. Cold water stung his cracked lips and chaffed cheeks as he lay on the ground burying his face in the pool.

Refreshed and rested, he made camp for the night. With his shelter, firepit, and campfire built, he began to search the woods for game. Hunger pangs returned as a fantasy filled with the aromas of a roasting grouse tweaked his appetite.

The sun sinking beyond the horizon chilled the warm afternoon. He had walked several hundred yards from camp when the sudden change reminded him that darkness would be coming soon. Through the growing shadows of twilight, he walked toward camp. Disappointment returned and pushed aside the contentment he'd discovered earlier.

His melancholy musings were suddenly interrupted by the sharp crack of a bough being snapped. The shade of evening was thick, obscuring the woods like a dense fog. Another limb snapped. He stopped, stood motionless, and listened as lesser sounds slowly approached. He drew the Colt from his holster and thumbed back the hammer. Like an apparition, a bull elk emerged from the darkness. It was huge, his giant rack of antlers spreading like barren tree limbs. The wily animal stopped. Joshua and the elk stared at each other. Joshua's heart pounded, knees became limp, and mouth turned dry as he raised the Colt and squeezed the trigger. The hammer slammed against the percussion cap but nothing happened; no exploding chamber, only a resounding metallic click. The elk didn't move. Joshua's thumb searched, fumbled, and then desperately cocked the hammer. The Colt bellowed as the elk turned away; however, the beast quickly disappeared as it ran into the darkness.

Joshua ran after the crashing sounds of conifer limbs being flung aside by the elk's antlers. "The bullet hit its mark. I couldn't have missed," he said, continuing to run after the crashing noises. He searched the heavy growth of pines, but fatigue and breathlessness slowed his pace. Being desperate to find the elk, he pushed himself until he could run no more. He stopped, leaned against a granite boulder and gasped for air. He tried to listen for the elk, but his own raucous breathing was all he could hear. When his pounding heart quieted and starved lungs became less demanding, he held his breath for a moment. He cupped a hand behind his ear and listened. There were no sounds other than a great horned owl hooting a welcome to the moon beginning to creep above the eastern horizon.

The darkness of night was settling across the mountains. Finding the elk before morning had to be abandoned. Disappointed and dejected, Joshua walked back to camp.

He replenished the firepit with more wood and crawled into his wickiup. He sat watching the flames shoot a spiraling trail of sparks into the sky. His thoughts were consumed by his failure to find the elk. His belly growled its protest and his mood fueled by self-pity became sullen.

While staring into the flames, he observed a light flickering beyond the firepit. Just for a moment, then it was gone, and then it appeared again. "What is that?" he whispered, pulled the revolver from his holster and thumbed back the hammer. There was nothing else he could do, just wait, hoping the fire would keep whatever it was away.

Over the following few minutes, Joshua watched the gleaming eyes moving about. All the time they were getting closer. He raised the Colt, braced it on his knee, aimed at the eyes, took a deep breath and squeezed the trigger. The Colt roared, its report echoing across the mountains. He crawled out of the wickiup and ran to where the animal lay.

"Well now, you've shot yourself a beaver." He picked up the fat rodent by his long, smooth, paddle-shaped tail and examined its chisel-like teeth. He marveled at how soft its brown fur felt, and how delicate was the webbing of its hind feet. He chuckled as he recalled one of Jim Bridger's brags. "You ain't findin' nothin' better than a juicy beaver tail," Bridger had said, "It tastes sweet as pork tenderloin."

Joshua skinned, gutted, and roasted the beaver on a green willow spit. He trimmed a morsel from the roasted carcass and popped it into his mouth. The flavor was a bit gamy, not quite like Bridger's brag, but good.

With a belly full of roasted beaver and his body racked by profound weariness, Joshua crawled into the wickiup. He listened to the wind, the eerie whistle of a bull elk bugling in the distance, and pondered tomorrow. Had he made a mistake, abandoning the game trail and heading out of the high country? The early snow had been frightening; yet, there should be enough time left before winter made travel impossible. And if he abandoned his quest to find Joel, where could he spend the winter?

If he headed back toward the northwest, the Yellowstone, and the Crow encampment in Montana, he might still find Joel before the deep freeze of winter. Could he survive the winter if marooned in the high country? That was questionable. Only three rounds remained in his Colt.

He lay on his bed of pine boughs in the wickiup, staring at the flames crackling in his firepit. Gradually, he began to make plans. He had to have snowshoes for the long trek across snow-covered mountains. A pair could be fashioned from green willows and strips of hide and sinew from the elk he had surely killed. He must find the elk, cut strips of meat for jerky and make coverings for his boots from its hide. To resume the quest for Joel was fraught with risks. Death from starvation, exposure, injuries, or hostile Indians might happen before finding him. But what else could he do? If the Army captured him, certain death by a firing squad awaited him. He would find the elk and build a pair of snowshoes in the morning.

Chapter 11

Medicine Hawk crawled behind a boulder into its shadow cast by the setting moon. He leaned against cold granite and gripped the quill-wrapped handle of his tomahawk. He listened and prayed Grey Bull would be asleep. He shivered from the cold wind whipping through the mountains and the chilling fear of the man he was stalking. With cautious movements, he crept around the boulder. He stopped and stared at glowing embers in a firepit Grey Bull had built. In the dim light of predawn, he could see a form lying beside the firepit. "Grey Bull," Medicine Hawk scarcely whispered and crept closer, clutching his tomahawk. The figure moved. Medicine Hawk halted and stood quiet as a cobra staring at a charmer blowing a flute. A groan came from the sleeping form. Suddenly, it leaped upright. "The Crow wicasa wakan walks in the hereafter," Grey Bull roared, raising his stone-headed war club. Swift as a diving falcon, an arrow zipped past Medicine Hawk and plunged its serrated head into the chest of Grey Bull. The light of disbelief flickered in the vicious stare of Grey Bull, but then vanished like the flame of a candle being blown away by a single breath. The fierceness of his face sagged. He slumped to his knees, grasped the shaft of the arrow, snapped it in two and flung it aside as he fell into his firepit.

Medicine Hawk turned to see whose bow had driven the arrow into the chest of Grey Bull. From the trees walked Joel accompanied by several Crow warriors, all of them tall, their hair worn in high pompadours and long braids. Their leader was a giant. His features, unlike the others, were massively proportioned. His cheekbones were high, broad, and separated by a large Roman nose. His countenance was resolute, expressed by heavy lips drawn in a straight line above a square chin. His eyes, deeply set, were eloquent like those of a war chief. He carried a long staff that was covered with buffalo hide and adorned with a string of eagle feathers. He raised his hand in a gesture of peace as he approached Medicine Hawk and spoke in Absaroke, the language of the Crow. "The dead Lakota called you a Crow *wicasa wakan*," he said, his voice low, rumbling within his immense chest. "How can this be so?"

Medicine Hawk, signing peace, replied in Absaroke, "I am Medicine Hawk, a *wicasa wakan* and Sun Dance chief."

"I am Big Belly, a chief of the Crow. How is it that you speak our language, Medicine Hawk?"

"The first six winters of my life were spent in the lodge of my father, Crow Dancer."

"The Crow people honor Crow Dancer. He was a brave warrior." Big Belly then turned and pointed his staff at Joel. "So, Medicine Hawk, why do you bring this white man to the medicine wheel?"

"For the protection of the Great Spirit *Wakan-Tanka*, the one you call *Acba-dadea*."

A young Crow warrior, born eighteen winters before, stepped forward. He had dark eyes and a slim, aquiline nose. His hair was dark brown and styled in the typical Crow tradition, which was a tall pompadour, stiffened by malodorous pomade, arching above his forehead. An earring with an elk tooth pendant dangled from each pierced earlobe, and he carried a long bow covered by the skin of a rattlesnake. Facing Medicine Hawk, he said, "It was the arrow of Plenty Coups that pierced the wicked heart of the Oglala."

Medicine Hawk nodded and pointed at Joel. "Wakan Dog and Medicine Hawk thank Plenty Coups. The Medicine Fathers have guided your hands."

A fleeting grin spread across Plenty Coups face. "The Medicine Fathers delivered the hated Oglala into our hands. His scalp will hang from the lance of Plenty Coups."

Joel, unable to understand the Absaroke language, wondered what Medicine Hawk and the Crow warriors were talking about. He tried to discern their mood by the tone of their voices but could not. Their language carried few inflections that could be considered pleasant or hostile. His and Medicine Hawk's fate was in the hands of these Indians. He remained silent; was reconciled to await whatever that would be with faith that *God* would be his protector.

Joel's resolute vigil ended as the heavy hand of Big Belly fell upon his shoulder. The deep voice of Big Belly spoke in pigeon English. "Why white man here?"

Joel lifted his face, trying to face the much taller Big Belly. "I am Joel Leslie, called by God to build a mission in Montana."

"Why do Joel Leslie have scars on eyes?"

"The Oglala blinded me."

Medicine Hawk intervened, explaining in Absaroke how Joel was captured and brought to the Oglala encampment on the Tongue. He told the Crow about Yellow Elk's vision; how Joel came to be known as Wakan Dog; how Lone Wolf and Grey Bull burned his eyes and cut his tongue. He concluded by telling how he saved Joel from the bear and the pursuing warriors led by Lone Wolf and Grey Bull.

"Aho," Big Belly said and pointed his staff at the spring running nearby. "Come, we will drink from the medicine pool, then we will share our pemmican. Medicine Hawk and Joel Leslie are welcome to come with us to the encampment of the Crow on the Yellowstone."

* * *

"I can see lodges," Medicine Hawk said to Joel as their ponies trotted into the valley of the Yellowstone.

It was during the bitten-moon of September, the Moon of Drying Grass. The sun was high, the day balmy. Big Belly's warriors yelped and prodded twenty stolen Lakota ponies with their lances. They were jubilant. Their foray into Red Cloud's land had been fruitful. Behind them lay one week since leaving the medicine wheel and the corpse of Grey Bull whose bloody scalp dangled from the lance of Plenty Coups.

During the first day, they had ridden down the western slopes of the Bighorns and out onto the sage covered Bighorn Basin. Their ponies' hoofs splashed across a shallow ford of the Bighorn River, taking them out of hunting grounds claimed by the Lakota. They reined their ponies onward toward the northwest.

Joel struggled to remain astride the lithe Indian pony. The dog-skin leggings made by Otter Woman had become worn, their crotch split and frayed. His buttocks burned. The hide of the pony's bare back scraped and gouged his rear-end. He raised himself, touched his throbbing butt and felt tender, weeping sores. He finally slipped to the ground unable to ride the pony any longer. However, he wasn't able to keep up with the others, because of a slow and faltering gait.

Plenty Coups wheeled his pony and rode back to meet Joel limping beside his horse. "Why Joel Leslie not ride sky-dog?" he said in pigeon English.

Joel bent over and pointed at his galled butt. "I fear my being able to ride is past."

"We build pony-drag for Joel Leslie."

As Plenty Coups headed for a grove of lodgepole pine, Medicine Hawk dismounted to walk beside Joel. A gust of cold wind whipped across their faces, its sudden appearance a portent of an approaching blizzard. Medicine Hawk's eyes narrowed and scanned northward toward the high plains of Montana Territory. He saw a massive cloudbank, its sooty base capped by a boiling gray haze. "A storm approaches."

Joel pulled his shirt tighter about his shoulders. "Aye, it is getting colder."

With the quickness of a prairie whirlwind, vicious gusts of wind laden with snowflakes lashed across the plain. Whirling dust clouds billowed upward, sullying the sun's brightness. Joel and Medicine Hawk cringed as sand blasted their faces and filtered between their lips, becoming muddy grit in their mouths.

Like a total eclipse, the sky grew dark and foreboding. The sun became only an orange orb behind a veil of dust and snow. "Can y'see Plenty Coups yet?" Joel asked and wiped muddy saliva from his lips.

Medicine Hawk peered toward the grove of pines and saw Plenty Coups emerge from the trees leading his pony that was harnessed to a travois. "Yes, Plenty Coups returns."

After Joel climbed onto the travois, Plenty Coups tied a heavy buffalo robe over him. They resumed their journey, heading into the howling northwest wind. They would have to make camp as soon as they could reach the shelter of the Pryor Mountains.

The travois swung side to side, its poles creaking with each step the pony took. Joel felt warm, snug as a papoose beneath the thick robe. He dozed, lulled by the rhythm of the swaying travois.

They camped to the south of Pryor Mountain that night. The snowing ceased during the night and as dawn brought the first light of day, the Crow broke camp. With Joel on the travois, they continued to ride toward their encampment in the valley of the Yellowstone.

The sun broke through at mid-morning. The night's accumulation of snow rapidly melted, turning the prairie soil into sticky gumbo. It clung to the horses' hooves and accumulated into globs on the pine poles as the travois cut dual scars across the prairie.

All day, the travois bounced over rocks, prairie dog mounds and narrow ditches eroded by wind and weather. Despite their being out of hostile Lakota country, the raiding party seemed to be in a hurry. Maybe the time of year when winter storms can barrel out of the north made the day more urgent. Or, just maybe the Lakota, angry over the theft of their ponies, would dare to pursue them. Many times, they had done just that. Often riding around the Crow, they would hide in a dry coulee or behind one of the solitary mountain peaks rising above the ascending Montana plain. And then they would erupt from their hiding places, screaming war cries as they charged into the Crow raiding party.

Joel discovered that riding a travois wasn't a comfortable mode of travel. Especially when the pony pulling it lunged up a steep incline or was goaded into a trotting gait. He found that a buffalo robe, comforting when shielding him from frigid winds, turned into a sweat bath beneath its wooly hide. The odor of his body, unwashed for weeks, seeped from beneath the robe. The stench was distasteful, which provoked dreams of bathing in a warm tub. Without being able to see, Joel was learning to listen to and smell everything around him. He listened to the rhythmic voices of Big Belly, Plenty Coups and Medicine Hawk. The Absaroke language had a pleasing sound filled with vigorous syllables and throaty intonations. One word repeatedly spoken by Medicine Hawk was Ac-ba-da-dea. He gave each syllable equal emphasis, welding the word into one that seemed to be a proclamation each time it was spoken. After pondering its meaning, Joel decided it must be one of a profound nature.

By evening, they had reached Clark's Fork of the Yellowstone. Fed by a confluence of waters high in the Absaroka Mountains, it ran swift, cold and tumultuous. The raiding party turned north, followed the river, and searched for the ford they had used for centuries. The river was running swifter and deeper than usual. Joel heard a low-pitched roar long before they reached the ford. It reminded him of the shallow rapids on the river Deveron that flowed near his home in Scotland. And as he listened to the Crow talking among themselves, he sensed their concern and their desire to get across the river before dark.

At dusk, they reached the ford. It had become raging rapids because of high water. The roar of the rapids told Joel that the ford was fraught with danger. To get the stolen ponies across without losses of horses and men would be unlikely. Big Belly called the men together. Their arguing voices increased in intensity, some apparently wanting to go ahead and take their chances. Most, however, didn't since the risks were so great. The arguing finally ceased when Big Belly's voice boomed his commands. Joel heard the raiding party running up and down the riverbank. After a few minutes, he smelled smoke and listened to the men talking as they butchered a deer one of the warriors had killed for supper. They would camp there for the night, hoping the high water would recede by morning.

Joel lay on the travois waiting for Plenty Coups to unhitch the pony. The tantalizing aroma of venison roasting over the fire tweaked his belly. His mouth filled with saliva. He swallowed and heard his gut growling in anticipation of the succulent meal sizzling on a spit. While savoring the idea, he heard someone unhitching the travois. "Medicine Hawk cook deer meat," Plenty Coups said, untying the buffalo robe.

"Aye, I can smell it."

"Joel Leslie sit by fire," Plenty Coups said, leading Joel

to the fire where they sat on a buffalo robe.

Medicine Hawk pierced a sizzling strip of venison with a sharpened willow stick. "You like deer?" he asked, handing the stick to Joel.

"Aye," he said and bit off a generous helping. He chewed, savored the succulent meat, swallowed, and bit off another piece. Like a hungry wolf, he consumed the venison. He licked the juices from the stick while waiting to be offered another helping.

"Joel Leslie is Eat-Like-Dog," Plenty Coups said.

Joel felt anger, sudden, ascending into his temples. He jumped up to face Plenty Coups. "I am not a dog! I am a man, a human being with a soul. The Lakota tried to make me a dog … they failed."

Plenty Coups stood up, straight, his head erect. "Plenty Coups not call Joel Leslie a dog. He is Eat-Like-Dog."

"Aye, so I do. But, I am not a dog."

"Eat-like-Dog is a name!"

Joel stood silent, pondering what Plenty Coups had called him. Eat-Like-Dog was disgusting. "I'll never be called a dog again!" He lunged at Plenty Coups. Plenty Coups spun away from Joel's blind charge. Joel sprawled on the ground. He jumped up. Medicine Hawk stepped between them. He grasped Joel by the shoulders and shook him. "Plenty Coups does not understand you. You do not understand Plenty Coups."

"I understand him. He called me a dog."

"No, he was giving you a Crow name."

"My name is Joel Leslie. I want no Indian name."

"You will not be given one," Plenty Coups said and walked away.

"You have angered Plenty Coups," Medicine Hawk said. "That is not good."

Joel grasped Medicine Hawk's arm. "I don't care. If he calls me a dog again, I'll kill him."

"Those are strong words for a wakan man."

"Aye, so they are."

When dawn broke, cold and clear the following morning, Joel crawled from under his buffalo robe. The night

had cooled his anger. Instead, he felt the bitter pangs of guilt.
He had threatened to kill, a terrible threat for a missionary to
make.   He decided to make amends, to apologize for his
outburst. "Plenty Coups!"

"He is not here," Medicine Hawk said. "He is catching
your pony."

"Please, tell him I wish to speak with him."

"Plenty Coups has been insulted. He will not talk with
you. Not today. Maybe never."

It was as Medicine Hawk said. Plenty Coups remained
silent; would not reply while helping Joel onto a pony. They
would have to ford the river before the travois could be
reassembled. The high water had receded enough by morning
for the fording to take place. The pony herd and the raiding
party splashed across the ford without incident. The coming of
darkness that evening found them camped on the north bank of
another stream called Stillwater Creek. Plenty Coups continued
his unresponsive attitude toward Joel.

Boulder Creek was their next stop the following night.
And then they rode into the valley of the Yellowstone at noon
the following day. In this valley on the southeast side of the
river was the encampment of Big Belly's band of the Crow. At
last, a refuge for Joel and Medicine Hawk, and the home of Big
Belly, Plenty Coups and their warriors were in sight.

The Crow have lived in this valley for many years. The
valley, carved by the Yellowstone River during several eons, is
sheltered by Sheep Mountain, Emigrant Peak, Mt. Cowen and
Blackmore Peak. The floor of the valley grows from a narrow
gorge into a wide, grassy plain along the winding river. The
river's banks are fringed with cottonwoods and willows whose
branches are laden during the summer with verdant foliage.
When the frosts of autumn settle into the valley, the trees soon
take on a mantle of brilliant yellow. Then, as icy gales of winter
lash the valley, the trees are stripped of color, leaving barren
limbs that sing forlorn songs until the Moon of Green Grasses
arrives. Suddenly, dormant grasses begin to turn green. These
lush meadows become vast grazing arenas for Crow ponies, elk
and deer.

From the distant encampment came high-pitched trills, a happy greeting by Crow squaws to their returning warriors. The nearer the raiding party came, the louder the welcome became. Young men and boys leaped onto ponies and galloped out to meet Big Belly's party. They raised bows and rifles above their heads and yelped their greetings as they circled the stolen Lakota ponies, yelling triumphantly for so many fine sky-dogs. It was a happy homecoming.

Chapter 12

Joshua trudged across a vast snowfield on crudely constructed snowshoes. They were cumbersome and difficult to walk on; nevertheless, they had carried him high into the Bighorns. His feet, unfeeling as two blocks of wood, had ceased to ache. He had hoped to insulate his feet from the austere coldness of the high country by wrapping rawhide around his boots. It was another mistake. The uncured hide had frozen into casts, brittle and unyielding with each step.

He flexed numbed fingers inside his mittens and gripped more tightly a staff he had made from a willow sapling. He was cold, so very cold.

His kepi, pulled low over his eyes, gave little protection from snowflakes whipping against his face. Spicules of ice encrusted his eyebrows, beard and mustache. He licked scabbed lips, cursed the blizzard sweeping across the mountain pass, and wished he had not found the bull elk where it had died in a thatched thicket of willows.

Why had he turned back and headed up country in search of Joel? It was another in a list of flawed decisions that numbered more than he could recall. *How many weeks had it been since he deserted Fort Laramie?* He couldn't say, having lost track of the days spent ascending the snowbound heights.

The wind was blowing snow so hard he was unable to see more than fifty yards. Oh, what he'd give for a compass. *What direction was he walking? Was he going in circles?* He only knew he was still climbing and had not reached the summit of the pass. Aye, it was supposed to be a pass according to the map Bridger had given him. Yet, he wondered.

Finally, the blizzard became so fierce he could go no farther, not today, not until the sky cleared. He had to find shelter. He spied a fallen tree whose barren limbs jutted skyward above the deep snow. With only his hands, staff and Bowie knife, he began to dig a snow-cave next to the dead tree. Within an hour he had burrowed his cave and covered the floor with pine boughs.

He cut dead wood from the tree, built a fire, and skewered a strip of elk meat onto his knife.

He held it over the fire, but his ravenous hunger couldn't wait for the meat to cook. Like a scavenger, he sat in his cave chewing raw meat and hardly noticed it had begun to sour.

Nightfall brought more snow, wind and misery. He sat near the entrance of the cave, staring at the firepit. There would be no sleep for him since the fire had to be kept alive throughout the night.

During the night, it seemed every muscle, bone, and sinew in his body began to ache. A rigor convulsed his muscles into spasms for nearly a half-hour. After the chills abated, his head ached and he began to cough. Each effort sent sharp, agonizing pain through his chest. His feet throbbed, eyes burned, and heart raced from anxiety and a soaring fever.

By dawn, the falling snow and winds had diminished. He felt some better, but continued to cough. He melted snow in his canteen and ate some more tainted meat.

As the sun eased over the eastern horizon, the snowfield became a blinding white world. He put on his snowshoes, pulled his kepi low, and started toward the pass.

All morning, he trudged toward the saddle between two towering peaks. He reached the summit of the pass at noon. Beyond the pass, the incline fell away toward open country. He could see a river in the distance coursing its way toward the north. "Thank God!" he cried, and slumped as pain clawed at his chest like the talons of a falcon.

He rested until the pain subsided. Then he ate more of the elk meat and drank from his canteen. The going would be much easier now, but he still had a long way to go before walking out of the mountains into the valley.

By mid-afternoon, he felt fatigued and more ill. He wiped his eyes, trying to clear his blurred vision. Even though he had reached a much lower altitude, he was experiencing more shortness of breath.

He looked over Bridger's map and decided the river was

the Bighorn. If it was, he would have open country between the Bighorns and the Yellowstone River. His fatigue and illness turned the hour urgent. He had to get to the valley and find shelter before night.

At four o'clock in the afternoon, he walked into the valley where shallow drifts leeward of the sagebrush became the only snow cover. He removed the snowshoes for faster walking and headed toward the river. His quickened pace produced an increased shortness of breath. Coughing seizures became more frequent, racking his chest with stabbing pains.

Near the river, he could see a shed. The sighting of shelter rekindled his efforts. He tried to walk faster, but his legs gave way. He struggled to get up, only to fall again. He heard voices, raised himself and looked around. Three men wearing fur caps and clad in buckskin were riding ponies along the river. "Here!" he yelled. "Help me!"

He struggled to his feet and ran toward the line of horsemen. But there were no horses, no mountain men wearing fur caps. "Where have they gone?" he cried, stumbling around with frantic eyes, searching. He braced himself, stood erect, and turned to walk toward the shed he had seen next to the river. But there was no shed.

"Delusions," he muttered and shook his head, trying to clear his befuddled brain.

The last light of day was yielding to the darkness of night as he staggered along the snow-covered riverbank. He had to find shelter, some place to spend the night. In the growing darkness, he slipped and sprawled onto a sandbar next to the river. The river was covered with ice except in the center where a swift current had kept it clear. His eyes caught movement. When he turned to look, a wolf leapt from a cave that some other animal had burrowed into the bank of the river. Two more wolves followed, all three running in long leaps away from the river. He watched them stop, turn around and look back for a moment. Then they disappeared into the darkness.

He cautiously walked toward the cave. Another wolf might still be inside. He leaned down and peered into the cave. It was empty with the exception of several bones that had been gnawed clean. Without hesitation, he crawled into the cave, felt the warmth and smelled the stench left by its prior occupants. He fell into a restless sleep stoked by a high fever and bone-breaking fatigue.

The following two days were spent in delirium as pneumonia sapped his strength.

On the third day after exhausting his canteen, he crawled to the river. He tried to break the ice with his knife, but it was too thick. He heard the gurgling current beyond the ice. His raging fever had built a thirst he had to quench. He slid out onto the ice on his belly, squirmed, wiggled and scooted himself toward the open water. He held the uncorked canteen at arms length and continued to slide toward the gurgling sounds. At last he felt frigid water flowing over his hand into the open canteen. He gulped from the canteen until his thirst had been quenched.

After returning to the cave, he ate the rest of the elk meat.   Sleep returned, but it was interrupted frequently by a hacking cough. He became more and more stuporous, arousing only for an occasional swallow of water.

Unaware of time, he languished in stuporous solitude for another day. He aroused as gentle hands sponged his face with cold water. He blinked and saw a bronzed face peering down at him. There was kindness in her hazel eyes and smiling face. "Mountain man not gone under," she said.

Joshua wiped his eyes. To his surprise she was still there, smiling at him. "Are ye real?"

"Mountain man big sick. You wait here, I go get Hook."

After she left, Joshua muttered, "Another delusion."

He slipped back into a stupor, longing for the delusion to be real.

"Who you be?" a man said.

Joshua opened his eyes and looked at the bearded man kneeling beside him. "Joshua... Leslie."

"I'm Jack Hooker, but most folks calls me Hook. What're you doin' here? You're near gone under."

Joshua shook his head. "My brother... Joel... the Lakota got him."

"Lakota? Ain't none here, just me an' my Shoshone

squaw."

Joshua smiled and nodded, but was too weak to speak again.

"Now don't you be frettin'. Me and my squaw have an elk on our travois. Soon as I unload him at the cabin, I'll come fetch'ya."

Joshua nodded and drifted back into a stupor. He did not rouse until Hook returned. With the help of his squaw, Hook loaded Joshua onto the travois. She covered him with a buffalo robe, and then led the travois pony while Hook straddled his roan mare. Within an hour, Joshua was lying on a bed in Hook's cabin. He was helpless, racked by fever, an unrelenting cough and frostbitten feet. While wondering if this was another delusion, he drifted between reality and fantasy.

During the ensuing night and the next day, Hook's squaw plied Joshua with frequent sips of willow tea, water, and hot elk broth. She smeared an herbal ointment on his feet and wrapped them in cotton muslin. Each time he convulsed with an outburst of coughing, she spooned a bitter concoction of boiled herbs into his mouth.

The following morning, he awakened as bright sunlight streamed through a glazed window above his bed. He was very weak but much improved. He felt his forehead and found it cool. His *crisis* had come, breaking the fever during the night. He looked about the room. Hook's squaw was asleep, sitting in a rocking chair beside the bed. She awakened when he turned over and began to cough. She poured her remedy into a wooden spoon. "Nay," he said, "no more."

"You drink for Lucy," she said, holding the spoon close to his lips.

"Lucy? That is your name?"

"No. Hook call me Lucy. He not like my name 'Water Too Deep'."

"How long have you been with Hook?"

"He gave six ponies to my father two winters ago."

"For six ponies, your father sold you to Hook?"

Lucy shoved the spoon against his lips. "You drink."

Joshua opened his mouth and accepted the bitter liquid.

He swallowed, grimaced and sputtered. Lucy laughed, her dark eyes twinkling as she began to unwrap his feet. He raised himself up on his elbows and watched her fingers gently peel away the muslin. The tops of his feet and toes were covered with blebs filled with dark fluid, but the pain was gone.

After Lucy redressed his feet, she turned to the hearth and a boiling pot. She filled a cup with broth and returned to spoon it into Joshua's mouth. "Nay," he said, reaching for the cup. "I can drink it."

Lucy sat in her chair, rocking, while Joshua sipped from the cup. "You like?" Her tawny lips curled into a pleasant grin.

"Aye, 'tis good."

"What you mean, eye?"

Joshua chuckled. "Aye is how we Scots say yes."

Lucy nodded, pointed at her eye and laughed. "Eye is yes? White man talk gives Lucy big laugh."

While Lucy was laughing, a yellow glint flashed from a pendant tied around her neck. Joshua stared at the pendant. He was certain it was bigger than the fifty-eight caliber minieballs he had probed out of wounds during the war. *That has to be a nugget of pure gold*, he thought. "Aye, our words can be confusing," he said, staring at the pendant.

Joshua's fascination with her pendant caused Lucy to glance down at the nugget. "You like?" she said, fondling the glob of gold.

"Aye, 'tis pretty. Where did ye get it?"

"Hook give me."

"Ah, of course." He raised up to get a better view of the nugget, and then looked about the cabin. "By the way, where is Hook?"

"Check traps—be back soon."

Like a beguiling Jezebel, the gold pendant was beginning to seduce Joshua. A raw nugget that big was worth more money than he could imagine. Wherever Hook had found it, there had to be more. *Millions—somewhere nearby there is a fortune.*

"You drink all of soup," Lucy said, interrupting Joshua's pondering. "When Hook get back, I make porridge."

He nodded and gulped down the soup now grown cool. She took the cup and wagged her head. "White man crazy, drink so fast no taste soup."

Joshua gazed at the log roof and dreamed of finding the gold. In his mind, the single nugget began to multiply. There must be hundreds, maybe thousands of them just waiting to be picked up. And Hook probably had more of them stashed away. Maybe they were here, in the cabin, hidden from the eyes of strangers. Could Hook be persuaded to tell where he had found them? If he could hold his fervor in check, Joshua would wait for the right moment. Perhaps even one when Hook would be in a boastful mood. Then the truth could be wheedled from him.

It was about midmorning when Hook shoved the cabin door open. His fur cap, fur parka and buckskin leggings were crusted with snow. He tossed several steel traps into the corner and began to unbutton his parka. "Well now, Joshua, you look like you're goin'ta live."

"Aye, Lucy is a good nurse. I am feeling much better."

Lucy glanced at Hook. "Feet not good," she said, wagging her head. "Toes all gone under."

"Froze 'em clean off, did he?" Hook said, pouring a cup of coffee.

"No," Lucy replied, signing with her hands. "Toes black—gone under—cut off soon."

Joshua winced and struggled to sit up on the side of the bed. "Nay, my toes ye'll not be cuttin' off. I'm a surgeon. I'll be the one to make that decision."

Hook sipped, squinting his eyes as he swallowed hot coffee. "Surgeon, you say? Can you cut off your own toes?"

"If need be, I can."

Hook laughed and slapped his leg. "By heaven above, this child has got to see that. I'll bet you a winter's pelts you caint do it."

"I'd take that wager, but I have nothing to bet."

"Just as well. You'd lose."

Chapter 13

Several weeks had passed since Joel and Medicine Hawk arrived at the encampment of Chief Big Belly. The Crow women had stripped the inner bark from poles of lodgepole pine and sewed tanned buffalo hides together to cover the tipi's skeleton of polished poles. They painted symbols on the tipi designating the lodge to be that of a medicine man. It was a pleasant, warm and comfortable home for Joel and Medicine Hawk.

One week after moving into their tipi, Medicine Hawk sat next to the firepit skewering chunks of buffalo onto a spit. Flames leaping from the firepit cast dancing shadows on the walls of the tipi above the bed where Joel lay. Medicine Hawk was worried. Ever since he and Joel had arrived at the Crow encampment, Joel had become reclusive. He seldom spoke to Medicine Hawk except when a need became desperate. He refused most of the food brought to him, no matter whether it was prepared by Medicine Hawk or the Crow women. When asked a question, his reply was either an aye or a nay. If a longer response was needed, he oft times shook his head, a gesture of not caring to answer.

Joel wanted only to sleep. He had discovered in his land of dreams that he was no longer blind. The worst part of the day or night was to awaken only to find the world of darkness that fate had brought to him. He no longer prayed. Why should he? God had deserted him. He felt isolated, cast into a dark dungeon by the red-hot blade of Lone Wolf. Every "why me" question he had uttered remained unanswered. At first, it was why did God allow him to be captured and taken from his mission? Next, why did God allow him to be tortured and degraded to being a dog in the eyes of the Lakota? Finally, the putting out of his eyes and the crippling of his tongue had taken away forever his being able to be a minister. His speech, once clear, burred by a Scottish accent that delighted his listeners, was distorted and almost unintelligible. Beneath the buffalo robe, on his mattress of grass, he languished, wishing that Medicine Hawk had not killed the bear.

In his melancholy state, Joel ignored all of the odors that wafted through their tipi: the mouth-watering aroma from venison, elk or buffalo roasting on a spit above the firepit and the sweet fragrance of smoke from kinnikinnick burning in Medicine Hawk's sacred pipe. Neither did he care about the heavy odor of sweating men as they gathered around Medicine Hawk to remember times past.

He had shut out all of the camp's sounds. The good-natured banter among the squaws preparing hides for tanning. The lively sounds of children playing went unnoticed. They could not compete with the dreams of his childhood. Once again, he and Joshua and Colie Condiff played scary games with their imaginary adversary, the troll that lived beneath the bridge of Castleton.

Medicine Hawk sat looking across the tipi at Joel. He watched the slow, steady rise and fall of Joel's chest, and his scarred and distorted eyelids partially closed by sleep. Medicine Hawk felt sadness, greater sadness than he had ever experienced. This washichun *wakan* man, an adopted son he had saved from death, seemed to be slipping away from him. His thoughts were always on how to return such a kind and gentle man to the world of reality.

Every morning after smoking the sacred pipe, he prayed to *Wakan-Tanka* for his adopted son, for the healing of his eyes, tongue and spirit. There had been no answer from the Great Spirit. Maybe there would be no message from the God of the Lakota now that Medicine Hawk had chosen to live with the Crow. Today he would pray to *Acba-Dadea*, The Great Spirit of the Crow, in the Absaroke language. Surely, *Acba-Dadea* would hear and understand his prayer.

Before filling his sacred pipe for the morning smoke, Medicine Hawk opened his medicine pouch. He pulled out a tiny flute he had carved from the leg bone of a swan when he was nine winters old. He raised the flute to his lips and began to play a song he had learned as a child. It was a song of healing called *The Midnight Song of All the Birds in the Universe*. The haunting melody, crisp as the song of a nightingale, flowed from the miniature flute. Joel stirred and was awakened by the strange new sounds. He opened his scarred lids and listened. The winsome strains flowing like a bubbling brook reminded Joel of the Scottish bagpipe his father played.

Medicine Hawk finished the song and placed the flute back into his medicine bundle. Joel didn't say anything, because his mind was in Scotland. Once again, he was watching lithe highland maidens dancing to a lively tune.

Discouraged by Joel's profound despair, Medicine Hawk left their tipi and walked toward the lodge of Spotted Eagle. Spotted Eagle was the grandson of Thunder Bear who was the brother of Medicine Hawk's father, Crow Dancer. Like Medicine Hawk, he was a medicine man and a chief of the Sun Dance. Medicine Hawk needed his counsel and his intercession with the Medicine Fathers for Joel.

He pulled his blanket more tightly about his shoulders. The hour was early, chilled by frost covering the bluestem meadow and the great circle of tipis alike. He quickened his pace as he glanced skyward. He saw the morning star flickering brightly in the eastern sky now being blanched by the approaching sunrise. He must hurry before the sun climbed above the horizon, bringing the time for morning prayers.

He headed directly toward a large lodge, avoiding the huge council tipi in the center of the encampment. The lodge's buffalo-hide covering was bleached white and adorned with colorful sacred designs. It was the tipi of Spotted Eagle, his wife and two daughters.

Medicine Hawk stopped in front of Spotted Eagle's tipi, leaned on his hooked staff and raised his hand in a sign of peace. Already awake and preparing for his morning prayers, Spotted Eagle stepped out of his lodge and greeted Medicine Hawk. "Medicine Hawk is welcome in the lodge of Spotted Eagle," he said, motioning for Medicine Hawk to enter.

Spotted Eagle's wife, Four Moons, seated beside the firepit nodded a silent greeting as Medicine Hawk sat down. One of Spotted Eagle's daughters, Willow Calf, awakened and peeked at Medicine Hawk from beneath her buffalo robe. Her younger sister Owl Eye continued to sleep hidden beneath the robe covering her bed. Spotted Eagle motioned for Four Moons to bring him his sacred pipe and pouch of kinnikinnick.

"Medicine Hawk brings great honor to the lodge of Spotted Eagle," Spotted Eagle said, laying several sticks of wood on the fire.

Medicine Hawk acknowledged Spotted Eagles compliment with a polite nod.

Four Moons handed the pipe and pouch to Spotted Eagle. "We will smoke," he said, "then we will talk."

Once again, Medicine Hawk nodded and waited while Spotted Eagle packed the pipe full of kinnikinnick, spooned a live coal from the firepit and placed it on the bowl of the pipe. He drew several drafts from the stem until smoke poured from his nostrils. The sweet fragrance of kinnikinnick filled the tipi as first he, then Medicine Hawk blew smoke to the sky, earth, and the four winds. Medicine Hawk returned the pipe to Spotted Eagle. "I come to your lodge with a heavy spirit," he said. "My adopted son, who has no eyes, is very sick."

"What is his sickness?" Spotted Eagle said while signing with his hands.

"His spirit lives in another place. He wills to not speak nor eat. Soon his spirit will leave his body, I fear. *Wakan-Tanka* has not heard my prayers."

Spotted Eagle stared at the firepit, wagged his head and remained silent for several minutes. He finally spoke without looking away from the fire. "What do you want to do?"

"Take him to the sweat lodge and try to bring his spirit into the hoop of the living two-legs. You have great power from the Crow Sun Dance, so maybe you can persuade *Acba-Dadea* to save him."

"We must pray first, then we will take the son of Medicine Hawk to the sweat lodge for purification."

They left the tipi and faced the sun now rising above the eastern horizon. Spotted Eagle raised his arms. He began to chant his prayer to *Acba-Dadea*. "Hey-hey-hey-hey! Hey-hey-hey-hey! Grandfather! Great Spirit—maker of everything— maker of the great hoop of the world. You have given the power of the bison to your children. It is from the bison that the hoop of the nation grows strong. It is into that hoop that the son of Medicine Hawk, the one who has no eyes has come. He is in despair, is sick and weak. It is for him, Grandfather, that I send my voice. Send us the power to cure the one who has no eyes. Aho! Aho!"

"Aho!" Medicine Hawk said, lowering his arms.

"Bring your son to the river," Spotted Eagle said. "I will prepare the sweat lodge."

Medicine Hawk walked back to his tipi. He felt at ease and free of apprehension over Joel's sickness.

Medicine Hawk laid his hand on Joel's shoulder and gently jiggled him. "Are you awake?"

"Aye."

"You grow weaker with each sun."

"Why didn't ye let the bear kill me?"

"So… you wish to walk in the hereafter?"

Joel remained silent for a moment and then turned his face toward the wall. "Aye, I do. I am no good to anyone. I am blind. Only ye understand my crippled speech. I am only a burden to ye."

"You have asked me many times why I saved you from the bear, from Lone Wolf and Grey Bull. I told you to ask *Wakan-Tanka*, but you said you would not. How can the Great Spirit answer if you do not speak to him?"

"I asked God, but got no answer."

"I told you that your God was not here, not where the Ancient Ones walked."

Joel felt anger throbbing in his temples. "Nay, ye don't understand. Ye are heathen. Ye do not know God. Ye pray to spirit beings that live in your imagination."

Medicine Hawk frowned, his heart stinging from Joel's rebuke. "Where is your God, Joel Leslie?"

"Well… I'm not certain… in heaven… no, he is everywhere."

"Everywhere?"

Joel turned to face Medicine Hawk. "Aye, everywhere."

Joel could not see the toothy grin spreading across

Medicine Hawk's face. "So we are arguing words, names and ideas about the Great Spirit. The Lakota call him *Wakan-Tanka*, the Crow call him *Acba-Dadea*, the Blackfoot call him *Natojewa*, the Ponca call him *Wakanda*. He is *Tirawahat* to the Pawnee, and you washichun call him God. The Great Spirit has shown himself to all of us in different ways according to our ability to understand."

"Nay," Joel said, "I cannot agree with ye."

"Very well—enough of this talk. This tipi stinks from your unwashed body. I am going to take you to the sweat lodge and a plunge in the river."

"The river? Nay, can't we heat some water here in the tipi?"

"The sweat lodge followed by cold water will cleanse your body and revive your spirit."

"I don't want to go," Joel said, wagging his head. "Why do ye want me to do this?"

"The sweat lodge ceremony is a tradition of the Sun Dance. It is done to purify the body and spirit."

"I am a Christian," Joel said, sitting up to face Medicine Hawk. "I have no faith in your Sun Dance."

"Your faith is not required. Come, Spotted Eagle is preparing the sweat lodge."

Medicine Hawk described the sweat lodge and its purpose to Joel as they walked toward the river. It purified and was a place for prayer and revelation. He described how the builders had cut twelve saplings and placed them in the ground in an upright circle. After bending the poles over and interweaving them at the top, they covered the frame with buffalo hides. When completed, it had the shape of a ball cut in half with its doorway facing toward the east. To the right of the doorway inside the lodge, they had dug a pit for stones that were being heated in an outside firepit.

Spotted Eagle raised his hand. "Medicine Hawk and his son that has no eyes are welcome to the sweat lodge of the Crow. After we strip naked, we will pour water over each other, then we will go into the lodge."

As Medicine Hawk led Joel into the lodge, Spotted

Eagle gave Joel a switch made from course grasses tied into a bundle. Spotted Eagle and Medicine Hawk sat down on either side of Joel. They sat in silence as four young men placed red-hot stones on flat rocks, carried them inside the lodge and placed them in the pit. After the fourth stone was placed, Spotted Eagle said, "Aho! Aho!, thank you Grandfather for hearing our prayers."

The four men then filled the pit with red-hot stones and closed the door-flap. The interior of the lodge was dark except for the glowing stones. Spotted Eagle reached for a bowl of water and a dipper carved from a buffalo horn. He splashed a small amount of water onto the stones. Joel felt the heat as steam began to fill the lodge. He heard swishing sounds as Medicine Hawk and Spotted Eagle began to spank themselves with their switches. "Joel Leslie must strike his skin with the switch," Medicine Hawk said. "It will make his skin sweat big."

Joel slowly struck the switch against his chest and thighs. Medicine Hawk and Spotted Eagle began to speak in their sacred languages as they prayed to *Acba-Dadea*. With their prayers said, Spotted Eagle poured a full dipper of water over the stones. Steam filled the lodge. Joel could not remember when he had been so hot. The air seemed heavy and laden with moisture. He struggled to breathe and bent over closer to the earthen floor where he found cooler air. Just when he felt the steam less oppressive, Joel heard Spotted Eagle pour another dipper of water over the stones. The stones hissed. More steam filled the lodge. Sweat stung Joel's eyes and dripped from his nose and chin. Rivulets of sweat coursed down his back, chest and legs. Slowly, the surface of the earthen floor around him turned into slick mud.

Spotted Eagle kept the stones hissing with two more dippers of water. As the heat began to lessen, he called for the men outside to open the door-flap. Joel felt a rush of cold air. At last, he could breathe, the air now light and cool.

"Is it over?" he asked, starting to stand up.

"No," Medicine Hawk said, pulling him back down. "We have three more sessions to go."

"I can not—it will kill me."

"Each session is easier," Medicine Hawk said. "You will see."

Spotted Eagle called for the door to be closed. He dashed another dipper of water into the steaming pit of stones. Once again, the lodge filled with oppressive heat. Joel did find the experience less painful as the second session progressed. Several minutes following the seventh dipper of water, the steam began to diminish. The second session ended with Spotted Eagle calling for the door to be opened.

Spotted Eagle used ten dippers of water during the third session. Another short intermission was followed by the fourth and final session. After steam rose from the tenth dipperful during the final session, Joel began to experience an exhilaration of a degree he had never known before. His body felt light, his head spinning. Strange things began to appear in the sky above him. Unable to see them clearly, he wiped his fingers across both eyes. He was no longer blind. There were images he had never dreamed of, let alone seen before. From the north, a great herd of bison streamed across the sky. The roar of their hooves was loud, its crescendo greater than the falling waters of Niagara. Leading the herd was an enormous white bull. Astride the white bison was a man, naked, his body painted white. His long hair and beard, white as his painted skin, streamed behind him. A red band of cloth tied around his head covered his eyes. He held a hooked staff covered with white buffalo hide fringed with eagle feathers in his hand. A voice louder than the stampeding herd thundered from a billowing dark cloud following the racing bison. "Behold, Sees Plenty!"

Joel replied to the voice by speaking strange words that neither he, Medicine Hawk or Spotted Eagle were able to understand. The spectacle faded into darkness when frigid air blasted through the open doorway. He rubbed his eyes. The darkness he had lived in since being blinded by Lone Wolf remained. He was still blind. He pondered the significance of his odd experience and decided he must have been hallucinating, overcome by the terrible heat in the lodge.

Joel felt the hands of Medicine Hawk and Spotted Eagle lifting him up. "Now we take a plunge in the river," Medicine

Hawk said, leading Joel out of the lodge.

* * *

The sky was cloudless and brilliant as Willow Calf hurried across the village grounds. In the parfleche bag she was carrying were warm winter garments and moccasins she had collected for Joel. The subtle passage of autumn's balmy days was nearly over. Soon the short and harsh days of winter would embrace the high country with icy winds and blowing snow.

Willow Calf hesitated at the doorway. Joel was sitting beside the firepit, clutching a tattered Hudson's Bay blanket around his shoulders. "I'm blind," he said to Medicine Hawk, "how could I have seen such things?"

"Greetings to Joel Leslie and Medicine Hawk," Willow Calf said, stooping to enter.

"Joel Leslie has experienced a great vision in the sweat lodge," Medicine Hawk said. "Sit by the fire and listen."

She sat beside Joel and listened to Medicine Hawk. "With the eyes of our Medicine Fathers you saw a great herd of bison released by *Acba-Dadea* from the North where the white giant lives. They kept coming for many winters, filling the sky with the thunder of their hoofs. Our four-legged brothers saw our people wandering naked and hungry. The Medicine Fathers spoke to the bison words of compassion for our people. Feed, clothe, and shelter the two-legs with your flesh, bones and hides, they commanded. This our brothers have done. The bison is our strength. Each of our people walks with the spirit of the bison inside them. In your vision, the Medicine Fathers have shown you this great truth. In times past, the white giant of the North would send to us a great white bull."

Joel raised his hand to interrupt Medicine Hawk. "Who is this white giant of the North?"

"He is the Grandfather of the North. His *power* is the cleansing wind sweeping from the white giant's wings."

"He is a bird?"

"Sometimes he is a great white goose. Usually we do not see him, only feel the cold wind from his wings."

Joel wagged his head. "I do not understand."

"In due time, the Medicine Fathers will reveal these

truths to you. Now the white bison comes on the wind from the wings of the Grandfather of the North. He is sacred and full of medicine.   No two-legs can ride the white bull, except one chosen by The Great Spirit. In your vision, a white man whose eyes are covered by the blood of dark spirits is riding the white bull. He is carrying a shaman chief's hooked staff covered with the hide of a white bison and adorned with eagle feathers. This vision has much medicine. Listen to what the Medicine Fathers have spoken to you, Joel Leslie. The Great Spirit has chosen Joel Leslie to ride the white bison. You are going to receive the Power of the Medicine Fathers. Your blind eyes will see plenty. You will be called Sees Plenty, a shaman chief of the Sun Dance."

"A shaman, a chief of your religion?" Joel said and then laughed. "That is impossible. I don't believe in your *Acba-Dadea*."

"What do you believe?" Medicine Hawk asked.

"In nothing—not anymore. Ye call me Sees Plenty just because I had an hallucination in that god-forsaken sweat lodge. Can't ye understand that I can't see a damnable thing? If there is a God, where was he when Lone Wolf and Grey Bull blinded me and maimed my tongue?"

"That is a strange question for a washichun *wakan* man."

"I'm not a missionary, not even a believer anymore."

"You cannot escape the truth of your vision," Medicine Hawk said, signing truth. "It will come to pass."

"I respect your words, but it will not."

Chapter 14

Joshua was looking forward to another of Hook's colorful after-supper stories, certain to be seasoned with embellished feats of bravery. As usual, they ate their supper in silence while Lucy kept their plates supplied with roasted elk and boiled Indian turnips. She ladled brown gravy over each new serving of meat and turnips, and kept steaming chunks of Indian fry-bread sizzling in hot bear grease. Joshua finally tore hot fry-bread apart and sopped the last remnant of gravy from his graniteware plate.

Hook belched and leaned back in his chair. With fingers gnarled and callused, he crumpled tobacco and packed it into the bowl of his once-white meerschaum pipe now stained brown from years of use.

Joshua sipped hot coffee and watched Hook search for a match to light his pipe. He judged Hook to be past forty but not much. Black hair streaked with gray fell across sinewy shoulders. Large grey-blue eyes flashed clear as a hawk's beneath heavy brows beginning to grow bristly. A rather large nose, slightly bulbous at the tip, leaned over a mustache that drooped over his mouth. Once cherubic cheeks bronzed by wind, sun and age peeked above a scrubby gray beard.

Lucy touched a flaming match to the tobacco curling atop the bowl of Hook's pipe. "By damn, Lucy girl," he said, sucked and blew several puffs of blue smoke. "You air the best damn cook in these here mountains."

"Aye, and that y'are," Joshua said, glancing over his shoulder at Lucy. Her hazel eyes, almost black in the dim lantern light, danced as she nodded her thanks for the compliments.

Joshua continued to watch Lucy, unaware of the story Hook was beginning to tell. He found her to be a comely young woman of medium height. She could be no more than twenty-five and was endowed with a figure that would be admired by any man whether Indian or white. The silver concho-belt tightly binding the waist of her buckskin dress emphasized an ample bosom and well-turned hips. She interested Joshua a great deal, but she belonged to Hook. He reminded himself of that fact once again and turned his attention to the story Hook was telling.

The tale was about a bear hunt Hook had gone on when he was seventeen. Being new in the mountains, he was uneducated to the power and cunning of a grizzly. While setting traps for beaver along Bull Creek in the Wind River Mountains, he encountered his first bear that zoologists had named *Ursus horribilis*. "Yessir, there I was," Hook said, pointing the stem of his pipe at Joshua. "All'st I could see was that critter all reared up with slobbers drippin' off his chin."

Not wanting to reveal that he had missed hearing the first part of Hook's story, Joshua said nothing.

"That was the biggest, most fearsome bear I'd ever see'd," Hook said, with his eyes popping. "Yessir, he were a good ten feet tall with them paws o' his slappin' the air. I pulled up my side-hammer Sharps an' jammed the barrel agin his chest an' yanked the hammer back. Afore I could pull the trigger, that grizz' slapped that Sharps right out'n my hands. That's when I got my first snoot-full o' grizz'. Never will forget that stink as he wrapped them paws around this child. I got one whiff afore he began to squeeze. I could hear my ribs snappin' like steppin' on dry sticks. All'st this child could do was reach for my Bowie. Never will forget that critter rarin' back and screechin' ever' time I rammed that blade 'twixt his ribs. That grizz' turned me loose and began to chaw on my arm. Them long claws ripped my duds apart until all'st was left were shreds."

Hook peeled off his buckskin shirt. He pointed first at the crosshatch of scars covering his chest, then at deep scars covering his left shoulder and upper arm. "He chawed meat off this child's shoulder and ripped hide with each swipe o' them claws. Well sir, I traded jab for jab with ol' grizz and was near done for when I felt the final jolt o' his heart agin my Bowie. Then he let go o' this child and tried to run off. Even a grizz' cain't go far without no heart."

Hook pulled on his shirt and reached for his pipe. He knocked the dollop of ashes from the bowl, eyed Joshua, and reached for his tobacco pouch.

"Your wounds must have been terrible," Joshua said, wagging his head.

"I reckon they was, but ol' grizz' helped get me well."

"He did? How?"

"Well sir, after washin' all the grizz-stink off in the crick, I cut out his liver an' poulticed up my hurts. I camped next to that bear and near' eat 'im up afore he began to turn sour."

"I find that amazing."

"It's the god's truth."

"I've read of such about Daniel Boone when he killed his first bear."

Hook began to chuckle and shook his head. "I heared 'bout that, but that bear weren't no grizz'. He were a black bruin. Reckon I could've kilt that critter with my bare hands."

Joshua glanced at Lucy. He could not hide his disbelief of Hook's brag. Lucy winked at Joshua and poured coffee into two graniteware cups. Once again, he was mesmerized by her gold pendant, from the flashes of light it was reflecting from the fireplace. Lucy walked from the hearth and handed Joshua a cup. His eyes followed the gold pendant swinging like a hypnotic talisman.

Lucy could see the lust for gold in Joshua's eyes, having seen it before in the eyes of Hook and other white men. It seemed to be a curse the white man could not resist. She felt it quite foolish and had only worn the nugget because Hook had demanded that she wear it.

Hook eyed Joshua's fascination with Lucy. He took the cup from Lucy, glanced back at Joshua and pulled at the cork in a brown crockery jug. A loud pop echoed inside the jug as the cork came free. "That's gold, y'know," he said, pouring whiskey into his and Joshua's cups.

"Aye, I assumed as much."

"I given it to her."

"So she told me."

"That figgers, I've seen you starin' at it."

"Aye, It must weigh a lot."

Hook sipped from his cup, sighed, knuckled his mustache and smacked his lips. "Five and a half ounces."

"How much is one that big worth?"

"I been tol' it'd bring over a hunderd bucks down at Brigham's town."

"Ah, that is a fancy price," Joshua said, hesitating to ponder Hook's bragging mood. He may be ripe for another boast. "Too bad y'don't have more of them."

"Reckon I don't, but I know where more of 'em is."

"Ye do?"

Hook sucked on his pipe and blew smoke at Joshua. "Yep, bet you'd like to know, too."

Joshua returned Hook's stare. "Would ye believe me if I said I didn't?"

"Hell no," Hook chortled, waving his pipe at Joshua's bandaged feet propped up on a keg with Shockley's flour stenciled in black on its side, "but you ain't goin' no place for a long time on those frizzed feet."

"Nay, I suppose not."

"Winter is 'bout to slam this country into a deep freeze that won't thaw 'til next spring. Y'ain't goin' nowheres, not until the Moon O' Green Grass. That's April, y'know."

Joshua wagged his head. "Nay, I'll be fit to ride a horse afore that."

Hook reared back his unshorn head and spewed rasping sarcasm around the pipestem clenched between yellowed teeth. "Haw. What horse? Y'ain't got no horse."

"You have two."

"Need 'em both. Ain't for sale."

Joshua reached inside his pocket, pulled out Bridger's map and spread it on the table. "Just where is your cabin located on this map?"

Hook ran the stem of his pipe along the Bighorn River until it reached a bend between Alkali and Bear creeks. "Right here," he said and pointed at the trail Bridger had pencilled up the middle of the Bighorn Basin. "What's that line for?"

"Jim Bridger's trail to the gold fields in Montana."

"I been there, up on Grasshopper Crick back in sixty-three. They was diggin' out a lot o' gold there an' over in Alder Gulch too."

"Is that where you found Lucy's nugget?"

Hook looked up at Joshua, smiled, and sucked another mouthful of smoke. "Naw, that glob peeked at me from the bottom of Beaver Crick," he said, spewing smoke with each word.

"Beaver Creek in Montana?"

"Hell no," Hook blurted, pointing his pipe at the Oregon Trail running between the Wind River and Green mountains. "Beaver Crick's down there on South Pass right here in Dakoty Ter'tory."

Joshua studied the map. *A fair distance from this place,* he thought. "How many days would it take to get to South Pass?"

The old ladder-backed chair, ofttimes fixed with rawhide, squeaked beneath Hook as Joshua watched him lean back and sip stale coffee spiked with rot-gut booze. "Seven, maybe eight when the weather's fittin'."

Toes blackened and without feeling wiggled within layers of unbleached muslin counting the weeks before geese would wing their way north. While contemplating the coming winter, its long nights and short days, Joshua wondered whether he could maintain his sanity. He felt once again the anxiety experienced when as a child he had counted the months, weeks and days until the arrival of special days, like his and Joel's birthday and Christmas. He glanced at Hook and pondered whether this man would remain his friend come the Moon Of Green Grass when April greened the mountains. And then there was Lucy, a woman of simple beauty whose eyes beguiled him the first time he saw her in the cave. Her face was smooth, the color of terra cotta faded by the summer sun. Sable braids trailed in front of her shoulders down to her waist. Her lips were full, curling upward a bit at the corners like a smile that never ceased. And he thought her nose to be perfectly balanced between high cheekbones that cradled those bewitching eyes. His musings concluded with the same question he'd asked himself over and over since Lucy found him. Why is a woman pretty as Lucy living with an ugly mountain man twice her age?

Joshua watched Lucy busy herself with getting the cabin ready to retire for the night. She draped woolen blankets across a rope Hook had strung across the room, dividing it in half. She and Hook would sleep on a bed of buffalo robes in the back half next to the fireplace. Lucy would spread Joshua's bed on the floor next to the front door.

It was a comfortable cabin made of peeled logs. The snow and frigid winds of winter were shut out by grass mixed with clay chinked between the logs. Its furnishings were meager but ample. The rocking chair, four ladder-backed chairs and a small table were pushed aside at night to make room for their beds. Just before retiring, Lucy blew out the oil lantern hanging from a nail driven into the end of open shelves Hook had built during the previous summer.

"Well, reckon its time to scoot under the robes," Hook said, winking at Joshua.

"Aye, I am weary and the whiskey has made me drowsy."

Hook held up the jug. "Have another snort. It's the only mistress you got tonight."

Joshua stood up, wagged his head and limped across the cabin toward his bed. "Nay, a mistress of any sorts I'm not needin'."

After Lucy blew out the lantern, Hook spoke to her in hushed tones. Joshua lay beneath heavy robes, distracted from sleep by Lucy's giggles and moans. After a few minutes, Hook began to grunt. *Hook sounds like an Angus bull mounting a yearling heifer*, Joshua mused, and then began to chuckle at Hook's strenuous efforts. *I hope the poor man doesn't have a stroke of apoplexy afore he's finished.*

After several minutes, Hook's grunting ceased. But sleep still did not come to Joshua. He lay awake, pondering all of the gold lying in Beaver Creek. For the first time since he deserted Fort Laramie, Joel's lot did not seem important. After all, some medicine man had rescued him, taking him away from the torture of the Lakota. Jim Bridger had assured him of that.

The following morning, after Hook left to run his traps,

Lucy began her task of changing the dressings on Joshua's feet. She knelt beside his right foot propped atop the Shockley's flour keg and peeled away the muslin wrappings. All of the toes were black and shriveled like dried prunes. Joshua's trained eye searched for the abrupt line of demarcation where healthy tissue suddenly turns dead. Lucy helped him examine each toe, making certain the line was sharply defined and extending the entire circumference of each toe. He found demarcation nearly complete on three toes of the right foot. Fortunately, only the big toe on his left foot was gangrenous and its demarkation complete. All of the swelling of both feet had resolved with only scabs where the gangrenous blebs had been.

Joshua was facing two options. He could wait for all of the dead tissue to slough away on its own or amputate each toe above the demarkation zones. Hook was right. He couldn't do the amputations himself. If it were to be done, either Hook or Lucy would have to do it.

After Lucy had washed, dried and rewrapped each foot, Joshua reached for her hand. "Thank ye, y'do have a gentle touch."

Her dark eyes met his for a moment. She nodded, smiled, quickly withdrew her hand and picked up the basin of soapy water. Joshua watched her open the door and toss the wash-water into the snow. She returned to the hearth, opened a large root bin and counted out several Indian turnips. She dropped them into an iron kettle of water setting on an iron trivet in the fireplace.

"What are ye cooking?"

"Beaver tail stew," she said, leaving the cabin.

She returned with a beaver carcass Hook had skinned and hung outside on the cabin wall. She laid the frozen carcass on the hearth to thaw while the turnips boiled.

"Beaver tail is quite good," Joshua said, reaching for a black, leather-bound volume lying on a shelf beside his chair. He lifted the book, blew dust from its cover and examined ornate gold embellishments covering its spine. At the top of the spine, gold letters spelled out the title, *The Book Of Mormon*. The year of 1830 was imprinted in gold at the bottom of the spine. *What have we here?* he thought, opening the cover. An inscription was penned on the flyleaf. *For my dear friend, James Hooker. May this first edition of the Book Of Mormon be for you an eternal pillar of fire. Joseph Smith, Jr.* "Where did Hook get this book?".

"Belong to Hook's father."

Joshua suddenly stopped turning the pages. Tucked between two pages was a folded sheet of paper, yellowed and brittle from age. He carefully unfolded the paper. It was a map bearing topographical lines drawn by an apparently skilled cartographer. The Sweetwater River and several creeks with their names neatly penciled along each stream meandered across the map. A series of elevations near the edge of the map were labeled Beaver Bluffs. To the southwest of the bluffs, four X's had been marked along Beaver Creek. At the bottom of the map was penned the signature of James Hooker and the year 1847.

More than ever, Joshua believed that Hook had more gold stashed someplace. No man could pick up one nugget and never return for more. He leaned back in his chair and envisioned hundreds of nuggets lying beneath the crystal waters of Beaver Creek. All of them waiting to make him richer than he'd ever dreamed.

Chapter 15

Joel lay on his back, staring into the blackness of his perpetual night. He wished to die, to end the torment that was sapping his strength like a blood-sucking leech. Like wintertime in Lapland, his sun refused to rise, to turn the night into day. He was alone with only memories to pluck him out of the depths of despair.

Where was Joshua? Why did he not come to rescue him from the abyss where his spirit was moldering? How many months had it been since he was taken captive by Lone Wolf? He had no idea. He had lost all sense of time. But surely Joshua would come soon. If he didn't, Joel was certain of his fate; he would soon descend into a hell of madness.

Joel no longer took notice of the daily incantations of Medicine Hawk. The rustling sounds of his eagle-wing fan, the aroma of smoke that he blew on Joel's eyes through a hollowed piece of a spikehorn-elk's antler, and the sounds of his flute playing songs of healing. And he wished the old medicine man would quit lecturing him about his sweat lodge hallucination. He wanted to be left alone, to dwell in his land of memories.

The pleasant timbre of Willow Calf's voice roused him from his sojourn into self-pity. "Joel Leslie," she said, gently nudging his shoulder.

He roused, turned to face the pleasing voice, and held up his hand to greet her. She grasped his hand and knelt beside his bed. "I have brought you some hot soup."

"I'm not hungry," he answered, and turned away.

She set the bowl aside. "What must we do? All you do is face the wall and curse your God because of your afflictions."

Joel didn't answer.

"We are your friends. Don't turn your back toward us."

He remained silent.

"You have turned away from Medicine Hawk. His heart is heavy."

Joel did not reply. Willow Calf wagged her head, picked up the bowl and poured the soup into the fire. He pulled the blanket over his head and began to sob as she left the lodge.

As he lay beneath the folds of his blanket, he muttered words of anger toward the Lakota that had tortured him and even at Joshua who had failed him. In his state of utter despair and rage, he crawled from his bed and began to search the lodge for Medicine Hawk's knife. He tore the blankets and robes away from Medicine Hawk's bed but found no knife. He ripped the bindings from Medicine Hawk's medicine pouch and scattered all of his sacred fetishes across the floor. He continued his frenzied search for a knife. In frustration he finally broke Medicine Hawk's hooked staff across his knee, slammed it into the firepit, and stood in the center of the lodge, flailing the air with clenched fists. "Why? Why?" he cried, and fell on his knees. "I can't even end my misery."

Medicine Hawk found him there, curled up like a newborn infant beside the firepit. Medicine Hawk glanced around the lodge and wagged his head. He knelt beside Joel and began to chant a prayer to *Acba-Dadea*. "Get away from me," Joel yelled, swinging blindly at Medicine Hawk. "I don't want your prayers. Why don't you let me die?"

Medicine Hawk slowly pulled his knife from its sheath. He placed the elkhorn handle in Joel's hand and walked from the lodge.

Joel's fingers gripped the handle. He raised the knife and pressed the cold blade against his neck. At last, he had the means to end the final act of this tormenting drama. One slash would bring down the curtain. One quick moment of pain to end all pain, then there would be nothing, no applause, no weeping, just blessed oblivion.

He lay next to the firepit with the blade pressed against the pulsating artery of his neck. His hand needed courage for the final act of deliverance, but his courage balked like a stubborn mule. Minutes passed. His hand strained but remained immobile as if it were sculpted from stone.

The sound of Plenty Coups' voice being lashed by the wind aroused Joel from his dilemma.

"I must speak with Joel Leslie," Plenty Coups said, stooping to enter the lodge.

Joel let the elkhorn handle slip from his hand. "Why?"

"You are poisoned."

"The Lakota gave me no poison."

"The poison is there," Plenty Coups said, touching Joel's chest. "When the tomahawk of Joel Leslie strikes Lone Wolf, the poison will be no more."

Joel looked up at Plenty Coups as if he were able to see into the Indian's eyes. *Ye must be mad. Me? Fight Lone Wolf? For heaven's sake, man, I'm blind.* He began to laugh at such an absurd idea.

"In a vision I saw the scalp of Lone Wolf hanging from your lance."

Joel stopped laughing and grasped a handful of his own hair. "These Scottish locks would hang from *his* lance instead."

"No, in my vision, you fought Lone Wolf in the Cave of the Winds deep in the mountain where the sun cannot see."

"Ye mean it is dark?"

"Yes... no light."

Joel extended and flexed his fingers as he pondered the idea of his killing Lone Wolf. *Over and over, in my own dreams, my hands have reached for Lone Wolf's neck, but my fingers refuse to obey. How can I take any man's life? I can't even kill myself.*

Plenty Coups grasped Joel's shoulders. "Have no fear."

"My eyes see only blackness."

"Lone Wolf will see only blackness in the Cave of the Winds."

"Even so, he is a warrior. I am not."

Plenty Coups plucked one of the eagle feathers from his hair. "Before the moon changes," he said, placing the feather in Joel's hand, "you will make your first coup. On that day, I will tie this feather in your hair. You will be a Crow warrior."

Joel ran his fingers over the feather while considering Plenty Coup's words. "Me... a warrior... I could not, even if I could see."

"You will be a warrior; the Medicine Fathers have spoken."

* * *

Each morning as the dawn crept into the valley, Plenty Coups and Joel met in the council lodge where they practiced fighting with tomahawks. Plenty Coups had replaced the heads of two tomahawks with practice heads made from many layers of tanned buffalo hide stitched together. But every jab or slash still inflicted painful bruises that quickly covered their head, arms, chest, and belly.

Joel learned to listen for Plenty Coups' movements; the subdued brushing of his moccasins against the clay floor, even his gasps, grunts, and raucous breathing. Gradually, Plenty Coups landed fewer painful blows as Joel stalked his sighted adversary.

One morning after Joel had avoided every slash and thrust by Plenty Coups, he graduated with one quick lunge. If the head of the tomahawk had been sharp steel, it would have killed Plenty Coups.

"You are ready," Plenty Coups said, rubbing his bruised chest. "Tomorrow, we will ride."

Joel wondered if he could best Lone Wolf in a hand-to-hand fight, even at the bottom of a deep cavern where Lone Wolf would be as blind as he. But there could be no turning back, not because of fear or blindness, not even if it were certain that his life would be ended by a slashing Lakota blade.

"We have become brothers," Plenty Coups said as he picked up his medicine bundle. He untied it, withdrew an ornate tomahawk and placed the quill decorated handle in Joel's hand. "This tomahawk is full of medicine. It will end the life of Lone Wolf."

* * *

The morning of their departure dawned beneath an ashen overcast. Joel and Plenty Coups urged their ponies to a trot as they and twenty warriors of the Fox Warrior Society rode away from Joel's lodge. The snowfield covering the valley was melting beneath a warm Chinook wind blowing down the mountain inclines. Joel could not see Willow Calf, Spotted Eagle, and Medicine Hawk waving farewell, but he did hear them voice their encouragement to him and the avenging warriors. The warriors broke into loud yelping sounds like stalking wolves. Their enthusiasm infused Joel with so much pride that he raised his tomahawk like a Scottish claymore sword above his head and yelled a Gaelic farewell.

For hours, their pace was steady as the ponies trotted through snow now turning to slush. Joel listened to twenty-two ponies beating the soggy ground with their muddy hoofs. Ice and mud clung to the sole of every hoof and grew with each step until a thick saucer of gumbo loosened and flipped away.

The farther they rode from the village, the more Joel questioned their foray into Red Cloud's domain. He was determined to face Lone Wolf, but how many Crow warriors would die or be captured and tortured by the Oglala? Why would twenty young men be willing to help him avenge the torture committed by Lone Wolf? Plenty Coups had faith in his vision, but why were the others there, riding toward a confrontation fraught with danger?

Plenty Coups reined his pinto closer to Joel's pony. "We will see the Tongue River after five suns."

"Maybe Red Cloud's village has moved."

"Red Cloud wars against the white fort on Piney Creek," Plenty Coups said. "He will not leave before all the white soldiers are dead or have returned to their fort on the Platte."

Joel faced Plenty Coups. "I pray your vision comes true."

"The Medicine Fathers do not lie," Plenty Coups said. "Lone Wolf will walk in the hereafter."

* * *

Willow Calf stood in the melting snow and watched Joel, Plenty Coups, and the warriors until they disappeared behind a snow-swept knoll. Her heart was heavy, weighted down by a worrisome spirit. As she stood gazing at the bleak winter landscape that had swallowed the raiding party, she whispered a prayer to Joel's God for his safe return.

She walked back to her father's lodge and the work that would hopefully chase away her feelings of helplessness.

Each morning as she went to the river with her axe to chop a hole in the ice so she could fill her bucket with sweet water, she eyed the northeastern horizon. Each day was the same—no yelping riders could be seen racing toward the village to tell of their victory over the Oglala.

Three weeks passed with Willow Calf following the same routine. Besides getting the water each morning and helping with daily chores, she assembled a shield for Joel's induction into one of the warrior societies.

In the village of Big Belly, there were five societies: the Lumpwoods, the Foxes, the Muddy Hands, the Big Dogs, and the Ravens. Since Plenty Coups belonged to the Foxes and he and Joel were being accompanied by twenty of their members, the Foxes would probably ask Joel to become one of them, if he counted coup by striking Lone Wolf with his tomahawk.

The warrior societies were a major influence in the village. They regulated camp life and decided when to hunt or move or carry out raids against their enemies. Each society loved to parade their successes and tease their rivals that failed to equal those achievements. Each society selected its own chief. He had to lead a war party, capture an enemy's horse, and make coup in battle. Whichever member achieved most of these was usually chosen to be chief.

It was late at night when Willow Calf finished stitching a sheet of rawhide over the shield's willow-shoot frame. The following morning, she and Medicine Hawk would paint and decorate it.

She awakened early. Another bitter storm had barreled into the valley during the night. Once again, the cold fingers of winter clenched the Yellowstone country with a frigid grasp that squeezed everything; the mountains, the valleys, and the forests of conifers and aspen. The north wind, howling with the voices of a thousand timber wolves, crackled the tipi cover of Spotted Eagle's lodge. Willow Calf wrapped the shield in a parfleche pouch, pulled a heavy buffalo robe around her shoulders, and walked toward Medicine Hawk's lodge.

Medicine Hawk held up the shield and flashed an approving smile. "This is a very fine shield," he said, caressing the rawhide. "It is just the right size."

She signed from the tip of her fingers to her elbow. "My father told me to make it this wide."

Medicine Hawk nodded and handed the shield to Willow Calf. "I will mix the paints." He began to set out several clay bowls. He poured powdered pigments of yellow, red, white, and black into separate bowls and stirred bear grease into each one.

He opened a parfleche pouch and withdrew the tail of a weasel. "The eyes of the weasel will see for him." Then he withdrew two eagle feathers. "The eagle will give him much power." After handing the tail and feathers to Willow Calf, he pulled the tail of a fox from the pouch. "The fox will make him quick and wise."

They worked all day on the shield. When it was finished, Medicine Hawk held it up and nodded his approval. "The spirits of this shield will protect my son from the arrows and bullets of his enemies. He will be a great shaman chief."

The shield was decorated with the painting of Joel's vision on its face: A white man with a red sash covering his eyes and riding a white buffalo, and a black cloud with jagged thunderbolts hovering above the buffalo. To either side of the buffalo, an eagle feather was attached. The tails of the fox and weasel dangled from the bottom edge of the shield.

"Do you think Joel will ever carry it?" Willow Calf asked.

Medicine Hawk laid the shield on Joel's bed and began to chant a prayer to *Acba-Dadea*. When he had finished, he sat down beside Willow Calf and patted her hand. "Joel Leslie will never return."

Willow Calf studied the old Indian's face as he stared at the flaming logs in the firepit. His hair, white as the snowshoe hare, framed his winsome features. Many winters had hollowed his cheeks and etched his face. "If Joel will walk in the hereafter, why have we made this shield for him?"

"Joel Leslie will die in the Cave of the Winds, but Sees Plenty will be born that day. He will carry this shield and count many coup."

Chapter 16

The night before he deserted Fort Laramie reeled into Joshua's mind; his downing several bottles of brandy and the drunken walk across the quadrangle to Colonel Maynadier's quarters. He couldn't recall having ever been that inebriated before, but it didn't compare to this day, this moment.

"Here, take another swig," Hook said, his voice echoing inside Joshua's head.

Whiskey splashed between his lips, seared his throat, and found its way into his pharynx and nose. He coughed. Raw booze spewed through his nostrils. Over and over, Hook drenched whiskey between Joshua's clenched teeth. "Nay," Joshua yelled and wagged his head trying to evade the steady stream pouring from the jug. "N'more."

"Stop wastin' my likker. Cain't whack off them toes yet."

It was either do as Hook commanded or drown, so Joshua gulped fast as he could. Within moments, the spinning world began to fade, spiraling like a whirlpool into the black hole of oblivion.

When Joshua awakened, nausea convulsed his belly into fits of retching. Inside layers of blood-soaked muslin, both feet throbbed with each heartbeat. A serpent of pain coiled itself around his pounding head. Every sound seemed to be accentuated. The steady squeaking of Lucy's rocking chair and the ticking of her mantle clock and the chopping sounds of Hook's axe splitting firewood goaded his pain into a crescendo of agony. By nightfall, seeming like an eternity, his misery began to ease.

Gold, the Jezebel of all men, continued its seduction of Joshua during his convalescence. He envisioned Beaver Creek on South Pass with hundreds of nuggets lying on the bottom of its crystal-clear waters. Hook had to have more gold stashed in the cabin, someplace where it wouldn't be discovered by Lucy. Lucy probably was unaware of its existence since Hook had promised her he wouldn't go searching for gold anymore. There had to be more nuggets. No man could pick up just one and never return for more.

One week after Hook and Lucy amputated Joshua's toes, she decided to help Hook run his traps. They left at first light, leaving Joshua to fend for his needs. Through the cabin's solitary window, he watched them walking along the river until they were out of sight. He sat down in Lucy's rocking chair and again pondered every bit of the cabin's interior. His gaze fell on the hearth, a wide strip of smooth river-stones extending from the floor of the fireplace. He squatted beside the hearth and examined each stone and the joints between them. After being satisfied that there was no hiding place there, he turned his attention to the planked floor. He discovered that all of the boards were securely anchored to each floor joist with wooden pegs. His search continued. For several hours, he examined the remainder of the cabin's interior; the flour keg, root bin, mantle clock, shelves, pots, pans, whiskey cabinet, and bedding locker. None produced any gold nuggets.

He sat down in Lucy's rocking chair, ready to give up on his search. He leaned back in the chair and gazed at the smoldering log in the fireplace. *Where... just where would I hide a poke full of gold... if I had a poke of gold? Hook is hiding it from Lucy, not anybody else. Ah, of course, not in here, not where Lucy knows every inch of this hut.*

The rocking chair continued to squeak as Joshua studied, trying to deduce an answer. The only logical conclusion was that the gold was stashed outside, probably in the storage shed. He hobbled on swollen feet to the glazed window and peered out at the frozen Bighorn Basin. The basin was blanketed by snow. The sagebrush had taken on a shroud of white. Their twisted branches were weighted down with saucers of white fluff that had collected with each snowfall. The sky was gray, obscured by a low overcast. Where the Bighorns met the flat basin, wisps of misty fog filled each ravine between phalanxes of conifers laden with snow. The leaden panorama contributed its bleakness to Joshua's mood.

He returned to the rocking chair, dejected, realizing that

he was a prisoner confined to that log-walled hovel in the middle of winter. And that prison was in the center of a basin turned hostile by a vast moat of ice and snow. He stared at his feet swathed in muslin. The bandages stained by a bloody drainage hid a toeless right foot and a left foot minus its big toe. He feared that months would come and go before he could venture outside to search for the gold.

The map! How stupid I am. He pulled the map drawn by Hook's father from the *Book Of Mormon*. After finding a sheet of paper and a pencil, Joshua hobbled to the glazed window. He unfolded the map, careful not to tear the sheet grown fragile from age. He melted the frozen frost on the inside of the window with the palm of his hand. After wiping the window dry with his handkerchief, he held the map against the glass and overlaid it with the paper. He carefully traced James Hooker's lines until the map had been transferred to the blank sheet. When finished he spread the copy on the table and compared it to the original. It was identical in every detail, even James Hooker's signature.

Pleased with his reproduction, he replaced Hook's map into the *Book Of Mormon*, and then carefully folded the copy and hid it in his wallet.

A bit of a celebration seemed in order. He retrieved Hook's whiskey jug from the liquor cabinet, and leaned back in Lucy's rocking chair. He popped the cork free, raised the jug to his lips and gulped. The whiskey burned his throat, and then his belly. He began to push the rocker to-and-fro only to stop for another swig of booze. As time passed, the jug's contents were consumed until Joshua set the empty jug on the floor and began to sing and dance to a highland tune. He was oblivious of pain, his feet being numbed by the whiskey. Finally, he collapsed and laid on the floor in a drunken stupor.

* * *

When Hook and Lucy returned, they found Joshua passed out on the cabin floor. Hook picked up the jug and turned it upside down. It was empty. He slammed the empty jug into the fireplace and grabbed a bucket of water setting on the table. He doused Joshua and yelled, "Why'd you drink up my likker?"

Joshua groaned, rolled over and tried to stand up. He lurched out of control and fell across the table. A table leg cracked as it broke away, causing him to tumble spread-eagled to the floor. Hook grabbed a fistful of Joshua's shirt and yanked him to his feet. "Answer me, you thievin' sonovabitch. Why'd you drink the whole jug?"

Lucy cowered in the corner, her eyes wide with fear at Hook's explosive behavior. She had felt his wrath before, whenever he would lose control. His fists were quick to strike out at her if he was provoked. When it came to his whiskey and the services he expected from his squaw, he was easily riled.

Joshua tried to steady himself, but was unable to dodge the fist ascending toward his jaw. Lucy heard teeth cracking together as Hook's knuckles crashed into Joshua's chin. His knees buckled and his body slammed against the floor. Bits of broken teeth mixed with bloody saliva spewed between purple lips that were beginning to resemble two knockwurst sausages.

Hook stamped on Joshua's bandaged feet and kicked him in the ribs. Lucy screamed and threw herself into Hook. "No! No!" she yelled.

"Get away from me, you Injun bitch," Hook bellowed, flinging Lucy aside. "I'm goin' to make this bastard pay. He owes me."

Hook grabbed Joshua's arm and gave it a hard jerk. "Get up!" He tried to pull Joshua's limp body to his feet. Joshua could make no response to Hook's challenge. Hook's fist, boot, and the booze had rendered him senseless. Hook kicked him in the ribs again and stomped out of the cabin. The door slammed as he headed for the shed where he stored his furs, meat for the winter, and cache of whiskey.

Lucy filled a pan with water and began to sponge Joshua's face. He moaned and grasped his chest where Hook's boot had smashed into his ribs. Nausea coursed through his belly and ascended into his throat as bitter vomit spewed from his mouth. He doubled up from the pain that was clawing at his chest with each retch of his stomach.

Hook returned to the cabin with another jug of whiskey. Without speaking, he sat down cross-legged in front of the fireplace. He uncorked the jug and began to take long sips that were interspersed with loud belches. He ignored Lucy and her caring for Joshua's needs. The flickering flames of the fireplace cast dancing shadows across the dismal scene; the scowling Hook, the intent Lucy, and the battered face of Joshua.

Lucy's dark eyes glanced at Hook. She felt anger and disgust for the pathetic silhouette of Hook slouched in front of the fireplace. She pondered how many times he had beaten her since her father had accepted the gift of Hook's six ponies. She tried to run away, back to her father's lodge, after the first time Hook had beaten her. He chased after her, caught her within minutes and gave her another beating. He threatened to shave her head and lock her up in the storage shed if she tried to leave again. The threat had worked. Fear had kept her in the service of a violent man.

As she washed vomit from Joshua's swollen and bleeding lips, she sensed the rage seething within his eyes, which were now open and trying to focus on her face. Hook reached for a stick of wood. "Woman," he yelled, tossing the stick into the fire. "Quit your fussin' over that miserable bastard and get me my pipe and 'bacca."

Lucy arose without a comment and fetched the pipe and tobacco pouch. After handing them to Hook, she started to kneel beside Joshua. "Get me a goddamed match," Hook bellowed. "You're Hook's squaw, not his."

She obeyed. She held the flaming match to Hook's pipe. He took several drafts, sucking the flame into the tobacco. He grabbed her wrist and pulled her down beside him. His mood grew more sinister as he looked into her eyes. She saw darkness, menacing and evil. "Now... Lucy girl," he said, his words brazen and threatening, "don't you get any idees about scootin' under the robes with that asshole. I seen how you've been lookin' at him, and he's been eyein' your butt like it were his'n."

Lucy's eyes glanced at Joshua. "I not do that."

"By god, you'd better not," Hook said, his eyes boring at her. "If you do, I'll cut off your tits, and his balls. Now get over there and clean up his stink so's we can get t'bed."

After Lucy had cleaned up the vomit, Joshua rolled over

and crawled toward the corner where she was laying out his bedding. While helping him get settled beneath the heavy robe, she whispered, "You need, you groan. I not sleep this night."

Lucy crawled into bed beside Hook and said nothing as his rough hands began to fondle her breasts. Now she knew that Hook's anger toward Joshua had little to do with the empty whiskey jug. It was she. It was Hook's obsession with Joshua's eyes ogling her and the gold nugget dangling from her neck.

* * *

Fear along with rage, boiling and filled with vengeance, took root in Joshua. No longer did he wish to remain under Hook's roof. His mind alternated between escaping the terror of Hook's presence and the need for his protection of Lucy. This dilemma arose during the ensuing week following Hook's outburst when Lucy told Joshua about the many times Hook had assaulted her. The violent and evil side of Hook was disconcerting. Joshua began to plan for their escape. He intended to take Lucy with him, whenever the right moment arrived. He would take both of Hook's horses and enough food to last until they could reach South Pass.

Very soon, Joshua came to a fearsome conclusion. Hook was quite capable of killing anyone, no matter who they might be. If murder suited his intent, he would have no compunction in carrying it out. So getting Lucy out of the clutches of Hook posed a quandary. Hook would not allow her to leave. He would sooner cut her throat than allow another man to have her. And that is how he would look at her running away with Joshua. If his plan were to succeed, Joshua decided he would have to kill Hook.

As the weeks went by, Hook never left Lucy alone with Joshua. He always insisted on her going with him to run his trap line. Joshua had about decided that his evaluation of Hook's intentions was in error. But that idea evaporated in early February when Hook abruptly announced that he was going to be gone overnight. He had to collect some traps too far away for him to get back before dark. "Lucy girl," he said, picking up his backpack, "I want all them beaver hangin' outside skinned and stretched when I get back tomorrow."

Lucy nodded and continued to scrub the pot in which she'd cooked porridge for breakfast.

Hook glared at Joshua. "You stay away from Lucy. She's my squaw, bought an' paid for."

* * *

Lucy continued to work in silence after Hook left. Joshua limped to the window and watched Hook walking up the riverbank. *So, Hook, you think you've set your trap. You say you won't be back until tomorrow? No, you'll sneak in here tonight expecting to catch Lucy in my bed.*

Joshua's health had been nearly restored. His feet had heeled, leaving scars where toes had once been. Only a limp remained when he walked. The ribs broken under the force of Hook's boot were no longer painful. His bruised lips and chin were healed. Several chipped teeth were the only remnants of that ordeal.

Several minutes after Hook disappeared into the morning fog rising along the Bighorn River, Joshua walked to Lucy's side. "You know what Hook is planning, don't you?"

Lucy nodded. "I know."

"He will accuse us, you and me, of bedding down together. No matter whether we have or not."

"I know."

"You know what I have to do?"

"I know."

"He will be back tonight, not tomorrow. We must leave right away."

Lucy turned to face Joshua. Her hazel eyes were filled with tears. She said nothing. Her lips trembled as tears trickled onto her cheeks. Joshua's arms reached out and drew her into his embrace. He patted her back, trying to comfort her as she sobbed against his chest. "It's going to be alright. Don't you worry, I'll get us out of here."

She pulled Joshua closer. "I *am* worried. This Lucy's fault. Hook watches me all the time; sees my eyes with Joshua in them. He knows I like Joshua."

"And Joshua likes Lucy... very much."

Lucy stepped back and wiped the tears from her eyes.

"What we do?"

"I'll saddle the horses. You pack enough provisions to last a week. We'll leave soon as you're ready."

Joshua limped toward the corral beside the storage shed. He opened the gate and whistled at the roan. "Come here, girl," he called and reached for a hackamore hanging from a peg on the shed wall. The roan perked her ears and raised her head. Joshua walked slowly toward her, holding the hackamore so he could slip it over her head. Suddenly, the sound of snow crunching under boots caused him to stop. He turned around just as Hook kicked the corral gate open. A smirk pulled his lips apart. Joshua saw the glint of steel in Hook's hand. Hook held up a long Bowie knife. "Well now, asshole, ain't you sceered o' catchin' another case o' pneumony out here in the cold? Ain't no never mind. I'm goin' to cut off your balls and stuff 'em in your dead mouth."

Joshua stepped backward and crouched to receive the charging Hook. Hook gave out a loud, "A-a-r-r," and leaped toward Joshua. Joshua stepped aside and swung the hackamore with a snap like a whip. The hackamore made of rough hemp slashed across Hook's face. He cursed, "Damn you," and pawed at his eyes. He staggered around, trying to focus them on Joshua. Joshua stood still, trying to control his raucous breathing. "Hey asshole," Hook bellowed, "y'ain't gettin' away from ol' Hook. Grab your balls cause I'm comin' t'get 'em."

Slowly, Hook started walking in a crouch toward Joshua. "You're plumb sceered out o' your wits, ain't ya? You're blowin' like a hoss with the heaves."

Joshua stepped away from the advancing madman. He began to swing the hackamore to meet the imminent charge. "Gotcha!" Hook yelled, waving the knife.

The two came closer; Hook with his knife slashing side to side, and Joshua swinging the hackamore like a slingshot.

"Stop," Lucy cried, pushing open the corral gate. Joshua glanced at her. She was holding his Colt at arms length with the barrel aimed at Hook.

"You Injun bitch! Get back in the cabin before I cut off your tits and make asshole eat 'em."

"Hook stop or Lucy kill."

Hook turned his attention to her. He took two steps toward her and wiped at his eyes. "Now Lucy girl, you ain't goin' to hurt ol' Hook, are you?"

"Hook step no more."

"What you aimin' t'do with that rusted piece of junk?"

"Lucy shoot Hook."

He scowled and straightened up. "Hell, that thing's been lyin' around ever since we found asshole. It won't fire."

Joshua eased toward Lucy. "Are y'willing to take that chance?"

"Hell yes, that Injun bitch cain't shoot, probably don't even know how to cock it."

Like a mongoose leaping for a cobra, Hook lunged at Joshua. His hand bearing the Bowie knife swept upward toward Joshua's crotch. The exploding Colt sent hot lead into Hook's left knee, spinning him around. The slashing blade barely missed its mark, only slicing the fly of Joshua's britches.

The bullet had shattered Hook's femur just above the knee. He tried to spin around for another lunge toward Joshua. The broken bone grated and Hook groaned as his leg gave way, causing him to drop the Bowie. Joshua kicked the knife away and seized Hook by the neck. Hook tried to breathe, but no air passed his lips. Joshua watched the hatred in Hook's eyes abruptly change to terror. His fingers clawed at Joshua's hands, trying to tear away their strangling grip. "So ye can kill a bear with your bare hands?" Joshua taunted the stricken Hook. "Well, how does it feel to be killed with bare hands?"

Joshua could feel the resistance within Hook dissolving. His face, now bloated and engorged, was turning from crimson to a purplish hue. His jaw relaxed, mouth fell open, and saliva drooled down his chin. The light of life in his eyes began to take flight like autumn leaves in the wind.

The oath Joshua swore at Edinburgh the day he received his medical degree surfaced from the depths of his memory. Over and over, he listened to his voice speaking those words of dedication: *Whatever house I enter, I shall come to heal.* His fingers began to loosen. Hook fell into the snow, at first unmoving, and then he began to writhe and cough.

Joshua picked up the hackamore and walked toward the roan. "I'll saddle the horses," he called to Lucy, "while y'pack the travois."

Hook struggled to sit up, but fell back into the snow. "You'd better kill me, 'cause I'll be comin' t'cut off your balls."

"With a compound knee fracture? Ye'll not be walking anytime soon, if ever."

"Even if I only got one goddamned leg, I'll be comin'."

After the horses were saddled and the travois packed, Joshua and Lucy carried Hook into the cabin. Joshua pulled off Hook's boot and slit his pant leg to expose the left knee and thigh. He found that the .44 bullet had entered about four inches above the knee and exited behind the knee where it left a gaping wound. The shaft of the femur above the knee had been shattered. Joshua leaned back, stared into Hook's eyes and wagged his head. "This leg will have to be amputated or ye'll be dead in a week."

Hook tried to sit up. "By god, no. Ain't goin' t'cut off my leg,"

"Ever hear of gas gangrene?"

"Reckon I have."

"It isn't a good way to die."

"Reckon not, but I'm takin' my chances, 'sides, ain't goin' t'get no gangrene."

"This kind of wound always results in gangrene. Your leg will be starting to rot within twenty-four hours."

"Just set the sonovabitch and let me be."

"That won't do any good, ye'll still get gangrene."

"Set it, and then get the hell out o' my cabin."

Lucy peeled bark from a willow staff to make a crutch while Joshua made splints out of boards used to stretch beaver skins. Then he handed the whiskey jug to Hook. "Drink—ye'll need it."

Hook pushed the jug away. "No, you just want t'cut it off. Get it set."

"This is going to hurt, maybe more than ye can bear."

"I can take it—do it."

With Lucy's help, Joshua quickly straightened the deformed knee. Hook groaned and hissed between clenched teeth. "Pull harder," Joshua said to Lucy who was tugging on a rope looped around Hook's thigh.

Joshua pulled on Hook's leg until the deformity disappeared. "Well, the break is reduced, for all the good that's going to do."

"Put on them splints, and then take that Injun bitch and get out."

Chapter 17

Joel, Plenty Coups, and the Crow raiding party had finally reached the banks of the Tongue River on the first day of December. They had found the land of the Lakota brutally embraced by the frigid arms of winter. It was so cold that the pine and spruce trees along the Tongue River were groaning and popping. The sap within many of them had frozen and was splitting their trunks.

Plenty Coups' belief that Red Cloud would remain on the Tongue close to Fort Phil Kearny had been dashed. They had moved, most likely to the Powder River Basin, because of the early onset of severe winter weather. It would have been foolhardy and replete with risks to ride farther into Lakota country. So, with exceeding disappointment, they began their trek back toward Crow lands.

All of them slumped astride their ponies, discouraged and weary from their long journey that had been for naught. Joel pulled the collar of his bearskin coat high around his neck and chin. The cold wind, lashing out of the north, stung his face and bit his ears. In a way he was disappointed that fate had deprived him of revenge, but he was relieved that a showdown with Lone Wolf had been postponed, if not altogether cancelled.

The shadows of late afternoon crept across the countryside as the raiding party reined onto the plains where General Connor's troops had battled the Lakota in 1865. The raiding party abruptly reined to a stop. Joel called to Plenty Coups, "What's wrong?"

"Prepare to fight," he said, raising his war club, "the 'Bad Face' Lakota are before us."

Joel reluctantly raised his tomahawk and called to Plenty Coups, "How many?"

"Ten! One is a 'shirt wearer'."

The raiding party moved forward in unison like a troop of cavalry. Plenty Coups shouted in a loud voice, "Death to the Oglala!"

From the Lakota came a shouting reply. "Death to the Crow!"

The roar of pounding hoofs and snorting ponies and yelping warriors filled Joel's ears. He could feel his pinto's heaving muscles as the little horse charged toward an unseen enemy. Fear squeezed his chest like the tentacles of a giant squid as he fathomed the hopelessness of a blind man daring to ride into the abyss of certain death. Above the din of mounted warriors racing toward each other, the screeching cry of a Lakota warrior pierced the high mountain air. "Hoka Hey! Hoka Hey!"

"Lone Wolf," Joel muttered, recognizing the voice.

A bedlam of sounds rolled over the grassy plain as the warring parties met. Screaming ponies and shrieking men joined together in strident mayhem on the battlefield where Connors' soldiers had fought the Lakota. And in the middle of the melee was Joel, slashing the air with his tomahawk, striking at a foe he could not see.

All around him Joel could hear the sickening thud of war clubs and tomahawks slamming against flesh and bone, and the muffled groans of men with mortal wounds tumbling from their ponies. And then quite suddenly he sensed an overwhelming exhilaration surging through him. In an instant, like dandelion seeds on the wind, his fear flew away.

From out of the din of battle, Joel heard the voice of Lone Wolf cry, "*Wakan* Dog! *Wakan* Dog must not die."

Joel yanked the reins and heeled his pinto toward the voice of Lone Wolf. He raised his tomahawk and charged as Lone Wolf yelled, "The *Wakanpi* live, no kill *Wakan* Dog!"

Joel swung his tomahawk with a vicious sweep as the two ponies collided. The steel head slammed into flesh, crunching bone as it imbedded into its victim. Joel heard the voice of Lone Wolf scream, "A-a-a-e-e-e." And then the handle of his tomahawk slipped from his grip as Lone Wolf fell.

Joel leaped from his pony. His groping fingers found his tomahawk and the lifeless body of Lone Wolf. Without hesitation, he yanked Lone Wolf's knife from its sheath and scalped his fallen enemy. He stood up, holding high the bloody topknot of black hair, and yelled his cry of victory. "A-H-H-H-

E-E-E-H, Lone Wolf walks without hair in the hereafter!"

It was only then that Joel realized the battle had ended. All of the surviving Oglala Lakota had retreated from the field the moment Lone Wolf died. There were no more sounds of fighting, no screeching ponies, singing war clubs, nor yelping warriors. Only the groans of dying warriors could be heard.

Suddenly all of the Crow warriors that had not died began to cheer. Plenty Coups grasped Joel's shoulders and began to praise him. "Sees Plenty is a brave Crow warrior. The *Medicine Fathers* sing this day. You have earned your first coup'."

* * *

The corpses of Lone Wolf and five Oglala warriors, the battlefield, and the burial scaffolds of seven Crow warriors standing in a grove of aspen along the Tongue River lay far behind the raiding party. The battlefield hadn't only claimed the life of Lone Wolf, but had also caused an abrupt transformation to come over Joel. During their homeward trip, he had pondered his sudden lack of fear, his miraculous victory over Lone Wolf, and his primitive elation at the moment his hands ripped away the scalp that now fluttered from his hooked staff. Suddenly his blindness had become insignificant. Something, some extraordinary force, seemed to have taken residence within his being. He was now convinced that his and Plenty Coups' visions were genuine. He was no longer a white missionary named Joel Leslie. He had become Sees Plenty, a Crow warrior.

Smoke hovering above the village of Chief Big Belly came into view as the raiding party topped a grassy knoll. Plenty Coups, riding beside Sees Plenty, gave the first victory cheer that echoed across the plain. All of the warriors, except one, joined into the exaltations. When the cheering stopped, the silent warrior reined his pony into a trot, while everyone else waited to enter the village. It was the duty of the silent one to tell the families of those warriors who wouldn't be returning that their brave sons had died in a battle with the Oglala Lakota.

Soon the cries of the bereaved families resounded from within the village. Within minutes, Chief Big Belly, Spotted Eagle and Medicine Hawk rode from the village to welcome home the raiding warriors.   Trilling squaws and cheering warriors of all five warrior societies followed them.

Within Sees Plenty arose a strange feeling he had never experienced before. Overwhelming power surged through every sinew of his body. Fleeting visions flashed, one after another, in his sightless eyes. He first saw himself astride the white bison racing across the prairie. Then an old coyote whose coat was grizzled from age trotted along the shore of a vast sea. Two green-headed ducks swooped down and lit in the sea beside the old coyote. Then he saw himself running with the speed of a pronghorn antelope across an arid land covered with purple sage. The darkness of night returned to his eyes as the visions vanished.

All of the cheering warriors and trilling squaws had ceased to sound their welcome. They were in awe of Sees Plenty; their perception of him had changed. Instead of a downcast and bitter white man, they saw him as a proud Crow warrior whose countenance revealed an air of distinction. He sat his pony like a chief whose chiseled face was uplifted and full of pride. Everyone remained silent, waiting for him to speak.

He raised high his hooked staff and waved the bloodied topknot of Lone Wolf. "Here is the scalp of Lone Wolf who the Medicine Fathers delivered into the hands of Sees Plenty," he cried in a loud voice.

Wave after wave of cheering arose from the chiefs, warriors and squaws as they accompanied the raiding party into the village.

* * *

As Medicine Hawk had predicted, Joel Leslie had ceased to exist following the battle with Lone Wolf. The man that returned was Sees Plenty, a respected Crow warrior who was destined to become a shaman chief. The change that had come over him was mysterious, impossible to explain by even Medicine Hawk. However, it had happened.

The visions Sees Plenty had experienced upon his return to the village were an enigma for him. With the exception of the white bison, he was unable to determine their meaning. He decided to ask Medicine Hawk.

* * *

Medicine Hawk sat down and warmed his hands over the fire. He dropped chokecherry bark into a steaming pot of water and stirred the mixture with his knife. He seemed unsure and reticent.   Then, with his eyes fixed on the dancing flames, he began to speak. "Many winters have passed since my grandfather, Man Of Absarokee, told me how the Great Spirit sent Old Man Coyote to earth to create the home of the Crow people. First, you must understand that Old Man Coyote was not a real coyote. He was an ancient Medicine Father. He loves to play tricks on people, to make us laugh when we are sad. But in the beginning, Old Man Coyote was lonely himself, because he had no children. That is why he made us, the Bird People, the ones called Crow by your white fathers."

Medicine Hawk studied Sees Plenty's face and saw the corners of his eyes crinkle as he pondered the enigma of Old Man Coyote. He patted Sees Plenty's hand and spoke to his bewilderment. "Old Man Coyote is a spirit being, so are the feathered water birds that helped him."

Sees Plenty nodded and said, "Aye, I understand."

"This is how I remember the story my grandfather told me when I was only four winters old. Old Man Coyote was sunning himself on a tiny island in the sea that reached from horizon to horizon. There was nothing there but the island and the sea. As he looked out across the vast expanse of water, two green-headed water birds swooped by him and landed nearby. 'What kind of water bird are you?' he called to the two drakes. 'We are diving birds,' one replied. 'Ah, that is good,' Old Man Coyote said. 'There is too much water here. I cannot swim very far, and this island will be covered with water very soon. I do not know how deep the sea is. Would you dive down to see for me?' One of them replied, 'I will; the sea is very deep, but I have dived to the bottom many times.' As Old Man Coyote watched, the green-headed water bird disappeared on his dive to the bottom of the sea. When the water bird surfaced, his bill was filled with mud. Old Man Coyote took the mud and formed it into the land. He looked at the land, but it was flat like the sea; so he shaped it into mountains, valleys, and rivers.   The mountains and valleys were barren, so he covered them with forests and grass. He looked at his handiwork and said that it was very good. The water birds splashed about and flapped their wings, because they were so happy. 'The land is wonderful,' one cried. 'But who will take care of the land?' cried the other."

"Old Man Coyote pondered their question and agreed that he had to create someone to look after such a fine creation. He sent both of the diving water birds to the bottom of the sea again to bring up more mud. From those mouthfuls of mud, he made a man, and then to please the water birds, he made more drakes of all varieties. But the man and the drakes moped around in a state of dejection. Old Man Coyote, being very wise, said, 'I will make the man a mate.' After he fashioned a woman from the mud, a water bird demanded, 'Make hens for us too.' He did, and while the drakes and the man were dancing with joy, Old Man Coyote howled and spoke to the man and his mate. 'I have formed you from mud and I have made this place for you and your descendants. You are the Bird People. Take care of your mother.' Then Old Man Coyote disappeared."

"Do y'mean to say Old Man Coyote is a god?"

"The medicine of the Great Spirit comes to us in many forms," Medicine Hawk replied. "Old Man Coyote is but one of them. The Medicine Fathers can speak to us from a bird, an animal, or even the rocks."

"Rocks can speak?"

"Only to one whose ears are open."

"That is a mystery," Sees Plenty said, signing with his hands.

"Sees Plenty answers well. We believe all life is a mystery, a never-ending circle. It is a sacred hoop where everything is spirit; the earth, the four-legs, the two-legs, and the feathered beings."

Sees Plenty nodded while staring at the flames leaping above the firepit. "Your fable about creation is similar to those of many people, but why did I have a vision of Old Man Coyote?"

"Would you have listened to the story about Old Man Coyote without having your vision?"

Sees Plenty nodded again. "What is the meaning of the other vision, the one where I'm racing across a sage covered plain?"

Medicine Hawk chuckled while pouring hot chokecherry tea into two buffalo-horn cups. "Our tribe of the Bird People is called the Mountain Crow," Medicine Hawk said, handing a cup of tea to Sees Plenty. "We live in the mountains except during hunts on the plains for bison and antelope. As soon as we have enough meat and hides for the winter, we come back to the mountains."

"But what are the Medicine Fathers trying to show me?"

"That Sees Plenty will not only be a medicine man and shaman, but will also find the bison and antelope for the Crow hunters. You will be the chief of the Foxes."

"A blind man will do this?" Sees Plenty said, wagging his head.

"This is true, but you must learn our ways. I will teach you about the sacred pipe and the Sun Dance. Willow Calf will teach you Absaroka, the language of the Crow."

"How did she learn English?"

"A white trapper lived with our people many years ago. We learned your language from him."

"When will she come to teach me?"

"After you undergo the piercing ceremony."

"What is piercing?"

"It is a mystery that you must experience. The only thing I can tell you is that from much pain comes wisdom."

"When?"

"Tomorrow."

Chapter 18

The fickleness of winter dealt harshly with Joshua and Lucy while they journeyed toward South Pass. They rode along the Bighorn River in a steady snowfall during the first day after leaving Hook's cabin.

When dawn slipped into the basin the following morning, the sky broke clear and cold. The horses struggled through snow up to their hocks until they made camp that evening near the mouth of the Greybull River. During the night, a Chinook howled across the basin. Its warm winds melted the snowfield and turned the silty soil into a quagmire of sticky gumbo. For two days, globs of gumbo clinging to the horse's hoofs and travois poles slowed them to a plodding gait.

Relief from the quagmire barreled out of the north the following night when another storm blanketed the basin with a new snowfield. While the sky cleared the next day, howling winds began to sweep the powdery snow into the sky. Seething clouds of the chalky stuff ascended until the sun became a sullied orange disc.

On the evening of the fifth day, after covering only seventy miles, they made camp next to a basin of thermal springs near the Bighorn River. The sky had cleared during the afternoon, and the cold north wind had yielded to warmer southwesterly winds.

While preparing to build a firepit, Joshua walked away from the hot springs in search of wood. The evening was calm; filled with the scents of conifers and sage that mingled with those rising from the thermal springs. While picking up driftwood along the river, he pondered the gold and how rich it was going to make him. His musings caused him to gaze toward the southwest. In the distance he could see where the high plains of the Bighorn Basin met the Owl Creek Range with their snow-streaked purple summits notching the horizon. It was still a long way and days to go before they would reach South Pass.

When he had gathered all the wood he could carry,

Joshua walked back to camp. Lucy was skewering chunks of elk meat and Indian turnips onto sharpened willow shoots. Joshua started the fire, anticipating the savory meal Lucy was preparing.

"Will Hook come to kill us?" Lucy asked.

"Nay, he is probably dead already."

"I think he will come."

Joshua could see the fear in her eyes. "Believe me, Hook will die a horrible death from gas gangrene. If he comes, it will be his ghost."

Lucy wagged her head but said nothing. For several minutes, she quietly gazed at the fog rising like smoke over the thermal springs. Joshua wanted to say something to allay her fears, but could not find the words. He knew Hook was dead or dying, but Lucy refused to accept that as fact. Hook had always returned from extended trips into the mountains to terrorize her. She couldn't escape then, nor could she believe that she was finally free of his cruelty now.

While Joshua was finishing his supper, Lucy walked to the edge of one of the springs and slipped off her fur-lined boots. She sat down on a stone ledge overhanging the pool and dipped her toes into the hot water. Gradually, she immersed her feet until the water crept above her ankles. "Water good, not too hot," she called to Joshua.

"Aye, it does look inviting."

"Come soak feet, make good again."

Joshua slipped off his heavy boots and sat down beside Lucy. The warm water of the springs was soothing to his aching feet; especially, to the toes remaining on his left foot. The heat rising from the pool brought relief to their jaded spirits, and a sweat to their faces. Joshua wiped his face and looked down into the pool. The water was so clear that he could see the crystallized sediment on the bottom. *Ah, a fine tub for bathing this would be*, he thought.

Apparently, Lucy had made the same decision. She stood up and began to undress. Joshua, embarrassed by her lack of modesty, turned away and gazed toward the clouds hovering over the western horizon. When he turned back, Lucy had walked to the shallow end of the pool. His eyes devoured her bronzed figure, her sable hair sweeping across her shoulders, and her well-rounded bosom tipped with dark brown nipples. Within moments, Joshua peeled off his clothing and slipped into the pool. Lucy walked farther into the warm water until her shapely hips slipped beneath the surface. She turned to watch Joshua wading into deeper water toward her. As he neared Lucy, she playfully splashed water toward him. He dodged, laughed at her frisky behavior, and swept a sheet of water into her face. Lucy giggled and lowered herself until the water lapped at her chin. Joshua stood still, gazing into her dark and seductive eyes. He squatted down so that his face was just above the surface. They each moved closer. Lucy's lips parted as Joshua reached for her waist. She laughed and feigned an attempt to escape his eagerness. He followed, more intent than ever. She began to swim away. He dove under the water and swam after her. He was discovering that the heat of his passion was surpassing that of the pool. She stopped and waited for him. His hands found her waist and pulled her into a tight embrace. Despite the heat of the water, the softness of her skin sent a chill through him. Her lips, open and eagerly seeking, met his as their heads broke the surface.

Following their romp in the warm pool, Lucy slipped into Joshua's bedroll where they lay in each other's arms. Joshua gazed up into the vaulted night sky and reflected on Joel's fate. With the arrival of spring, he would go find him. But, first, he had to find the gold before someone else discovered the riches lying in Beaver Creek.

The following morning, they reined their horses along the Bighorn until they reached a deep canyon. Joshua peered into the narrow gorge that the river had carved through the mountains during many aeons of time. The wide banks of the river abruptly became towering inclines of stone that ascended on a nearly vertical course for hundreds of feet. He listened to the distant roar of waters cascading over rapids and around boulders. Following the river was not possible; so, after studying Bridger's map, he decided to follow the trail Bridger had marked over the mountains east of the gorge.

The trail was primitive, having had little use since Jim

Bridger set up stone markers to designate its course. The forty-mile trek over the mountains took three more days before they reached the last ridge high above the alkali flatland south of the Owl Creek mountains. While watering the horses from a spring-fed pool, Joshua pulled out his binoculars. As far as he could see, the great expanse of semi-arid lands stretched out before them. Wind-eroded ridges lay on the horizon like sleeping elephants. Across the flatland below, the only remnants of the last snow were clinging to the tortuous branches of greasy sage. Far to the southeast, a herd of antelope with their white rumps flashing in the sunlight galloped up a ridge. Not far behind them raced six mounted brown and white pinto ponies.

"Come here and take a look," Joshua said to Lucy who was minding the horses. "I see six men chasing a herd of antelope."

Lucy grounded the reins with a rock and walked to where Joshua was still glassing the distant ridge. He pointed at the ridge silhouetted against the horizon. "There they are," he said, handing her the binoculars.

Lucy held the glasses in front of her eyes and watched the riders galloping over the ridge. "Chief Washakie's Shoshone, my people," she said.

"Then, they should be friendly."

Lucy handed the binoculars to Joshua. "No, my father make Lucy go back to Hook."

"Hook is dead."

"Hook will come."

"No! He will not," Joshua blurted. "If he did, no man would force his daughter to return to such an evil man."

"My father take six ponies from Hook. I belong to Hook."

Joshua glassed the ridge again, his eyes searching for more Indians. "I swear," he said, barely more than a whisper, "no man will take ye from me."

Those words had barely left his mouth when Joshua remembered his vow to find Joel, no matter the cost. The reasons for the delay were easily explained. Frostbitten feet, pneumonia, blizzards, and the rescue of Lucy from Hook had been the culprits that would impede any man. When winter released its grip on the high country, then he would head toward Montana. There was still time to find the gold.

Not being able to build a fire for fear of it being seen by the Shoshones, they made a cold camp that night near the Wind River. While Joshua and Lucy chewed peppery sweetness from cakes of pemmican, their hobbled horses grazed on succulent clumps of last summer's grass along the riverbank.

In the dim twilight of evening, Joshua studied his map. South of the Owl Creek Range, Bridger had drawn a sweeping line depicting the course of the Wind River across the flatland until it ended in the Wind River Range of mountains. He had penciled in the convergence of Beaver Creek and the Popo Agie River that in turn emptied into the Wind River. Also, he had drawn the route of the Oregon Trail across the southern half of Wyoming and had placed an X where it crossed the continental divide on South Pass. *There's my pot o' gold*, he mused, tapping the mark with his finger.

They broke camp and reined their horses toward the southwest the following morning. The terrain was gray and foreboding with no life in it. Wiry sagebrush grabbed at the bellies of their horses and entangled the travois until it became hopelessly snared. They tied their bedrolls and two bags of pemmican cakes and jerky behind their saddles, and left the travois behind. They crossed the wide expanse of sage toward a barren and windswept rocky ridge. Beyond that ridge, they rode toward another, and then another one beyond that ridge. There seemed to be an endless stretch of flatlands divided by meandering ridges.

It was harsh country they were travelling, pushing their ponies toward the Wind River mountains shrouded by low wintertime clouds. The sage had given way to sweeping meadows of tall grass that whipped and swayed in the winds swirling down from the mountains. Joshua pulled up atop a grassy knoll. He raised his binoculars and glassed the terrain rising toward tapering summits on the southwestern horizon. "I've not seen any more of your people."

"They here, follow all day."

Joshua lowered the glasses. "Here? I haven't seen them."

Lucy pointed back toward a ridge of rocky outcroppings. A covey of partridges, with their wings humming, had risen from the rocks and were winging down the slope away from the ridge. "Two Chief Washakie braves hide in rocks."

Joshua glassed the ridge. "I don't see anything."

"They hide there," Lucy said, pointing at a scrub pine growing between two boulders.

Joshua peered through the lenses at the pine swaying in the wind. He could see no Indians, only the gray and red rocks jutting from the ridge, and the lone pine. He decided Lucy had seen no Shoshones, only ghosts that had been spawned by her fears.

As Joshua lowered his binoculars, Lucy leaned forward and heeled her ponies flanks. "Hah!" she yelled. The pony lurched into a gallop.

The roan, spooked by Lucy's sudden departure, leaped in pursuit of her galloping pinto. Joshua grabbed the saddle pummel to keep from falling off his charging mare. He yelled into the wind blasting against his face. "Lucy, stop! What are ye doing?"

Lucy abruptly reined her pony about and pointed toward the rocky ridge. "I no go back to Hook," she yelled.

Joshua looked back at the ridge. Two Indian braves were frantically kicking their ponies' flanks as they galloped through high grass toward them. Joshua wheeled the roan around and slapped her withers, over and over, with the reins. He heard the braves yelping like hungry wolves as their ponies slowly gained on Lucy and him. He yanked his Colt from his holster and recalled that only two loads remained, and they might not even fire.

Joshua was encouraged by the speed of Lucy's pinto. His roan was slowly falling behind her fleet little horse. Each time he looked back over his shoulder, the Shoshones were closer. Then in a sudden move, the two braves separated. They reined their ponies to either side of Joshua's roan. Joshua whipped the roan in a frenzy of lashes with the reins. The little mare responded with a burst of speed. The braves continued their yelping cries while trying to outrun Joshua. He held the Colt close to his chest trying to conceal it from the Indians. The brave to Joshua's right reined his pony, closer and closer, until he was alongside the roan. He reached for Joshua's reins as the other Indian heeled his pony faster in pursuit of Lucy. Without any hesitation, Joshua whipped the barrel of the Colt toward the brave chasing after Lucy. The heavy revolver lurched in his hand as the black-powder load exploded. The brave reeled and slumped onto his pony's withers. Suddenly, the roan wheeled as the other brave yanked at Joshua's reins. While falling from the spinning mare, he leveled the Colt at the Indian and pulled the trigger.

After the Colt fired, all Joshua could see was blue sky and all he could feel was the wind as he hurtled backward off the roan. He slammed against the ground with a sickening jolt that stole all of his senses, except the pain in his back that accompanied the sounds of a thousand cicadas singing in his ears. Gradually, his vision returned. Lucy was bending over him. Her lips were moving, saying something, but he could not hear her voice. She splashed water from her canteen on his face several times. Her voice seemed far away when he finally heard her say, "They rubbed out, gone under."

Joshua slowly raised himself into a sitting position. Lucy poured water into her hand and washed his face. He looked at her, grinned, and kissed her fingers. She giggled, was relieved that he did not appear to have been badly injured. She pointed at the second brave he had killed. "Him rubbed out." Then she pointed at the other brave lying crumpled nearly fifty yards away. "Him rubbed out. I no go back to Hook. Joshua shoot good."

They made a cold camp that night where Beaver Creek empties into the Popo Agie River. Joshua's Bowie knife was their only remaining weapon. The emptied Colt was useless. He and Lucy spent a restless night. Joshua wondered when more of Chief Washakie's braves would come to kill him and take Lucy back to her father. After Lucy slipped into her bedroll, Joshua draped a buffalo robe around his shoulders and began his watch for the night.

The night was clear, and so frigid that the cold seeped through the buffalo robe like raindrops sinking into dry sand. Joshua shivered and hugged himself trying to retain some warmth. The temperature plummeted as the earth's heat radiated into the clear night sky. His feet began to ache, an omen he had become all too familiar with during the blizzard high in the Bighorns. He began to pace around their campsite in a wide circle while trying to keep alert. He wondered if any Indians would be foolish enough to be stalking them on such a severe night. Probably not; however, he could not take a chance on crawling into the bedroll with Lucy.

What does a body think about while trying to keep from freezing to death? Joshua's mind meandered through a maze of thoughts like a rabbit raiding a vegetable garden. He sampled family, friends, food, bad times, good times, treasures lost, riches to be gained, highland lasses lifting their skirts with dancing knees, and finally he settled on the tender shoots of love that had been nourished by Lucy's kisses. The intoxicating presence of her lying naked beside him within the snug warmth of their bedroll had massaged his desires to a level he had not known. Oh, aye, he had a bit of a fling with young Becky Watson, a highland lassie, one spring day beneath the old bridge of Castleton. But he had only experienced her wet kisses and listened to her panting in his ear before cousin Colie interrupted their interlude of passion. What a disappointment he felt as Colie leaned over the bridge's banister and peered down at them, snickering at his discovery. "What ye doin', Joshua?" Colie chided. "Just wait 'til I tell Becky's papa." Well, that was the end of his and Becky's under-the-bridge affair.

With his mind trying to shut out the cold, Joshua continued to walk around camp like a sentry walking guard. Fatigue became another adversary, stalking his tracks and turning his legs into burdensome limbs. Each time his thoughts drifted toward his lying down, he would straighten up and slap a mitten against his cheek. His vigilance, now dulled by overwhelming tiredness and bone chilling cold, had waned like bubbles in flat ale. With his eyes concentrating on every step he took, Joshua ambled on like a sleepwalker exploring his dreamland.

On he walked, oblivious of the chorus of a pack of yelping timber wolves that were stalking an aged bull elk on the other side of the river. Finally, he roused from his trance when Lucy tugged on his sleeve. "You sleep now, I watch."

Chapter 19

The odors of kinnikinnick, wood smoke, and sweating men engulfed Sees Plenty. Pain like the talons of a great bird clawed at his chest. Spotted Eagle had just pierced the skin below each collarbone with two sharp awls of bone. After tying two ropes of sinew dangling from the ceiling of the lodge to each awl, Spotted Eagle raised his arms and prayed to *Acba-Dadea*.

When his prayer ended, the sounds of pulsating drumbeats and chanting singers commenced. Pain tore at Sees Plenty's chest as several men yanked on the ropes, pulling him upward until his moccasins cleared the floor. Agony, searing and consuming, coursed through him until urine trickled down his thighs and dripped from his moccasins.

For nearly an hour, he fought to stifle the scream that was building from the depths of his belly. It finally ascended upward, convulsed his diaphragm, slammed into his throat, and hissed between clenched teeth. Over and over, muffled screams battered his will to show no pain, but to no avail. As he slipped deeper into the yawning abyss of nothingness, his screams filled the lodge.

The velvet blanket of unconsciousness enfolded and smothered the pain. The land of oblivion into which he had entered was suddenly filled with a great light. He reached up and tried to touch flames leaping from the sun that was so close it nearly filled the sky. Then out of the sun raced four stallions: one black, one white, one sorrel, and one Paloose. Lightning flashed from their nostrils and thunder boomed each time they neighed. Chiefs wearing war bonnets of many eagle feathers rode the black, white, and sorrel stallions. But the rider astride the Paloose was a strange being with the sinewy body of a mighty warrior and the head of a coyote.

While the chiefs reined their stallions back into the sun, the Paloose trotted up to Sees Plenty. "I am Old Man Coyote," the rider said and yanked off his coyote hood, revealing chiseled features that glowed like burnished bronze. "On the day that the

Bird People cease to walk the sacred way of the Sun Dance, I must bury the bones of their brother the bison beneath the tall grass of the prairie. And their land will wither away until it becomes an island of misery. They will live in square lodges and beg like camp dogs for meat."

Old Man Coyote's words, replete with sadness, moved Sees Plenty. "What can I do?"

"The Sun Dance chief that will ride with me into the sun can save the Bird People."

"I will ride with Old Man Coyote."

"Sees Plenty can never dismount."

"I am willing," Sees Plenty said, and leaped astride the Paloose.

When Sees Plenty awakened, gentle hands were sponging his wounds with cold water. He was in his lodge, having been carried there by Spotted Eagle and Big Belly after the bone awls had ripped through the skin of his chest. "Is that ye, Medicine Hawk?"

"Yes."

"I'm sorry I screamed."

"Every warrior screams. It means nothing."

"The pain was fierce."

"Did you receive your vision?"

"Aye, I did. I met Old Man Coyote."

"Ah, that is good, what did he say?"

"That Sees Plenty can save the Bird People from much trouble."

"Then, that is what you must do, my son."

* * *

Sees Plenty sat on a buffalo robe next to the firepit, longing to hear the cheerful timbre of Willow Calf's voice again. A blizzard that lashed the village with severe winds and drifting snow had kept her from coming to teach him his language lessons. How he missed her presence that filled his day with joy. For three mornings, he had listened to the howling winds and knew Willow Calf wouldn't be coming. But today promised to be different. The winds had ceased to howl and the sun had risen to warm the walls of the tipi.

His musings were interrupted by the sounds of snow crunching beneath someone's moccasins.

"To see you makes my heart sing," Medicine Hawk said as Willow Calf entered the lodge. "Sees Plenty has been moping like a sick pony for three suns."

"Aye," Sees Plenty said, "the days are lonesome when ye aren't here."

"I have missed both of you too," she said, sitting down beside Sees Plenty.

"Before Willow Calf begins her lesson, I have something to show both of you," Medicine Hawk said, untying an old pipe bundle decorated with needlework of dyed porcupine quills.

Willow Calf nodded and Sees Plenty signed as he spoke. "Aye, what is it?"

"The Medicine Fathers taught the Ancient Ones to use the sacred pipe every day," Medicine Hawk said and withdrew a pipe with a carved stem and pipestone bowl from the bundle. He caressed the pipe and chanted a short prayer.

When his chanting ceased, Medicine Hawk placed the pipe in Sees Plenty's hands. "This pipe belonged to my grandfather, Man Of Absarokee, now it belongs to Sees Plenty. The smoke from your pipe will please *Acba-Dadea* very much."

Sees Plenty ran his fingers over the pipe and felt the intricate carvings on the bowl and stem. Even without being able to see the designs, he knew it was a work of art. He sensed that Medicine Hawk was bequeathing a treasured possession to a son. "Tonight, my father," he said, lifting the pipe, "we will smoke this sacred pipe before we pray."

Medicine Hawk grinned, nodded his pleasure, and reached for Willow Calf and Sees Plenty's hands. "You make your father's heart soar like a hawk, my son."

* * *

The colder days of winter were beginning to change. Ice clinging to barren limbs of cottonwood, willow and aspen had begun to melt. Clumps of ice and large drops of water pelted the melting snow beneath the trees. The first moon of the changing season would soon fill the dormant trees with budding new life.

Like the trees, it was time for the warrior societies to replenish their numbers with young men that had distinguished themselves in battle. The Foxes voted to induct Sees Plenty into their society.

They sent Plenty Coups to Sees Plenty and Medicine Hawk's tipi to inform him of their descision. Sees Plenty and Medicine Hawk welcomed him to sit beside the fire and share their hot chokecherry tea. Plenty Coups sat erect with his shoulders squared. "I come in the name of the Foxes," he said. "Before the face of the bitten-moon changes, the drums of the Foxes will sound and our singers will sing to *Acba-Dadea* the name of Sees Plenty. On that day, you will be a Fox and my brother."

Sees Plenty signed his gratitude and acceptance without speaking. Medicine Hawk grasped Plenty Coups' and Sees Plenty's hands and voiced his pride. "The Medicine Fathers will sing on that day."

As Plenty Coups had said, three nights later when the final sliver of light had faded from the moon, the Foxes gathered in the council lodge. A ceremonial fire in the firepit lighted the interior of the lodge when Plenty Coups and Sees Plenty entered. They had walked from the river where they had taken a plunge into the cold waters of the Yellowstone following a session in the sweat lodge.

The head singer chanted his greeting to Sees Plenty and the drummers began to sound a slow cadence as Plenty Coups conducted Sees Plenty toward the center of the lodge. The mixed aromas of sweet cedar and sweet sage Spotted Eagle had sprinkled into the fire greeted them. The drumbeats suddenly stopped. Spotted Eagle lit the sacred pipe and blew smoke to the Medicine Fathers, Mother Earth, and *Acba-Dadea*. Then he placed the pipe in Sees Plenty's hands for him to repeat the ritual.

Following the sacred pipe ceremony and a prayer by Spotted Eagle, Medicine Hawk stepped up to Sees Plenty. He held up the shield that he and Willow Calf had made for all of the warriors to see. And then he explained the meaning of each component before slipping the shield onto Sees Plenty's left arm.

Drums abruptly began to sound a quick beat. The dancing moccasins of a warrior wearing a fox-head hood took up the cadence. As his dancing gyrations carried him around the lodge, the singers joined into the ceremony with a song filled with the same pulsing rhythm. The dancing warrior spun and oscillated up to Sees Plenty where he suddenly stopped dancing. He pulled off the fox-head hood, slipped it over Sees Plenty's head, and in Absaroke invited him to do the dance of the Foxes.

Having been taught the dancing steps by Plenty Coups, he began to dance. The pulsating rhythm of the singers and drummers was intoxicating. He sensed the surging energy coursing through every sinew of his body. His moccasins pummeled the earthen floor and his hooded head bobbed up and down as he danced and danced and danced.

Soon all of the Fox warriors except one were dancing with him. Spotted Eagle watched Lone Elk, the son of Chief Big Belly, who was standing in the shadows with his eyes glaring at Sees Plenty. Like his father, Lone Elk was very tall. But he had inherited the willowy facial features of his mother who was the sister of Plenty Coups' mother. Unlike Plenty Coups, his demeanor was harsh, intimidating and arrogant. A stiff pompadour arched above a sloping forehead that bulged into a ridge beneath thin brows. A slender aquiline nose arched prominently between haughty hazel eyes that hardened his features. Now they appeared more menacing in the dim firelight.

Before the ceremony ended, Lone Elk slipped unnoticed by everyone except Spotted Eagle from the lodge into the moonless night.

* * *

Lone Elk and Spotted Eagle rode their pintos into the mountains. Spotted Eagle had agreed to sponsor his vision quest after Lone Elk swore that he would not return until the Medicine Fathers had given him a vision.

Since early childhood, Lone Elk had grown up in the shadow of his father and his cousin Plenty Coups. His father had been the principal chief for all of Lone Elk's life. Big Belly's warrior shirt bore tassels of hair taken from every clan member of the Mountain Crow, which was an honor no other chief had attained. Plenty Coups, whose Absaroke name was *Aleek-chea-ahoosh*, had attained early recognition when only nine winters of age. Like many Crow boys, he aspired to experience a vision. He was rewarded for his persistence when he had a vision foretelling the future of the Crow nation and his own destiny in becoming a great chief.

Lone Elk had gone to the mountains on vision vigils several times, but his lack of discipline had always brought failure. He refused to fast, always secreting a few strips of jerky with him to stave off hunger pangs. He never pushed himself into any physical discomfort. While others danced until falling from exhaustion during the annual Sun Dance, he would dance only a short time before lying down to rest. If he could find a shortcut in any undertaking, he would take it.

He had harbored resentment and jealousy of Plenty Coups for many winters. These feelings had grown because of his anger over Plenty Coups relationship with Sees Plenty, a detestable white man in Lone Elk's eyes. Now Sees Plenty was getting all the recognition to which he, Lone Elk, aspired. Sees Plenty had experienced two visions and had killed a hated Oglala in spite of being blind. He had undergone the piercing ritual of the Sun Dance and had been inducted into the prestigious Foxes warrior society. And Willow Calf, the prettiest maiden in the village, was spending hours with him every day. Lone Elk was so furious that he had vowed to even the score by any means.

Lone Elk spread his bed of cedar boughs in a grove of quaking aspen near a spring-fed pool. He stripped down to his breechcloth, leggings and moccasins, and then built his evening fire. He and Spotted Eagle smoked and chanted prayers for a successful vigil. Spotted Eagle promised that he would return with Lone Elk's pinto after three suns.

Like a devoted vision seeker, Lone Elk sat on his bed of sweet cedar. He gazed through budding aspen branches at the brilliant blue sky that was veiled with wisps of high, cirrus clouds. A golden eagle soared on outstretched wings high above. He watched the graceful bird gliding on high mountain currents and pondered whether it might be his Medicine Father. But the eagle's wings carried it farther and farther away until it was lost from view.

Lone Elk felt a shiver slithering up his back, so he reached for more wood to renew his fire. Evening shadows falling across the mountains were bringing cold winds that moaned among the aspen. A sudden gust swirled sparks from his firepit into the air. He shivered again. It was getting colder by the minute as the sun sank beyond the land of the Crow.

He arose from his bed and searched for more dead wood. It was going to be a miserable night. He didn't care if Spotted Eagle had camped nearby and would see him building such a big fire. After all, he was the son of the chief. Why should he have to suffer as much for a vision?

With the fire rekindled into a roaring inferno, Lone Elk sat down and warmed his aching hands. Soon pangs of hunger pinched his belly. He tried to ignore them, but the thoughts of the sweet, peppery taste of jerky became his master. He tried to kill his desire by chewing a twig of cedar, but the aromatic wood burned his lips and tongue.

On into the night, his misery continued. The moon arose and ascended into the sky, but sleep would not come to bring relief. His resistance to suffering collapsed before midnight. He put on all of his clothes, sat beside the fire, and chewed on strips of jerky.

While staring into the flames, he decided to invent a vision. He was certain that he could create one better than Plenty Coups or Sees Plenty had experienced. And he could snip off the tip of his little finger to prove his discipline and perseverance. It would hurt, but not for long. Why not? Having made his decision, Lone Elk curled up beside his firepit and went to sleep.

Out of the shadows of his innermost being danced a warrior whose shield was bright as the rising sun. Singers pounded their drums and chanted in the shadows beyond the leaping flames of his firepit. A great spotted eagle swooped out of the dark, overcast sky and perched on the top of a forked cottonwood pole to the east of the firepit. Lone Elk leaped up and stared at the white-headed bird with gleaming yellow eyes. "I see you! I see you!" Lone Elk yelled.

The eagle remained mute while the bare-chested and barefoot warrior, who was blowing a whistle made from an eagle's wing bone, danced around the pole with rhythmic steps. Eagle plumes fluttered at the end of his whistle and dangled from his fingers. He was wearing a long skirt made from the hide of a white buffalo that was tightly cinched around his waist by an otter skin belt. As the dancer gyrated closer to the flaming firepit, Lone Elk gasped, "Sees Plenty!"

The booming voice of the eagle startled Lone Elk. "Behold the son of Old Man Coyote!"

"No," Lone Elk said, backing away from the dancer. "He is a white man."

"He is the son of Old Man Coyote!" the eagle exclaimed, flapped its great wings, ascended into the overcast, and was gone.

Lone Elk awakened. The firepit was dead. A frigid wind was spitting minuscule flakes of powdery snow out of the inky sky. He wiped sweat from his face and muttered, "No. No. He is a white demon."

Chapter 20

The forested slopes of the Wind River Mountains loomed to the northwest. A bitter north wind blasted Joshua's and Lucy's backs, stung their ears, pulled tears from their eyes, and whipped their ponies' manes and tails like unfurled guidons. They had been following the tortuous course of Beaver Creek for two days. Now they had reached a stretch of rocky bluffs overlooking the creek from the east. A scattering of pines dotted the bluffs. To the west, rugged foothills covered with rocky outcroppings and pines and chokecherry bushes overlooked the gulch where Beaver Creek twisted its course from the Northwest.

As they rode into the gulch, the gale force wind abruptly ceased, leaving the roaring sounds of the wind above them. The noonday sun, languishing above the southern horizon, warmed their weary spirits and embellished the solitude of this haven tucked below the prevailing mountain winds.

Joshua slipped from his mare and retrieved the copy he'd made of James Hooker's map from his wallet. He compared the landmarks indicated by Hooker to the surrounding terrain and decided they had arrived at the right place.

Lucy swung her leg across her pinto, slid to the ground, and led the horses to the gurgling creek. Its surface was crusted with a skim of ice in the center that became denser toward each bank. The heavier ice was murky with embedded pine needles and leaves captured by the never-ending cycles of snowfall, freeze, and thaw. The horses, eager to taste the sweet mountain water, began to stamp the ice with their hooves. It did not require many stomps until the ponies began to snort for air as they sipped the waters of Beaver Creek.

Hoping to find a better place to make camp, they headed their ponies upstream. The ground was covered with glazed snow that grated like breaking glass as each hoof broke through the crusted surface. Their search carried them up the gulch toward the mountains and the headwaters of Beaver Creek. The snow became deeper the higher they went until they neared an oxbow where the creek looped around a grove of barren willows. This place, sheltered from the winds by the high bluffs, became their campsite.

With the sun sinking beyond the horizon, the chill of night descended into the gulch. Joshua buttoned his parka and pulled the collar high about his neck as the temperature plunged. The gulch, warmed by the sun during the day was freezing at sundown when frigid mountain air settled into the valley.

They gathered deadwood and built a fire to ward off the bone-breaking cold. Darkness descended so quickly that the tree-covered slopes slipped from view within minutes. As they sat down next to the fire to eat their pemmican cakes, a man called to them in a squeaky voice from the darkness. "Allew, the camp."

Joshua slipped his hand inside his parka and grasped the handle of his Bowie knife. "Who are ye?" he yelled.

"This child be Jean LaRoche."

"I know this man," Lucy whispered. "We call him Bird Face."

"What sort is he?" Joshua said, peering into the darkness.

"You watch, Bird Face bad," she whispered, "him eat sky-dogs."

Joshua jerked his head around and stared at Lucy. "He eats what?"

"Sky-dog," she said, pointing at their horses. "Pony!"

Growing impatient with their delay, LaRoche stepped into the light of their campfire. Joshua was amazed at LaRoche's runty, short stature and an elfish face that had been bronzed and wrinkled by years of trudging across the Rocky Mountains. His beak-like nose separated dark, beady eyes that gleamed like an animal's in the firelight. A bulky bearskin coat, which accentuated his dwarfish stature, reached down to the toes of his fur boots. His swarthiness was emphasized by long gray hair that dangled across his shoulders from beneath a motley fur cap. He carried a Hawken muzzleloader, which was longer than LaRoche was tall, slung across his shoulder. "Allew," LaRoche squeaked again. "It is very cold. May I share your camp?"

Being reluctant to share their camp with him, Joshua hesitated. LaRoche stepped closer to the fire, but stopped when he recognized Lucy. "Ah, is that you Alouetta?" he asked, squatting down about ten feet from the firepit, and then continued as he eyed Joshua. "And who might you be, mon ami?"

Joshua did not answer. Lucy nodded, picked up the pouch of pemmican cakes and tossed a cake toward LaRoche. It landed in the snow causing LaRoche to dig for his supper. He wiped the cake with his mitten and grinned at Lucy. "Where is Hook?" he asked, glancing at Joshua before biting into the pemmican.

"The man is dead," Joshua said, before Lucy could answer.

"Hook dead?" LaRoche said, chewing pemmican. "Oh no, he is very much alive."

"That's impossible," Joshua replied, still grasping his knife hidden beneath his parka. "How do you know this?"

LaRoche glanced at Lucy and then Joshua. His lips twisted into a smirk as he pondered Joshua's answer. "A busted leg could not kill Hook. He is stronger than a griz'."

"Gangrene will kill anyone, even a grizzly," Joshua said, pulling out his Bowie and laying it atop the log he was sitting on. "He wouldn't let me amputate. Hook is dead."

"Ah, but he isn't dead," LaRoche said, eyeing the Bowie's blade. "You see, I cut off his rotting leg two days after you left him to die."

Joshua glanced at Lucy and saw eyes filled with fear. "Even so," Joshua said, turning to face LaRoche. "Once gangrene advances, amputation usually fails."

LaRoche said no more while finishing his pemmican. After the cake was gone, he licked his fingers and began to chuckle. "Oh, mon ami, I cut it off well above the rotting wound. Believe me, Hook is alive."

Joshua wagged his head in disbelief of LaRoche's story. He had seen too many cases of gangrene during the war to believe such a tale. Forty-eight hours after that type of injury would be too late. The thigh would have been gangrenous by then, requiring a disarticulating amputation of the hip joint. He was certain the grubby hands of LaRoche were not capable of such a feat. And whiskey would hardly be an adequate anesthetic for a surgery of that magnitude. Hook was dead.

LaRoche waited for Lucy to offer him another cake of pemmican. When he decided there wouldn't be anymore, he pulled out his harmonica and began to play a lively tune. After playing the song through, he jumped up and began to dance while his squeaky voice sang out the words. "Alouetta, gentille Alouette, Alouette, jeteplumerai. Jeteplumerai la tete, Jeteplumerai la tete, Et la tete, Et la tete, Et la tete, O!" He danced closer to Lucy as he continued to sing, "Alouette, gentille Alouette, Alouette, jeteplumerai." When finished, he squatted in front of Lucy. "Remember how we danced together that night, my little alouetta, my little lark? You remember, the night Hook drank too much likker?"

"I no dance with Bird Face anymore," Lucy said, turning away. "You bad man."

"Oh, my little lark, you did not think I was so bad that night."

Joshua laid his hand on the Bowie. His voice was sharp as a cleaver as he spoke. "That is enough, LaRoche. Make your bed and I'll have y'gone by first light."

LaRoche nodded, stood up, walked to the other side of the firepit and picked up his Hawken. He kicked away the snow and lay down beside the fire, hugging his long-gun as if it were his lover. "A la bonne dreams to you, Scotsman, and to you, Alouetta."

Joshua stayed awake all night, determined to keep an eye on the repulsive wee French weasel. As the cold night crept by, slow as a wingless walkingstick, he pondered LaRoche's words. There wasn't any question about Lucy's feelings toward LaRoche. She obviously not only feared but detested the half-breed Frenchman. Finally, Joshua decided LaRoche was merely trying to provoke him for reasons known only by the wee varmint.

Just before dawn faded the eastern sky, Joshua tossed more deadwood into the firepit. The dry wood flared within moments. He stared through the flames at the place where LaRoche had made his bed. He wasn't there. Joshua stood up and walked around the firepit, but there was no trace of LaRoche. He was gone. When? How could he have missed seeing the departure of LaRoche? If LaRoche could apparently leave with the stealth of a mountain cat, he might return with equal slyness at any time to do murder or maybe seize Lucy. The thought was disconcerting.

* * *

During the months that followed, Joshua's concern over LaRoche abated. Lucy cut willows and weaved the limber shoots into a wickiup on the oxbow of the creek. She also provided them with fresh fish and meat. She fashioned spears by peeling bark from willow shoots and tapering the ends until they became as sharp as war lances. She stalked the open water near the center of the creek for cutthroat trout.

With a thrust quick as any warrior, she impaled each trout and tossed it into the snow. She also built willow snares to catch the beaver that populated several ponds, which the furry critters had built by damming the creek with aspen cut down by their sharp teeth.

Each day that was free of falling snow, Joshua searched along Beaver Creek for gold. He decided that winter was no time to glean nuggets from the creek. Seeing the creek's graveled bed through the murky ice was nearly impossible. He needed a tool to clear away some of the ice, so he devised a crude axe by fastening his Bowie knife to the end of a sturdy willow stick.

One of the places marked by an X on Hooker's map was at the tip of the oxbow. He spent several weeks chopping holes in the ice, but none of his efforts were rewarded. The gravel bed revealed no glitters of yellow, only a tan and gray monotony of smooth pebbles and stones.

Finally, Joshua's patience waned until frustration turned him surly. Lucy allowed him to sulk realizing that he had to work out his disappointments himself. She watched him spend days comparing Hooker's map to the topography of the gulch. But he never seemed confident that he had found the places

Hooker had marked. She wondered why he no longer seemed interested in her. It had been weeks since he had crawled into the bedroll beside her for any purpose other than sleeping. She had been replaced by his obsession with finding Hooker's gold. She was fearful that the white man's passion for the yellow metal would consume him.

At the first sign of spring, his frustration reached a turning point. The day dawned clear and sunny, and rapidly warmed the gulch with another thaw. As usual, Lucy had gotten up early to smoke trout over the fire for breakfast. Joshua laid in bed, sulking over the many weeks of failure.

Lucy walked down to the creek to get water. She discovered that the ice along the bank was breaking up with sizeable chunks floating downstream. She ran back to the wickiup. "Joshua!" she called. "Come, the creek is melting."

Joshua slipped out of bed. "The ice is breaking up?" he asked, pulling on his boots.

She stooped down to enter the wickiup. "Yes, aye," she said, "ice go fast."

Joshua and Lucy ran to the creek and laughed at the chunks of ice rolling downstream. They walked up and down the bank along the oxbow, peering into the clearing stream. "Ah, ha, what a day. What a bonny day," Joshua repeated, over and over. And then he fell silent staring into the creek. Next to the bank, scattered over a sand bar on the creek bed, were several yellow pebbles that were no bigger than peas. "Saints, be glory," he muttered, bending over the bank to get a better view of the bottom. He pointed at the find. "See them, Lucy," he cried, and jumped into the frigid water.

The depth of the creek as it circled the oxbow was deep, much deeper than it appeared. Joshua sank up to his chest, pushing aside chunks of ice. He was oblivious of the numbing cold as he squatted down beside the sand bar. He raked his fingers through the sand. Like peas being shelled from their pod, several yellow pellets popped out of the sand. One by one, he gleaned the nuggets as easily as picking ripe chokecherries from a bush. He continued to gather nuggets until his lungs cried for air. He raised up, thrust his head above the water, heaved in a draft of air, and then returned to the bonanza on the bottom of Beaver Creek.

Joshua worked the sand bar until his fingers ached from the cold. His eager pawing of the sand bar sullied the water until he could no longer see the bottom. Unable to continue, he crawled from the creek with his fist clutching a handful of nuggets.

Like the sudden change in the mood of a manic-depressive, Joshua ascended out of abject depression into reckless elation. Lucy marveled at the immediate change that came over him. That morning, he refused to even get out of bed. Then after he crawled out of the creek with a fistful of gold, he sat on the bank only long enough for the murky water to clear. At which time he would plunge back into the creek. Within a short time, he was exhausted and shivering. He was so cold that his teeth chattered behind purple lips. Joshua crawled into the wickiup clutching his gold. "Yellow metal no leave," Lucy chided, covering him with her buffalo robe. "Why you go crazy?"

"Don't y'understand?" he said as Lucy massaged his shivering legs. "I've got enough gold in my hands to buy ye anythin' y'want. Saints preserve us Lucy, but there's more gold lyin' on the bottom o' that creek than I'd dreamed of."

During the ensuing weeks, the last remnants of snow and ice melted. The gulch rapidly changed into a haven of verdant new growth. The once barren willows, aspen and cottonwoods began to sing in the wind as new leaves unfolded. Clusters of berries began to form on the wild chokecherry bushes. They would begin to ripen as the warmer days of summer turned them from green into juicy red treats.

Lucy's parfleche pouch no longer contained pemmican cakes. It had become a repository for all the gold nuggets Joshua was gleaning from the creek. He worked from the first light of day until darkness blotted the creek bed from view. This frenzy continued for several more weeks, then Joshua's elation began to subside as the number of nuggets gleaned for the day progressively diminished. Almost as quickly as the gold had appeared, it vanished. Up and down the creek, Joshua searched, but the gravel bottom refused to give up any more nuggets.

So tired that his bones ached, Joshua returned to camp after spending an entire day without finding a single nugget. He collapsed in front of the wickiup so exhausted in body and spirit that he fell asleep. Lucy shook his shoulder several times before he roused. "Joshua eat," she said, handing him the roasted leg of a rabbit she had snared that morning.

"Nay," he said, wagging his head. "I'm too tired to eat."

"When we leave? No more yellow metal."

Joshua wagged his head again. "Leave? Nay, there has to be much more gold." He pointed to the north. "The mother lode is up there. That's where all these nuggets came from."

Lucy sat down beside him, reached for his hand and rubbed it over her belly. Joshua turned to face her, his brows lifting as his eyes spoke the question. She nodded. "I grow big soon. When we leave?"

"Oh, Lucy," Joshua said, reaching for her. He looked around at their meager shelter. They had survived the winter, but another winter would bring increased hardship for Lucy and the child she was carrying. Then his eyes turned back to the headwaters of Beaver Creek. *There's a vein of gold up there in the side of this gulch that would make a thousand men rich.*

"I tell ye what we can do," Joshua said, hoping Lucy would agree to his proposal. "The Oregon Trail is only a few miles south o' here. Freight-wagon trains will be comin' along now that it's summer. We could buy a saw and some tools from them and I could build us a bonny cabin afore winter."

"You no go find Joel? Snow all gone."

Joshua stared at Lucy. He hadn't even thought of Joel since finding the gold. He turned away and gazed into the night.

"When we go to land of Crow to find Joel?" Lucy asked.

"After I find the mother lode," Joshua replied, "we'll go find Joel."

"Summer fly away, then big snow come."

Being angry about Lucy's frustrating questions, Joshua stood up and tore a leg from the roasted rabbit. He walked down to the creek to eat his supper in solitude. With the need to go find Joel and with Lucy being pregnant and the summer being halfway gone, how could he stay here to guard his discovery? Men riding the Oregon Trail were bound to find this place sooner than later.

He squatted beside the creek and gnawed on his rabbit leg. He listened to Lucy singing as she went about stoking the fire for the night. It seemed to be a tender song, a lullaby most likely.

Joshua decided whether they left for Montana or stayed here, he needed a rifle and ammunition. His Colt was useless without caps, bullets and powder. Hostile Indians and men like LaRoche roamed across the high country. And with a new baby on the way, Lucy would not be able to provide them with food. He would have to hunt for game to carry them through the coming winter months.

More reasoning convinced him that to take Lucy on such a long journey at this time would be irresponsible. After all, he had to think about the child too. He tossed the rabbit bone, gnawed clean, into the creek and started back to tell Lucy that the search for Joel would have to wait.

Chapter 21

The mountains and valley were tinted with vivid, verdant hues. Winter's gray patchwork of dormant aspen groves had been erased. Now their once naked branches were arrayed with green leaves humming in warm, spring breezes.

Willow Calf walked toward the tipi of Medicine Hawk and Sees Plenty carrying a rawhide bucket. After her tutoring session with Sees Plenty, Four Moons had asked her to get water from the river.

The day was fair, filled with the fragrances of flowering Indian paintbrush and bitterroot. Children were busy playing a game of stick and ball. Their energetic laughter and the jovial banter of several squaws decorating parfleche boxes that would be filled with pemmican lightened her mood.

Each day that she visited Sees Plenty to teach him the language and customs of the Crow, Willow Calf's heart ached for his sightless eyes and afflicted speech. But today was going to be different. He had promised to play a song on his flute, one that Medicine Hawk had taught him.

In spite of his scarred eyes, she thought Sees Plenty to be handsome. His beard, mustache and hair had turned nearly white during the moons of winter. White traces interwoven with strips of red cloth hung in braids down to his shoulders. He had grown robust and muscular. Anxious to hear Sees Plenty play his flute, Willow Calf hastened toward the tipi now bearing a pictographic motif over the doorway. Spotted Eagle had painted a picture depicting Sees Plenty's vision of a naked white warrior astride a white bison. His eyes were covered with a red sash tied around his head. In his outstretched hand was a hooked staff covered with white buffalo hide fringed with eagle feathers. *Acba-Dadea* had spoken. Sees Plenty had been chosen by the Medicine Fathers to be a shaman chief of the Crow nation.

As Willow Calf neared the tipi, she heard the rough scuffing of moccasins behind her. Without looking she knew the feet in those moccasins belonged to Lone Elk. For several moons he had been hanging around the tipi of Spotted Eagle waiting for each appearance of Willow Calf. He seemed to be smitten, his eyes ogling her tall, trim, well-proportioned figure. He followed her wherever she went, always keeping at a distance so as to not anger Spotted Eagle.

Willow Calf considered him to be weird, one to be avoided.   So,   as   always,   she   continued   to   walk   without acknowledging Lone Elk's presence.

Sees Plenty stepped from the tipi and stood erect in his buckskins, waiting for Willow Calf. He could not see the snarling face, the anger flashing in the eyes of Lone Elk, but he did hear him slapping his palm with an antler-handled quirt.

Lone Elk's eyes, steeled with rage, glared at Sees Plenty. Over and over, the quirt snapped as it ripped across Lone Elk's palm.

"Greetings to Sees Plenty," Willow Calf said in Absaroke.

"Greetings to Willow Calf," he said, signing as he spoke. "Ye are welcome to our lodge."

She hesitated, and then spoke in English. "Would you walk with me to the river before your lesson? The day is so fair and I must get water for our lodge."

"Aye," he said, reaching out his hand. "Let me carry your bucket."

"It's not heavy, I can carry it," she said, grasping his hand. They walked in silence for a short way toward the river, and then he asked, "Lone Elk was following ye again?"

"He follows me everywhere."

"Does your father know about this?"

"I don't know."

"Ye must tell him."

"Lone Elk will not harm me. Do not worry."

She glanced back at Lone Elk, saw him spin about and trot toward a herd of ponies grazing in the meadow.

"The Indian paintbrush has covered the meadow with a blanket of orange," she said, returning her attention to Sees Plenty.

"Would that I could see this place that has become my

home," he said, his voice sounding pensive. "The sounds of the river remind me of my home near the river Deveron in the north of Scotland."

"You miss your home?"

"Aye, I do miss the cottage where I grew to manhood, my mother, hunting grouse with my father and brother and the deer hunts with all my kin. I long to taste the fare from my mother's table: the crowdie cheese, cakes, scones, shortbread, kippered herring, finnan haddie, and heather honey. How sweet and heady is heather honey. A bit poured over shortbread is heavenly, aye 'tis food for the angels."

"Scotland sounds like a paradise."

"In a way it is, but it can be cruel too. Winters are long and can be harsh. The winds blowing from the North Sea are often of gale force."

They walked on in silence toward the sounds of the river. He could feel the gentleness of Willow Calf's hand grasping his arm, guiding him along the trail. Again, Sees Plenty pondered what this young Indian maiden walking beside him looked like. Since the day of his piercing, he had tried to imagine how her features matched the sounds and scents of her presence. He knew that she was tall, almost as tall as he. He envisioned her body to be lithe, as willowy as a deer stepping quietly from the forest. The delicate sounds of her moccasins treading across the floor of the tipi denoted nimbleness and poise. The essence of her presence was pleasant, tinged with the aroma of smoke from cooking fires. But he found the most striking thing about her was her voice. How mellow and soothing it was to his ears. Yet when she laughed it had a light and airy timbre, not unlike the ladies in the shops of Edinburgh. How often had he wished to touch her cheeks, nose, chin, lips, all of her face and hair just to prove how beautiful she was? Every day when she came to teach him, he had to squelch that urge. As this thought came to him again, he almost yielded to the temptation. But, no, that would be unacceptable conduct, a breach of tribal customs.

The shrill whinny of a foal searching for her mother awakened Sees Plenty from his reflections. He sensed the river was nearby; the rumbling sounds of its swirling current now a steady din. "Ah," he said, sniffing the fragrances of spring. "Why don't we have our lesson here, beside the river?"

"I don't know," she said, concerned that her tarrying very long away from the encampment would bring criticism upon them. "I must not bring dishonor upon my father."

He nodded, accepted her caution, but thought, *A wee urge may change her mind.* "Please, we can make the lesson short. I'll even play my flute very loud so everyone can hear."

She laughed, the corners of her hazel eyes crinkling at the tone of Sees Plenty's plea. "Before I get water, we will sit beside the river for your lesson."

Sees Plenty seemed tentative, being preoccupied with his envisages of Willow Calf during his lesson. He stumbled over syllables, apologizing frequently for his bumbling behavior. "What is wrong?" she asked. "Are you not well?"

Sees Plenty apologized again. "I'm sorry, I am fine. It's just that I...."

Willow Calf waited for him to finish, but he remained silent, staring at the river with sightless eyes. She reached for his hand. "Tell me."

"I have been with you most of the winter," he said, hesitated, and turned to face her. "I know your voice, your laugh, your touch, the sound of your moccasins. I sense the kindness of your spirit, but without eyes, I cannot see your face. I have accepted my blindness; however, I long for this one thing, to know the face of Willow Calf."

They sat beside the river, engrossed in their individual thoughts. Sees Plenty pondered whether he had offended Willow Calf; however, she only felt great sadness for the frustration of his blindness. Finally, she lifted his hand to her face. Without speaking, he traced his fingers along the angles of her jaw and the delicate fullness of her lips. Slowly, he stroked the bridge of her nose and the curve of each brow. His fingers, at the pace of a snail, explored each cheek. He savored the exquisite softness of her skin until his fingers found the tears spilling from her eyes. He cupped her chin in his hand and lifted her face. "Aye, my dear Willow Calf, ye are more beautiful than

I had imagined."

She nodded, feeling embarrassed by his flattering words. No other person had ever called her beautiful, except Spotted Eagle and Four Moons. She eased his hand from her chin. "Now I want to hear your song," she said, wiping the tears from her eyes.

Sees Plenty raised the flute to his lips. The piercing strains of his courting song wafted through the cottonwoods and willows and across the meadow to finally reach the jealous ears of Lone Elk.

* * *

The anger within Lone Elk seethed like a simmering pot of chokecherry tea. He vowed within himself to never divulge the true nature of his vision; instead, he would invent one to suit his purposes. If he could convince Spotted Eagle to believe his contrived story, then the village's chief of the Sun Dance might accept a gift of ponies. Then he would allow Lone Elk to take Willow Calf for his wife. So the time had come for him to go ask Spotted Eagle to interpret his invented vision.

Spotted Eagle, unlike many of the Crow men, did not wear his hair in the pompadour style. Instead, it was parted in the middle and hung without braids down past his waist. He appeared taller than he was because of his very erect posture while standing or sitting cross-legged. His fingers were slender and talented in the art of painting pictographs. For most of his forty-seven years, he had kept a running record of the village history by painting their story on buffalo robes. His work was considered by the Crow to be the most talented of all their painters. He was working on a robe depicting the visions and piercing ceremony experienced by Sees Plenty when Lone Elk tapped on the lodge and called, "Is Lone Elk welcome?"

"Lone Elk is welcome," Spotted Eagle said, looking toward the door-flap.

Lone Elk entered and sat down across the firepit from Spotted Eagle. "I have decided to ask you to interpret my vision."

"You had a vision?" Spotted Eagle said without looking up from his painting.

"Yes."

"Why did you not reveal that to me when I came with your pony?"

"I was afraid you would not believe me."

Spotted Eagle leaned back from his pictographs and eyed Lone Elk. "Why should I believe you now?"

"Will you hear my vision?"

Spotted Eagle laid his feather brush aside and nodded without speaking.

Lone Elk related his true vision in great detail, but with significant fabrication relative to the dancer and the message spoken by the eagle. Lone Elk was the dancer instead of Sees Plenty, and the eagle proclaimed that he, Lone Elk, was the son of Old Man Coyote. When his tale was finished, he asked Spotted Eagle to give his interpretation of the vision.

Spotted Eagle, like Medicine Hawk, was a descendant of a long line of Crow medicine men and Sun Dance chiefs. Since visions were a vital ingredient in the Sun Dance religion, they were always considered to be true. But this vision was very perplexing to him. Lone Elk was no stranger to Spotted Eagle. He knew the son of Big Belly for what he was, a lazy and haughty man who would lie if it served him to do so. He gazed into the flames leaping above the firepit without responding until Lone Elk began to fidget with the fringes of his buckskins.

Spotted Eagle finally spoke without looking away from the firepit. "You say that your skirt was made from the white bison?"

"Yes."

"The spotted eagle said you were the son of Old Man Coyote?"

"Yes."

"This is a profound vision. The dancer is a holy man, a chief of the Sun Dance whose Medicine Father is Old Man Coyote," Spotted Eagle said, then he faced Lone Elk. His piercing eyes bored into the young warrior as he continued to speak. "If you were the dancer in your vision, you must walk the sacred path."

Lone Elk could not endure the penetrating gaze of

Spotted Eagle. His eyes darted away and stared at his own hands. "I *was* the dancer," he lied, without looking at Spotted Eagle.

Lone Elk departed the lodge of Spotted Eagle confident that his fable had been believed. He walked out into the meadow where the village ponies were grazing to count the ones that belonged to him. There would be no need to wait. He would pick out three of the sleekest pintos for his marriage gift to Spotted Eagle.

His heart was light and dancing with the headiness of his fantasies about Willow Calf. He envisioned his first night with her. How soft and delicate her skin would feel to his exploring hands. Her kisses would smother him with the intoxication of the white man's devil water. And there would be tomorrow morning after Spotted Eagle accepted the ponies. He would walk by Sees Plenty's lodge and fling insults at him. No longer would he allow Willow Calf to see the hated white man. The thought of it all lingered like wild honey on his tongue.

The following morning, shortly after sunup, Lone Elk walked out into the meadow with three hackamores. After catching and haltering three black and white pintos, he led them across the village grounds toward the lodge of Spotted Eagle. He stopped in front of Plenty Coups' lodge to boast of his expected success. "Plenty Coups, come see my wedding gifts," he called.

Plenty Coups stepped out of his tipi and signed a greeting to Lone Elk. "Who are the sky-dogs for?"

"Spotted Eagle," Lone Elk said, then pointed at the ponies. "Are these not the finest sky-dogs in our herd?"

Plenty Coups walked around the ponies, nodding his approval of their quality. "Owl Eye is a good choice."

"No. I want Willow Calf."

"Willow Calf will not wed you," Plenty Coups chortled. "She is promised."

"No, you lie!" Lone Elk screeched.

"It is true," Plenty Coups said. "Medicine Hawk has spoken to Spotted Eagle and Four Moons."

"Medicine Hawk spoke for Sees Plenty?"

"Yes, two suns ago."

"Sees Plenty has no sky-dogs to give Spotted Eagle."

"He has six."

"Where did he get six sky-dogs?"

"From the Lakota the day he killed Lone Wolf.

"I will kill that white man one day," Lone Elk snarled, and led his ponies back to the meadow.

Chapter 22

Joshua tied the roan to an aspen and began his fourth day of waiting for one of the freight-wagon trains that rolled across South Pass carrying supplies between Fort Laramie and Salt Lake City. In a poke Lucy had made from beaver-skin, he had brought gold nuggets to trade for a rifle, ammunition, supplies, and tools.

Since the days of summer pass so quickly in the mountains, their cabin had to be finished within several weeks. For three days he had camped beside the Oregon Trail to wait for the ox-drawn Conestoga wagons, but none had come lumbering up the deeply rutted grade. Maybe this would be the day that they would come.

Every day of his waiting vigil, he had explored surrounding outcroppings for wall rock that might contain veins of gold ore. And he had walked several dry creeks searching for ore bearing float rock that had been scattered by water erosion. All of his exploration failed to discover any evidence of gold, but he was unable to stop his relentless quest until the wagon train arrived.

Shortly before noon his search was interrupted by the raucous sounds of a bull train ascending the trail toward the summit of South Pass. The rising din of loud cursing, cracking bullwhips, and grinding steel-rimmed wheels against the rocky trail drifted over the pass like waves breaking on the north shore of Scotland. He dropped a chunk of quartz and ran up the slope toward the aspens where the roan was tied.

By the time he reached the grove of aspen, each gulp of air burned deep within his chest. Wheezing like a wind-broken horse, he collapsed on the ground and waited for the wagon train.

As the first of a string of ten wagons came into view, Joshua jumped up, waved and called to the leading bullwhacker. "Hello!"

The bullwhacker eyed Joshua's faded army britches,

frayed kepi, and tattered buckskin shirt. "Hello!" he answered, cracking his whip above the leading yoke of oxen. The dumb oxen ignored the whacker's whip and the gibberish that he continued to yell at them.

Wanting to start a conversation, Joshua bragged on the bullwhacker's beasts as they leaned into hauling their heavy load up the steep grade. "A finer string of oxen I've not seen."

The bullwhacker spat and tongued his chaw. "The only fit one is ole Baldy there," he said, aiming the handle of his whip at one of the leading bulls. "The rest done pulled too many o' these grades. That's why we got ten critters instead o' eight pullin' each wagon."

"Where's the wagon-master?"

"You're lookin' at 'im," the bullwhacker said, doffing his old Greek fisherman's cap.

Joshua eyed him and thought such a huge man could probably out pull any of his oxen. "Are y'of a mind to do some tradin'?"

"Whatever y'want, I got it."

Joshua pulled out his poke and hefted it in his palm. "I need a rifle, some tools, and supplies."

The wagon-master's voice boomed, "W-h-o-a—h-u-p the train!"

Following a few minutes of haggling, Joshua waved goodbye to the wagon-master and proceeded to load his purchases on his travois. He had a new Winchester carbine, ammunition for it and his Colt, a broad axe, pickaxe, shovel, two hammers, buck saw, wedges to split logs, a keg of nails, two oil lanterns, a gallon of lamp oil, a box of matches, a coffee pot, two tins of coffee beans and two one-gallon jugs of whiskey.

He chuckled while lashing down his supplies. The wagon-master's eyes had popped like a greedy owl eyeing a mouse when Joshua poured the nuggets out of his poke. "Where in hell did you get all this gold?" he had asked while studying each nugget. "Won it gamblin'," Joshua had lied, but he feared the wagon-master hadn't believe him.

* * *

Before the first snow swept across South Pass, Joshua

and Lucy had finished their dugout shelter. The cabin was half cave and half shanty. They had hurriedly burrowed the back of the shelter into the bluff near their wickiup on the ox-bow bend in Beaver Creek. With the exception of a narrow doorway, they closed the front with a stone fireplace and peeled pine logs chinked with mud and pine needles. The roof of aspen poles, chinked and covered with a layer of sod, would hopefully keep the interior warm and dry during the coming winter time.

With the dugout ready for winter, Joshua turned his efforts back to looking for the mother lode above Beaver Creek. As he walked up the creek, headed for an outcropping of quartz jutting from the face of one of the bluffs, the sky was suddenly filled with gaggles of long-necked water birds. Throughout the day, wave after wave of Canada geese winged their long Vee formations across the pass and out over the vast badlands of the Red Desert.

Once Joshua had reached the quartz formations, the clatter of his pickaxe blotted the tenor of honking geese from his ears. All he could or cared to hear were the grating noises made by the chisel-blade of his pickaxe prying into fissures of the quartz wall. By dusk he had filled a gunnysack with rock specimens that he would peer over after supper.

After tying the sack behind the cantle of his saddle, he stepped into his stirrup and reined the roan down Beaver Creek toward the cabin. It had been a good day with a number of quartz specimens showing promise. He was certain that tomorrow or the day after would reveal to him a vein that would make him the richest man in Dakota Territory. His happy mood brought a tune to his heart and a whistle to his lips as the roan sauntered toward home.

His gaiety was interrupted by the report from a rifle echoing across the ravine. "Whoa," he said, reining back the roan.

His eyes searched the inclines, but could see nothing amiss. He listened, but couldn't hear any unusual sounds; no deer, elk or bear trying to escape a hunter's rifle. He sat the roan and continued to peer up and down the ravine while listening for the intruder. Not hearing or seeing anything unusual, he nudged the roan's flanks with his heels. "Get up Roanie, we'd better be gettin' on home."

Lucy met him as the roan trotted up to the cabin. "You shoot gun?"

"Nay, I didn't."

"Maybe Hook here?"

Joshua stepped out of his stirrup, wagging his head at Lucy's obsession. "Hook's dead, I tell you."

"Bird Face say him alive."

Joshua pulled the sack of rocks from the roan and started for the cabin door. "Bird Face may be a butcher, but he's not a surgeon. He's a liar."

Lucy's fear of Hook was not appeased by Joshua's persistence. She became downcast and irritable, and refused to accept all of Joshua's efforts to reassure her. He finally stopped trying and devoted his energies to breaking into the vein of ore that he believed to be coursing through the quartz outcropping.

The end of the week found Joshua clawing fragments of rock embedded with gold from an ore-bearing fissure that his pick had broken into. He was ecstatic with his discovery, but quickly realized that the ore bearing rock would have to be pulverized to release its riches. It wasn't going to be as easy as picking nuggets from the bed of Beaver Creek.

He squatted in the excavation he had dug and pondered what to do. He recalled reading about an arrastra dragstone mill, which is used to pulverize ore, while he was a student at Edinburgh University. It was a simple apparatus, but it would be very difficult to construct. And he had no way to quarry a large enough block of stone to make it from either. Hiring one of the bull trains to freight in a disassembled stamp mill would be the best solution. The longer he contemplated the problem, the more discouraged he became. The ore would have to be assayed first and it might not be rich enough to undertake such a mammoth task. And to buy a mill would cost more than all the nuggets Lucy had hidden in their parfleche.

The distant high-pitched whistle of a bugling bull elk broke his thoughts. It reminded him of the approaching harsh months of winter when getting food would be almost impossible.

If he, Lucy and the expected baby were to survive until the return of warmer days, he must find and kill an elk. Mining gold would have to wait.

* * *

Joshua and Lucy lay beneath their warm buffalo robe, listening to night winds sweeping across the mountains, howling packs of timber wolves, trumpeting geese, and the bugling of a rutting bull elk. The fireplace was a scintillating glow in the darkness, and the heady aroma of roasted elk meat hung heavily within the cabin.

Joshua heard the slow, rhythmic breathing of Lucy and realized she had fallen asleep. He turned to look at her face silhouetted by the orange and red flames dancing in the fireplace. For many nights, he had crawled into bed too weary from working the mine for anything but sleep. And then came the three days of hunting that ended when he killed the elk whose carcass he had quartered and hung to cool on the outside wall of their cabin. All during the hunt, he had yearned to get back to their bed where Lucy's softness once again snuggled against him. How he had missed her gentle submission, but she had changed. She had become cold, distant in thought, and uninterested in his caresses. While the bitter lump of sadness lodged in his throat, he tenderly stroked her swollen belly. Then he felt it, the new life within her womb as it nudged his hand. The thrill of it overwhelmed him. She awakened as he held his ear next to her belly, listening to the wee heart beating inside. He continued to listen while Lucy's fingers caressed his bearded cheek. For the first time in months, he forgot about the gold, the mine, and getting a stamping mill.

During the ensuing weeks, life was good. Lucy's mood lightened and she became her old self. Joshua didn't go near the mine he had begun. Instead, he stayed close to the cabin, fishing for trout, chopping down aspen, and sawing and splitting firewood. Lucy often watched him working and in a quiet way would nod her approval. She seemed to believe that maybe he had recovered from the gold fever that had been consuming him.

Then as the first snowfall of winter settled through the barren aspen limbs to powder the ground, their tranquillity was broken. High above on the bluffs to the east came the report of a rifle that echoed up and down the ravine. Joshua stopped splitting wood and gazed up at the summit to the east. He had forgotten the gunshot he and Lucy had heard several weeks before. But now he wondered anew who the shooter might be. The first answer that came to mind was the greedy-eyed wagonmaster who leered at his gold nuggets on South Pass. It might be him or someone else that he could have told about the gold. He dropped the axe and walked to the cabin. Lucy watched as he shoved cartridges into his Winchester. "What you going to do?" she asked.

"I'm going to find whoever fired that shot."

"Hook?"

Joshua eyed Lucy for a moment and then embraced her. "Hook is dead," he said, with gentleness in his voice. "Please stay in the cabin. I'll not be gone long."

Joshua reined the roan southeast along Beaver Creek until he was able to ascend the slope to the east of the bluffs. A light snowfall continued until he reached the summit where a cold northwesterly wind lashed his face with flakes that stung like a hundred ants. He urged the roan on into the rising gale that was launching the season's first blizzard.

Following an hour of riding into the lashing teeth of winter, Joshua found the remnants of a slain elk. The antlered head and bloody offal lay partially covered with snow where the shooter had butchered his kill. The snow was too deep to find the tracks of a horse or shooter, nor the trail he left carrying the elk to his campsite. He gazed into the mounting storm and decided the search would have to wait. With anger and disappointment, he reined the roan toward home and the warm fire Lucy would have waiting for him.

The roar of the frigid tempest blowing across the Pass continued for the following two days. Lucy's taciturn mood returned. She spoke of her fears for the coming of Hook to vent his revenge upon them. As far as she was concerned, the one-legged taskmaster was lurking in some cave eating the elk he had killed while planning murder and mayhem.

Lucy's renewed obsession worried Joshua. Whenever

the blizzard abated, he must go find whoever killed the elk. If by some miracle Hook had survived, he intended to kill him. Then and only then would Lucy give up her obsession.

The morning after the storm abated, Joshua saddled the roan and Lucy's mare. She insisted upon accompanying him for fear that Hook might come while Joshua was away.

There was no use in their returning to the site of the intruder's kill, because the snow would still obscure his tracks. Instead, Lucy followed Joshua as he reined the roan up Beaver Creek toward his mine. Going there first had no logical explanation, but he feared someone discovering it more than worrying about Lucy's fantasy.

The day had dawned clear, cold and still. The winds had calmed before the sun bowed the eastern horizon and turned the snowfield into a glaring mirror. In the quiet cold, every noise seemed amplified. The horses' hoofs punching into the snow, the popping of freezing tree sap in the aspens, and the horses blowing; all of these reverberated, filling the ravine with sound.

When his excavation into the bluff came into view, Joshua reined back the roan. "Wait here," he said, pointing at a hobbled horse, pack mule, and smoke spiraling upward from a wickiup campsite near the creek.

She pulled the Colt from her pocket. "Lucy kill Hook."

Chapter 23

The warm days of spring were turning hotter as the first days of summer crept into the Yellowstone Valley. The quieter days of winter, when the men in the warrior societies had busied themselves with making bows, arrows, lances and shields, were but a memory. Their working sessions had been filled with the boasting of their feats in battle or in hunting buffalo, bear, elk and deer. Now, every man, woman and youngster were busy with preparations for the village to be moved to their summer encampment on the high plains. Soon, the warrior societies would send out scouts to find the great buffalo herds, and then the hunts would begin.

Sees Plenty and Willow Calf walked toward the river. Both seemed pensive as each pondered that this would be their final day spent next to the Yellowstone. Tomorrow, the journey to the high plains country would begin.

As the morning sun crept upward, warmer breezes rustled the aspen and cottonwoods. The first cicadas out of their burrowed nests in the ground were clinging to tree limbs while singing their high-pitched arias. The scent of smoking campfires and the aromas of venison and elk being roasted on spits drifted across the village.

When they neared the river, Sees Plenty had to push aside the branches of chokecherry bushes with the hooked staff Plenty Coups had made for him. The drooping branches were so laden with clusters of reddening berries that they almost obstructed the pathway to the river.

The once roaring river, filled to its banks by melting snowfields in the mountains, was now gentler as the receding waters whispered over stones dotting the riverbed. Willow Calf led Sees Plenty toward their favorite place beneath aspens beside the river. As they walked closer to the murmuring waters, Sees Plenty sensed that there might not be another opportunity for them to be alone. There would be little time for lessons during the hunting season. Every woman of the village would be involved with butchering, drying meat and preparing hides after the men had killed the buffalo.

"Why are you so quiet?" Willow Calf said.

Sees Plenty reached for her hand. "Medicine Hawk tells me that ye'll be very busy once the hunts begin."

"Yes, everyone will be working very hard."

"Then this will be our last lesson?"

"Until we return for the winter season, yes."

"I will miss being alone with you," he said, squeezing her hand.

"The days will be long," she said, stepping closer. "I shall be lonely for Sees Plenty, also."

The scent of her nearness kindled his yearnings. Slowly, he drew her closer. He could hear his pulse pounding in his ears as her softness pressed against him. His staff fell, clattering against the rocks on the riverbank as he pulled her closer and found her lips eagerly searching for his. Over and over, they kissed and clung to each other as if there would be no more stolen moments beside the river.

"I love you more than I can express in either of our languages," Sees Plenty whispered, and kissed her again.

"Oh, Joel... Sees Plenty," she said between kisses. "I love you too."

"I asked Spotted Eagle for permission to...."

"You did?"

"Aye."

"What did he say?"

"That Four Moons and Owl Eye would help you build our lodge."

"Our lodge? Are you asking me to wed, Sees Plenty?"

"Aye, will ye?"

"Yes, aye, yes, I will."

He drew her nearer and whispered in her ear. "My dear Willow Calf, you have made my heart soar like an eagle."

Squaws trilling and men yelling in the village suddenly interrupted their reverie. "What is happening?" Sees Plenty said, releasing his embrace.

"They are welcoming a visitor—we must hurry back."

When they reached the village, a man playing a lively tune on a harmonica was riding into the encampment astride a speckled Paloose stud. Babbling squaws and warriors were curiously stroking and pointing at the black and white patchwork covering the Paloose's rump and flanks.

Sees Plenty and Willow calf mingled with the gathering crowd as Big Belly walked from his lodge to greet the visitor. The man's scrawny frame was cradled in an old Spanish saddle with very short stirrups that conformed to his legs quite well. His swarthy face was nearly covered by a short-cropped beard that hid a receding chin, but failed to cover a prominent Adam's apple that bobbled as he spoke. His sharp nose, which hung over a bushy mustache, took a downward turn at the tip like the beak of a flamingo.

"Greetings, mon ami, Chief Gros Ventre," the man called, doffing his motley fur cap.

Big Belly raised his hand. "Greetings Bird Face LaRoche. Where did you get speckled sky-dog?"

"From Nez Perce; is he not a very handsome horse?"

"I not believe Bird Face. Too many moons to land of Nez Perce."

"For two Crow ponies, I will trade you this fine Paloose."

Big Belly grunted, "Humph." He walked around the Paloose, stopping to feel the muscles of each of the stud's legs. He opened the horse's mouth and ran a finger over each tooth. "I tell you Bird Face LaRoche, this sky-dog see many winters. Him not worth two ponies."

"No, mon ami, "LaRoche replied, sliding off the Paloose. "He is only three winters old, and he's a Paloose, a very rare breed."

Big Belly stared down at the runty half-breed dressed in fringed buckskins with a red *ceinture flechee* sash drawn tightly around his waist. "Ride him," LaRoche said, handing the reins to Big Belly, "then we'll talk."

Big Belly leaped astride the Paloose and heeled his flanks. The stud began to prance about the grounds like one of Buffalo Bill's show horses. While calling his sales pitch,

LaRoche ran after the prancing animal. "Look at Chief Gros Ventre. What a fine looking chief. The Paloose is a chief's horse. No other Crow chief will have such a fine mount."

LaRoche's flattery caused Big Belly to thrust out his chest and sit the stud straighter. The Paloose was larger than a pinto by two hands, which made him a much better mount for the titanic chief. Big Belly rode him around the encampment several times, each circuit becoming faster until the stud was stretching into a charging gallop. Big Belly finally reined him to a sliding stop in front of LaRoche.

"Is he not worth two ponies?" LaRoche called.

"Sky-dog run good, but too old for two pony. You go pick out one pony, we trade."

"I'll include that fine *la jineta* saddle if you will trade two ponies."

"No want saddle, stirrups too short. Go pick one pony."

"Oh," LaRoche groaned. "I cannot. What will everyone say about your fine noble horse? That he is not worth more than one little Indian pony? I tell you what I will do, just for the great Chief Gros Ventre. I will pick out one pony after we smoke and you listen to the message I bring from Red Cloud. Will you do this, mon ami?"

Big Belly jumped off the Paloose and thumped LaRoche on the head. "I not listen. The Lakota are thieves. They steal hunting grounds from Crow."

"Red Cloud calls Gros Ventre the greatest of Crow chiefs," LaRoche crooned.

Big Belly stood more erect and glanced across the campgrounds at the tipi of Medicine Hawk and Sees Plenty. His eyes narrowed as he pondered what to do. "Big Belly will speak with Medicine Hawk. Then I will decide if we smoke and talk."

LaRoche tilted back his head and lifted his brows. "Medicine Hawk, the Oglala *wicasa wakan*?"

"Medicine Hawk is Crow."

LaRoche avoided the gaze of Big Belly for a moment and then he spoke. "If Chief Gros Ventre will only listen to the words of Red Cloud, the Paloose is his."

Big Belly slowly nodded and pointed at Medicine

Hawk's and Sees Plenty's tipi. "We smoke and talk in medicine lodge of Sees Plenty and Medicine Hawk."

Sees Plenty and Willow Calf walked with the crowd as they followed Big Belly and LaRoche toward the lodge with Sees Plenty's pictograph painted over the door-flap. "Who is this Bird Face LaRoche?" Sees Plenty whispered to Willow Calf.

She explained that his father was a French-Canadian fur trader who had lived with the Crow during the winter of 1832. The following winter, he had lived with the Oglala Lakota where he fathered Bird Face with a Lakota squaw.

Misfortune came to Bird Face at the age of ten. While his father was setting beaver traps high in the Absaroka Mountains along the Yellowstone, a grizzly killed and buried him. The Oglala found only shredded remnants of his bearskin coat where the bear had dug up and eaten his moldering corpse.

After Big Belly called his greeting, Medicine Hawk stepped out of the tipi. He tapped his hooked staff against LaRoche's cap and leaned down to face the haughty little half-breed eye-to-eye. "Bird Face is a fool to come to the land of the Crow."

"Oh, mon ami, Medicine Hawk," LaRoche whined. "I come in peace to bring Chief Gros Ventre a gift from Chief Red Cloud."

Medicine Hawk stood up straight and folded his arms across his chest. "A Lakota gift?"

"It is true," LaRoche said, pointing at the Paloose. "Chief Red Cloud sent me to give that fine horse to Chief Gros Ventre."

Big Belly punched two fingers into LaRoche's chest. "Bird Face tongue is forked; he is a liar."

"No, no, the Paloose is yours," LaRoche said, handing the reins to Big Belly.

Big Belly grasped LaRoche by the arm and shook him. "Bird Face lies. He want two pony for speckled sky-dog."

LaRoche began to cringe, trying to make amends with Big Belly. "You misjudge me. Did I not give you the Paloose?"

"Now you run," Big Belly snarled. "Go back to your lying brothers."

"I will, but hear Red Cloud's words before I go."

"Speak! Then Bird Face run like antelope before his scalp hangs from the lance of Big Belly."

"Chief Red Cloud speaks these words to Chief Gros Ventre," LaRoche said. "If the Crow will kill all of the bluecoats and burn the fort they are building on the east bank of the Bighorn River, they will be forever welcome to hunt the land of the Lakota."

Anger flashed in the eyes of Big Belly as he glared at LaRoche. "That land was made for Crow by Old Man Coyote, the creator of our home, our bison, our water birds. You tell Red Cloud these words. When Big Belly sees the last Lakota ride back to the Black Hills he will fight the bluecoats."

"I will tell Chief Red Cloud your words," LaRoche said. He then addressed Medicine Hawk. "I will also tell him that Medicine Hawk lives with the people of Chief Gros Ventre."

Medicine Hawk looked down at LaRoche and spoke with defiance in his voice. "Tell Chief Red Cloud my words. The one called *Wakan* Dog has been given a vision by The Medicine Fathers. He will be a *wicasa wakan* and a Sun Dance chief of the Crow people."

A smirk lifted the bristles of LaRoche's mustache as he chortled his reply. "So, the preacher lives... but it is too bad, mon ami... his brother will soon be dead."

"How do ye know this?" Sees Plenty yelled, his blind eyes searching for the half-breed runt.

The crowd stepped aside as Willow Calf led Sees Plenty toward LaRoche.

"During the Moon Of Popping Trees, I shared your brother's camp on Beaver Creek."

"Beaver Creek. Where is that?"

"Near the Oregon trail on South Pass."

"Ye are a liar," Sees Plenty said, grabbing a handful of LaRoche's buckskin shirt.

"No! I swear it is the truth. I found your brother for mon ami, Jack Hooker."

"Who is he?"

"A mountain man. He claims your brother ran off with

his squaw."

Sees Plenty slowly lifted LaRoche off the ground until the terrified runt's fetid breath blew hot against Sees Plenty's face. "Ye are lyin' through your blood-sucking teeth. I ought to kill ye," Sees Plenty whispered.

"I speak the truth," LaRoche squeaked. "Hook is going to kill both of them."

Sees Plenty released his grip. LaRoche's retreat from the encampment was as swift as his short legs could carry him. A chuckle rose from the depths of Big Belly's barrel-like chest as he watched LaRoche disappear into the grove of cottonwoods that lined the Yellowstone River. "Bird Face run like weasel," Big Belly yelled, slapping his thigh with the Paloose's reins.

* * *

The day after LaRoche ran to save his scalp, Big Belly and the chiefs of each of the Crow's five warrior societies led their clans toward the northeast. It would take the better part of a week for the village to reach the confluence of the Bighorn and Yellowstone rivers. It would be there that they would establish their summer encampment east of the Bighorn River.

All of the tipis were disassembled and loaded onto travois. Everyone had a pony to ride, with the exception of infants and very small children. The children were transported on the travois and each infant snuggled in a cradleboard strapped to its mother's saddle horn.

Behind the chiefs, rode all of the warriors of the five warrior societies. The first society was the Foxes. The Lumpwoods, the Big Dogs, the Muddy Hands, and the Ravens followed them.

Clouds of dust soon rose into the sky over the long procession. Lone Elk reined his pony next to Medicine Hawk's pinto. "For many winters," Lone Elk said, "my father has spoken like an old squaw in our councils. He refuses to fight the bluecoat devils. One day I will be principal chief. Then it will be different."

"Your father is wise," Medicine Hawk said, signing with his hands.

"He is a coward. I should be...."

"A principal chief is chosen," Medicine Hawk interrupted. "First, he must be a chief of his society."

"After we raid the fort on the Bighorn, I will be chief of the Foxes."

"There will be no raid," Medicine Hawk said. "Chief Big Belly will not fight beside the Lakota."

"The bluecoats take our land and we do nothing. Why don't we kill them like the Lakota?"

"Because there are more bluecoats than buffalo," Sees Plenty said, riding beside Medicine Hawk. "If you fight them, more will come until all of the Crow are walking in the hereafter."

"Why do you live with the Crow?" Lone Elk shouted. "You are a white man."

"Sees Plenty is Crow," Medicine Hawk said.

"No, he is white. He will never be Crow. One day I will kill you, white man," Lone Elk yelled at Sees Plenty as he heeled his pony's flanks.

Medicine Hawk and Sees Plenty rode on in silence, each pondering his own thoughts. Finally, Medicine Hawk voiced his concerns. "The Crow have never fought the bluecoats. Every tribe that battles them have lost much of their lands, and their way of life is flying away like smoke in the wind. I believe whichever path we take, whether it be war or peace, all Indians will lose."

Sees Plenty had not heard any of Medicine Hawk's words. He was deep in thought about Joshua, the sniveling Bird Face LaRoche, and the man LaRoche called Hooker.

Chapter 24

The blended aromas of elk meat sizzling on a spit and aromatic cigar smoke welcomed Joshua and Lucy as they neared the intruder's campsite within a grove of aspens. The camper's canvas-covered wickiup was swathed within a cocoon of snow. Just beyond the campsite, a chestnut gelding and a long-eared pack mule strained at their hobbles. Beneath a cross-pole mounted between two aspens swayed the carcass of an elk.

"Hello, the camp," Joshua called, reining back the roan.

A man's resonant voice answered. "Who's there?"

"That not Hook," Lucy said, tugging at Joshua's sleeve.

"I'm the man that opened that mine up there on the bluff," Joshua said, stepping out of his stirrup. "What are y'doin' here?"

"Reckon I'm after the same as you, "the man said, crawling out of the wickiup.

"This mine belongs to me."

"I'm Louis Fontaine," the man said, brushing snow off of his long, bearskin coat. "Afore we get tangled up, I'd like t'know who I'm talkin' to."

"Henry Watt," Joshua lied, not wanting his identity to be revealed.

Louis pulled away the heavy woolen scarf covering his nose and chin. "Well, Henry, reckon I owe you an explanation."

Joshua eyed Louis's tawny features accented by a black beard and mustache and saw that he was a mulatto of no more than twenty-five years. "Aye, Louis, that y'do."

"I heard about your gold down at Fort Bridger."

"Damned wagon master," Joshua said, wincing over Louis's words.

"You and your squaw are welcome," Louis said. "I've got meat and coffee ready."

"Looks like ye're well equipped," Joshua said, pointing at a packsaddle and packing crates.

"Yes, I plan on being up here for quite a while."

"Where are y'from, Louis?"

"New Orleans; how 'bout you?"

"Scotland," Joshua replied, then grinned as he nodded at Lucy. "Lucy is from here, these mountains."

"Ah, Lucy, I'm pleased to meet you."

"Are you buffalo soldier?"

"No, I'm a geologist."

"What is ge-ol-o-gist?"

Louis pulled a chunk of ore from his pocket. "I study rocks like this piece of quartz."

Lucy frowned, but said nothing. Joshua continued to question how a man of color from New Orleans could be educated and a man of property as well. It was difficult to accept in a land where anyone of African descent had been denied these for nearly three-hundred years. He finally said, "Where were ye schooled?"

"Paris."

"Paris?"

"Yes, my father, Jaques Fontaine, took me to Paris when I was twelve."

Joshua stared at Louis in disbelief. "Blackjack Fontaine... the pirate?"

Louis ignored the question; instead, he poured coffee into their cups and spoke frankly about his sojourn into the mountains. "I sold my share in a Nevada mine because I wanted to see new places and find new adventures. I was on my way east when I stopped for supplies at Fort Bridger. That's where I learned from the suttler about the wagon master trading for your gold. I had to see for myself. That's why I'm here."

Joshua continued to consider what he should do. Louis wasn't going to go away, not now, not after he had found Joshua's mine. "You know anything about stamp mills and arrastras?"

"Yes, I do."

"I may need one."

"Ah, rightly so," Louis said, pulling a notebook from his pocket. "I took the liberty of looking over your mine, and I did an assay on your ore with my field kit." He opened his notebook and pointed at his recorded findings. "You can see there is an abundance of granular gold running clear through the ledge. You've got one hell of a gold find, Henry."

"Aye, I thought I might."

"Would you be interested in a partner?" Louis said, shoving the notebook back into his pocket. "I've got the know how; you've got the mine."

"Maybe, I'll think on it."

"An arrastra and a stamp mill will cost ten thousand dollars plus the cost of gettin' them here. I'll put up the money for half interest."

Joshua gazed into the eyes of Louis, searching for the substance of the man. Could he trust the son of one of the most vicious pirates that ever plundered the high seas? Probably not, but what other choice did he have? None that was attainable. "Equal partners?"

"Equal partners it is," Louis said, reaching for Joshua's hand.

* * *

With Louis Fontaine's promise to return with the needed mining equipment in several weeks, Joshua assaulted the depths of his mine with renewed vigor and determination. He was certain that the mother lode, a vein of pure gold might be opened with the next swing of his pickaxe or a black-powder charge tamped into a hole or crevice. Fontaine's instruction on using the explosive power of black powder would make the mining much quicker, but it was still grueling and dangerous work. Oh, yes, the mine had already proven itself – Fontaine had assured him of the high quality of ore residing within the strata of quartz running through the mine. That good news had merely stoked Joshua's fancy. Even if the find was good, it still wasn't the mother lode. He was determined to discover it before Louis returned. There would be no time for anything except working the mine.

Days came and went as he labored more and more hours—seldom taking a break except when Lucy came to the mine with hot coffee, pemmican cakes and fry bread. He even lost his taste for whiskey, which had calmed his growing frustrations before Fontaine had arrived. Lucy tended his increasing infirmities brought on by arduous labor and very little rest. She massaged his aching muscles and bandaged his bleeding and blistered hands. But, he would not stop—the lust for gold was consuming him.

After several weeks of a frenzied struggle, his judgment began to slip. In spite of exhaustion, he could only sleep a few hours before awakening. He would rise, demand that Lucy get his breakfast ready while he saddled the roan and replenished the mine's lanterns with oil. Fatigue was sapping his strength and clouding his mind. He started to make bad decisions, not the least of which was deciding to discontinue shoring up the mine's ceiling. He just couldn't take the needed time to cut down the pines and hew more shoring timbers from them. His flawed reasoning could not recognize the mounting danger—the deeper he burrowed into the mountain, the greater the hazard became. With each yard of excavation, the forces exerted by the mountain began to multiply. And the rock-crushing energy exerted by black powder explosions tended to loosen the mine's overhead structure.

Six weeks after Louis had headed for Denver astride his chestnut gelding, Joshua arrived at the mine at first light. The threatening sky was overcast with low gray clouds. A frigid wind, sweeping down the valley, pelted his face with stinging flakes of snow. He peered back in the direction of the cabin, but the valley was obscured behind a curtain of blowing snow. A late winter blizzard was in the making. But since blizzards are quite common on South Pass, he reasoned that there was no need to halt his work. There was plenty of firewood in the cabin. Lucy would be fine.

Joshua entered the mine and lit two lanterns. He hooked the bail of the first one onto a wall peg near the entrance and headed for the diggings at the end of the shaft. He hung the second lantern on an overhead hook and picked up a sledgehammer and rock drill. It was time to drill a hole in the quartz, pack it with black powder, and fracture it with a blast. Once the hole was drilled, packed with powder, and a fuse lit, he quickly stepped backward and crouched down awaiting the explosion. The resulting blast was more than he had anticipated. The cavern erupted in an earth-shaking tremor. The earth beneath him shuddered and lifted with a rumbling heave. Several pieces of quartz pelted him as he cowered next to the floor of the shaft. Suddenly, the overhead gave way. Shoring timbers cracked as the ceiling of the mine collapsed. The cascading shower of rocks slammed against him, pinning him to the floor of the shaft. After he gathered his senses, he found the mine to be dark as a moonless night. He tried to move his legs, but pain halted his efforts. The mineshaft was cold, dark and foreboding. He reached out his hand in the darkness, searching for whatever had pinned his legs to the floor. He discovered that an intact shoring timber next to his head hadn't collapsed. It had prevented the failed overhead from crushing him. He soon discovered that he was imprisoned in a small space within the collapsed mineshaft. He clawed at the rocks, but could not free his legs.

Joshua felt short of breath—the air was foul. His right leg throbbed. Nausea convulsed his belly. Reality seemed to come and go like a nightmare interrupted by sleepless moments. Awareness returned when he heard the scraping of a shovel as it scooped away rubble just beyond his place of entrapment. Soon, he heard the familiar voice of Lucy, "Joshua—Joshua!"

"Aye" he managed to utter. "Here I am."

"Do not walk in hereafter. Lucy save Joshua."

At least an hour passed before Lucy had cleared enough rubble to free Joshua. He immediately realized that the tibia and fibula of his right leg were badly broken just above the ankle. If the fractures were not reduced and splinted, he would be severely crippled. But that would have to wait until they got back to the cabin.

Lucy helped Joshua hobble out of the mine to the aspen where his roan was tethered. With her supporting his fractured leg, he managed to climb into the saddle. She untied the roan, handed the reins to Joshua, and then mounted her own mare. They headed toward the cabin. The trail lay beneath deep drifts of newly fallen snow. The gale blowing from the north was sculpting the mountainside with drifting snow like desert winds building sand dunes in the Sahara.

After struggling through drifts, they finally reached the cabin. Lucy helped Joshua inside where he collapsed on the bed. "Shed and feed the horses," Joshua said, "then with your help I'll be needin' t'set my leg."

Lucy knew what had to be done. She had a clear memory of how they set Hook's fracture. "Lucy get rope, willows for splints and whiskey—you drink big."

Enough whiskey to dull the pain would be needed. That amount would make him incapable of helping Lucy reduce the fracture. Before uncorking the whiskey jug, he went over the necessary procedures with her. "Around my thigh, ye must tie the rope. Then secure it to the head bedpost. Ye must remove the boot. If the swelling is too great, cut away the boot. Grasp my heel with your left hand and my foot with your right. Then ye must pull hard as y'can until the ankle straightens. After it looks straight, splint it with several willows."

"Lucy fix," she said, handing the jug to Joshua.

"That's a bonny lass."

He pulled the cork and began to guzzle from the jug. The day Hook and Lucy amputated his toes came to mind as he struggled to swallow fiery drafts of whiskey. After several minutes of dousing his stomach with booze, the room began to spin. Not wanting to pass out, he set the jug on the floor. "Ye can go ahead now."

The ankle was too swollen for Lucy to save the boot. After splitting the thick horsehide boot top, she pulled the boot and woolen stocking from his foot. The ankle was markedly swollen and had an angular deformity that turned the foot inward. She methodically followed the directions Joshua had given by grasping the heel and foot and pulling hard as she could.

The pain roused Joshua. He gritted his teeth and moaned, trying to tolerate the misery that was excruciating in spite of the booze. It seemed like an eternity before both Lucy and he felt the broken bones slide into place. While she splinted the foot and leg, Joshua fell into a deep sleep.

When he awakened, the cabin was cold and dark. Only a few glowing coals in the fireplace gave any light to the room. He felt the familiar warmth of Lucy lying beside him. He reached for her. She moaned. "What's wrong?" he asked, laying his hand on her thigh.

"You have a son."

"A son!" he said, trying to get up. "It's too soon."

"Him come while you sleep."

A wave of elation followed by apprehension swept over Joshua. The baby was premature, so much so that its survival was in question. He was certain that the early birth had resulted from the mine accident. If Lucy hadn't gone to the mine with coffee and pemmican, she would not have exhausted herself rescuing him. The extreme effort required for her to set his fractured leg had been the final factor that had precipitated her premature labor and delivery. The sorrow and guilt for causing this to happen to Lucy overwhelmed him. "I'm so sorry," he murmured. "Let me hold our son."

* * *

Joshua sat in front of the fireplace sipping whiskey to dull the pain in his right leg, and his soul as well. While gazing into the flames, he tried to shut out Lucy's blanket-wrapped form huddled in grief beside the hearth. Through the alcoholic haze that clouded his thoughts, he dwelled on all of the anguish that had descended upon them since Louis had left for Denver. Four months had passed and he still hadn't returned with their stamp mill and arrastra. The pain in his fractured leg was constant, but not as tormenting as the loss of their son. The premature infant had died after a three day struggle to survive. The snowbound high country was reluctant to relinquish its gold without payment in full.

"I'm goin' back to the mine," he said, setting the jug aside. "I've got to get the shaft open again."

"Your leg not healed."

"I'll go mad if I don't."

"Lucy help."

Joshua reached for her hand. "No, you lost too much blood."

"I stronger."

"No, not yet, maybe in a couple of weeks."

Joshua was up at first light, hitching a travois to the roan. Being unable to step into a stirrup, he intended to ride the travois back to the mine.

Joshua spent the day at the mine trying to clear the caved-in shaft. Frequent swigs of whiskey kept his pain at a tolerable level, but he could work for only a short time without resting his swollen leg.

He had cleared much of the shaft when a jagged chunk of quartz broke loose from the ceiling, slammed against his head and ripped open his scalp. Addled and with blood streaming down his face, he crawled out of the shaft, sat beside the mine entrance and tried to clear his scrambled wits. Too much whiskey and the blow on his head had sent the world spinning around as if he were on a carousel.

At least an hour went by before the merry-go-round slowed enough for him to stand. He wiped clotted blood from his eyes and saw that the sun was beginning to slip beyond the western skyline. He staggered to the aspen where the roan was tethered and hitched the travois poles to her saddle. He climbed onto the travois and reined the roan toward the cabin.

It was almost dark and getting very cold by the time Joshua reached home. He unhitched the roan and led her to the creek where he axed a hole in the ice. While she sipped from the creek, he kept looking at the cabin. Something was amiss. There was no smoke rising out of the chimney.

"Lucy!" he called, limping toward the cabin. "I'm back."

There was no answer, no sounds at all. He pulled the door-flap aside and called to her again. "Lucy!"

"Oh... Joshua," she said, her voice weak and barely audible.

Joshua found her lying on the floor next to the hearth. "My god, what's wrong?" he said, kneeling beside her.

"Hook," she whispered.

"Hook was here?"

The all too familiar odor of human blood sickened

Joshua as Lucy pushed back the buffalo robe that covered her nakedness. Revulsion and rage gripped him. Both of her breasts had been mutilated by Hook's slashing blade. A massive quantity of blood that had gushed from her wounds had congealed into an enormous burgundy puddle, which surrounded her on the sod floor.

Joshua lit a lamp, quickly evaluated her injuries, and found that all of the active bleeding had ceased. During his examination, he kept repeating, "I shouldn't have left ye alone."

Lucy had already lost a sizable quantity of blood during the premature labor and birth of her child. Now Joshua was certain that the additional hemorrhage from her wounds had propelled her into a critical situation. He found her face to be pallid and covered with clammy sweat. Her eyes were sunken, anxious, and had lost their luster. Her pulse was rapid and almost imperceptible to his fingers. She was in a state of profound shock and close to death.

He hastily elevated her legs atop stacked firewood and covered her with buffalo robes and blankets. He built a fire in the fireplace and brewed hot willow tea. Then he sat beside her, spooning hot tea between her lips. A flood of emotions surged through him as he continued his vigil. The guilt for leaving Lucy alone and not believing that Hook had survived, consuming rage for the deranged Hook, and profound sadness for his imminent loss filled his mind with hatred and vengeance.

A pall of helplessness enveloped him like a freezing winter's mist. He had never felt so inadequate. He had nothing, no medicines, no means of reversing Lucy's critical state. Words were all he could give to her to ease her suffering. "I love ye Lucy, more than life. Don't leave me, I can't survive without ye. When ye are well, we will leave this place and go find Joel." On and on, he spoke softly while caressing her hand and face.

Lucy smiled, looked at him and whispered, "Lucy... love... Joshua."

Then the end came like the puff of a breeze that momentarily flutters a curtain and then wanes into stillness. Through misty eyes clouded with sadness, Joshua watched the light of Lucy go out. He shivered. Deep inside his being, the cold fingers of death had touched his soul. For hours, he sat beside her, unable to turn loose of her hand, to let her walk away into the hereafter.

Morning dawned after a sleepless night. He wrapped Lucy in her blanket and carried her on the travois to the place where they had buried their son. It was a peaceful site on the bluff overlooking their cabin. While covering Lucy's grave with stones to discourage plundering scavengers, he saw smoke billowing up from the ravine. The cabin was on fire. He had no doubt that Hook had set it ablaze and would be waiting to ambush him. But reason had been replaced by a raging desire to do vengeance. Joshua unhitched the travois and grimaced from pain as he stepped into his stirrup. He heeled the roan's flanks and reined her down the slope toward the burning cabin.

By the time he reached the cabin, only a pile of smoldering rubble remained. Lucy's mare lay next to the creek, dead from a slash that had severed the carotid artery in her neck. Joshua cranked a round into the chamber of his Winchester and eased himself to the ground. "Hook!" he shouted and listened as that hated name echoed up and down the ravine.

"Here I am, asshole," Hook yelled. "Up here."

Joshua looked up and saw Hook balancing himself on one leg and a crutch atop the bluff. "That Injun bitch gave me the gold y'stole after I cut off her tits." Hook waved Joshua's parfleche of gold nuggets over his head. And then the gulch echoed with his taunting laughter.

"You murdering sonovabitch!" Joshua yelled, aiming his Winchester at Hook. He squeezed the trigger, but nothing happened when the hammer fell against the firing pin. He cranked in another round only to have the same result.

"After I cut up that Injun bitch, I filed down the firin' pin on your rifle." Hook began to laugh again, taunting and venomous. "Now, you just wait right there, asshole. I'll be down there in a minute t'cut off your balls and jam 'em in your dead mouth."

Joshua slung the useless Winchester into the creek. "I'll be here."

While waiting for the one-legged Hook, Joshua pondered the situation. It was certain that Hook wasn't going to grant a fair fight. The range of Joshua's Colt was no match for Hook's rifle. So, the need for a different twist of his own to turn the advantage became evident. Fortunately, Fontaine had left a packing crate of mining tools and supplies, which included several sticks of dynamite, detonating caps, fuses, and a box of Cuban cheroots. And the crate was still there, leaning against a tree stump.

Joshua armed six sticks of dynamite, tied them together and carefully slipped the bomb into the pocket of his parka. He pulled the Colt from his holster, spun the chamber and found each round to be ready and primed. Then he sat down on the tree stump, lit one of Fontaine's cigars, and waited for Hook.

He didn't have to wait long before hearing the hoof beats of a horse. It was Hook astride a cantering chestnut gelding. Hook had his Winchester cradled across the pummel of his saddle and an Army Colt jammed under his belt. He reined to a halt about fifty yards away, sat the skittish chestnut and glared at Joshua. "Well, asshole," Hook chided, "after I kill you, I'm goin' t'dig up that whore and feed both of ya t'the buzzards."

Joshua didn't say anything; instead, he reached into his pocket and pulled out the dynamite bomb. "What y'got there, asshole?" Hook said, caressing his rifle.

Joshua touched the fuse to his cigar. "Dynamite!"

"What the hell is dynamite?"

"Oh, some Swede invented it last year."

As the fuse began to spew sparks, Hook levered a round into his Winchester. "You're dead, asshole!"

Joshua threw the bomb at the chestnut and dove to the ground. Hook's rifle bellowed just before the dynamite slid to a stop beneath the gelding. His bullet missed Joshua, but exploding dynamite cratered the ground and tore into the unfortunate chestnut before Hook could get off another round.

Joshua wrestled the heaving earth, praying that the dynamite would do its job. Then a shower of horseflesh, including hooves, head with bridle still in place, and saddle catapulted through the trees. Where the chestnut gelding had once stood, wisps of smoke curled upward out of a deep crater.

Joshua jumped up and looked around for Hook. He finally spied the mangled, one-legged corpse reposing amid the branches of an aspen. It seemed to be a fitting place for the evil monster, since several buzzards were already circling overhead.

The most fortunate fallout of the explosion was that the parfleche, which Hook had secured behind the cantle of his saddle, had survived unscathed. However, Joshua's elation at recovering all of his nuggets turned into despair when he discovered Louis Fontaine's notebook and wallet inside Hook's saddlebags. The discovery explained why Fontaine had failed to return. Hook had apparently been stalking the area for several months, and had waylaid the unfortunate Fontaine for his chestnut gelding. There would be no stamp mill and arrastra arriving from Denver.

Joshua hitched the travois to the roan and headed her for South Pass where he met another train of freight wagons. After purchasing a new rifle and replenishing his supplies that had been consumed by the fire, he moved into the wickiup he and Lucy had built.

Working the mine diminished while his consumption of booze grew. A jug of spirits became his companion during the daytime and his mistress at night. Neither grief nor all of his misfortunes that were growing with each day were lessened by work or booze. Since Louis Fontaine had fallen victim to the murderous whims of Hook, there wouldn't be any machines with which to work his gold ore. And with the birth of spring weather, the dreaded rush of gold seekers had gotten underway. Scores of them, like bees seeking sweet nectar, were prospecting every gulch and quartz outcropping all across the pass.

He decided to abandon the wickiup and move into the mine, reasoning that his pile of ore had to be guarded day and night against pilfering prospectors. Many a dawn found him sitting in the entrance, cradling his Winchester and sipping from a jug of bourbon. But all of the whiskey in Kentucky could not dull the pain resulting from his losses and his abandonment of Joel. Yet, the prison of his lust for gold would not release him, not until the mother lode was his.

Chapter 25

Chief Big Belly and Sees Plenty topped a rise west of Fort C. F. Smith. They sat their ponies while the cautious chief shielded his eyes against the rising sun now casting long shadows beyond several haystacks north of the fort.

Sees Plenty sensed the summer morning to be charged with the pungent scents of new-mown hay, horse corrals, cooking fires and parched soil that had been revived by an early morning shower. He listened to shouting officers and cussing troopers who were haltering and saddling rebellious mounts down in the fort's corral. These familiar sounds and aromas of a frontier fort caused him to ponder the reasons for their mission. While Big Belly wanted to assure the bluecoats that the parties of armed Crows hunting buffalo nearby were not hostile, his only desire was to find out what had happened to Joshua. Had the half-breed LaRoche lied about Joshua and the mountain man Jack Hooker? The fort's commanding officer or Jim Bridger might know.

"Bluecoats pick good spot for fort," Big Belly said, scanning the log and adobe stockade that was perched atop a plateau less than two-hundred yards east of the Bighorn River.

"Aye, they always do."

Big Belly tied a strip of white trade cloth to his hooked staff. "We wait here for bluecoat soldier," he said, lifting high his peace signal.

Two troopers carrying a white flag rode out of the stockade astride prancing black geldings. They spurred their mounts across the river ford and up the Bozeman Trail toward Big Belly and Sees Plenty. Big Belly signed peace. "Tell soldier chief that Crow Chief Big Belly want talk peace."

"Follow us," growled one of the troopers.

All of the cussing troopers and bellowing noncoms fell silent when Big Belly and Sees Plenty entered the fort's north gate. They all stared wide-eyed, like kids at a circus, at Big Belly who was dressed in his finest chief's attire as he rode past them leading a black and white piebald pony. A soldier with captain's bars on his shoulders and a smoldering cheroot jutting beneath a waxed handlebar mustache, walked out of his office to meet them. "Welcome to Fort C. F. Smith," he said around his cheroot.

Big Belly pointed at the piebald pony. "Big Belly bring soldier chief spotted sky-dog. We talk now?"

"Well now, chief," the captain said, walking around the piebald. "This is a fine looking animal. I appreciate your giving him to me. Come into my office."

Big Belly eyed the small office beyond a single doorway. "We talk here."

The captain chuckled at Big Belly's caution. "Sure, right here will do fine."

Big Belly jumped from his Paloose stud and pumped the captain's hand like Sees Plenty had taught him. "I am Big Belly, a chief of the Mountain Crow."

Kinney grimaced from the power of Big Belly's grip. "I'm Captain Kinney, commandant of Fort C. F. Smith."

Big Belly grinned, dropped Kinney's hand and pointed at Sees Plenty. "That Sees Plenty, a Crow medicine man."

Sees Plenty slid from his pony to meet Kinney, who frowned while eyeing his scarred lids, opaque corneas, and features bronzed by the summer sun. "I've never met a medicine man before," Kinney said, reaching for Sees Plenty's outstretched hand.

"Good morning, Captain Kinney. I believe we've met before at Fort Laramie."

Kinney, startled by such precise English being spoken by an Indian, stammered his reply. "We... ah... we've met before?"

"Aye, during the cholera epidemic."

"My god man, you sound like Major Leslie?"

"Nay, his brother Joel."

"The preacher that...."

"Aye."

"Damn," Kinney said, peering at Sees Plenty. "Who in hell blinded you?"

"Lone Wolf, a Lakota."

"Damn, bet you'd like to kill that bastard."

"I did."

"Christ, how'd you do that? A blind preacher killin' an Injun."

"*Acba-Dadea* guided my tomahawk."

Kinney gawked at Sees Plenty and chewed on his cheroot trying to comprehend what he had just heard. "Well now, that's some Injun, that *Acba-Dadea*."

"Would ye be knowin' the fate of my brother?" Sees Plenty asked, ignoring Kinney's ignorance.

"Well, reckon Bridger could answer that for you."

"Would Mister Bridger be about?"

"Yeah, he rode in last night."

"I'd like to speak with him."

"I'll send for him, and when you're ready, I'll have a detachment escort you back to Fort Phil Kearny."

"Nay, there is no need for that. As Chief Big Belly said, I'm now a Crow medicine man."

"Christ, you can't be serious."

"Aye—I am—the Crow are my family now."

Kinney wagged his head. He then spoke to Big Belly. "Now, Chief, just what is it you want to talk about?"

"This Crow hunting ground." He turned around while pointing in every direction. "Our warriors hunt bison everywhere. Crow not fight bluecoats; we kill bison and Lakota. You not kill Crow; we not kill you."

"Sure, Chief, we won't interfere with your hunters."

"Them good words. We make deal. You keep spotted sky-dog."

* * *

Sees Plenty waited in Captain Kinney's office until he heard the familiar voice of Jim Bridger calling his name. "Preacher Leslie, damn you're a sight for sore eyes."

"Aye, and the sound of your voice to my ears."

"Reckon y'want t'know what happened to your brother."

"Aye, I do."

"Well, reckon he ain't dead like y'most likely heard."

"Do ye know a man by the name of LaRoche?"

"Sure as hell do. Why y'askin'?"

"He said that Joshua was livin' on South Pass with the squaw woman of a mountain man by the name of Jack Hooker."

"Ain't knowin' about no squaw, but I know Hook and he's a mean sonovabitch."

"LaRoche claimed Hooker was going to kill Joshua."

"Reckon he might if Doc run off with his squaw. Lets set a spell and I'll tell y'everthing I know."

Bridger began with Joshua's desertion and concluded with their encounter in the Bighorns. "The last I seen o' Doc Leslie was him ridin' away on ol' Mule wearin' my duds. Mule got away from him later and showed up back at Fort Phil Kearny about two weeks after that. Reckon I ain't knowin' what's happened since then, but he wouldn't be the first white buck t'get his urges roused by a purty Injun squaw."

Sees Plenty nodded. "Aye, 'tis true."

"Reckon y'found a Crow gal for yerself," Bridger said, slapping Sees Plenty on the shoulder. "Well son, them's a handsome lot. What might be her name?"

"Willow Calf, the daughter of Spotted Eagle."

"Knowed Spotted Eagle an' Four Moons a lot o' winters. They's good people."

"Aye."

Bridger nodded, "Well, when the Crow take y'in, you're one of 'em. Reckon you'll make 'em a good med'cine man."

Sees Plenty and Chief Big Belly rode out of Fort C. F. Smith and headed for the Crow encampment. Big Belly was pleased with Captain Kinney's promise not to interfer with the Crow's upcoming annual hunt., but Sees Plenty was troubled by Bridger's story. He was certain that Joshua had been killed by Hooker or he would have come by now. However, his spirit soon began to soar. *Tomorrow will be a day for much singing and dancing. Spotted Eagle, Medicine Hawk and I will send smoke and prayers to the medicine fathers, asking them for a successful hunt. But first, before the hunt begins, Willow Calf will become my bride. Aye, it will be a good day.*

* * *

Medicine Hawk and Sees Plenty stood in front of Spotted Eagle's tipi waiting for Willow Calf and her family to join the wedding party. When she stepped through the doorway, many squaws gasped and young maidens giggled. Medicine Hawk described her to Sees Plenty: "Your bride is fair as a swan on the wing. Her hair shines like the raven and hangs to her waist in braids tied at the ends with eagle plumes. She wears a bighorn-skin dress that has been bleached until it is white like the snow-hare. It is ornamented with many elk teeth, and much quill and beadwork. It is a dress worthy of the bride of a medicine man."

After smoking and praying to *Acba-Dadea*, Medicine Hawk recited the wedding ritual while Sees Plenty and Willow Calf stood facing each other. Much gift giving by all of the villagers followed the ceremony, and then the dancing began. The celebrants danced and danced and danced until fatigue ended the festivities.

The rhythmic drums suddenly stopped and the dancers melted into the dark August night leaving Willow Calf and Sees Plenty alone. Willow Calf took Sees Plenty's hand and they walked to the tipi that her mother, sister and she had made.

Sees Plenty savored the texture of Willow Calf's skin, her softness, and her gentle voice cooing endearing words as they lay together for the first time. The lodge was heady with the aromas of tanned buffalo robes and sweet cedar smoke from dying embers in the firepit. The miseries of times past and his despondency over the loss of sight and a wayward brother vanished like fog in the wind when he found the eager lips of Willow Calf. At last, all of his emotions gained release and joy filled the lodge of Sees Plenty and Willow Calf.

* * *

Lone Elk was not a happy warrior. All of his efforts to win Willow Calf had brought him nothing but more hatred towards Sees Plenty. His eyes glared like a Mexican bull facing a tormenting matador each time Sees Plenty walked past. He ached to feel the crunch of cartilage beneath his hands and to watch blind eyes bulge as his fingers strangled the white demon that had taken Willow Calf from him. Today, he might get the chance. Sees Plenty was to lead the Foxes on a scouting foray to find another buffalo herd. One more successful hunt was needed to get enough meat and hides for the coming winter.

The chill of night waned as the August sun climbed over the eastern horizon. The hunting party had already covered several miles since the first light of dawn had crept onto the high Montana plains. Sees Plenty was riding beside Plenty Coups at the head of the party as they ascended the incline of a plateau. Sees Plenty sensed the eagerness of his little horse and the tenseness of his own hands. Something within him was whispering like the whine of a coyote sniffing the entrance of a prairie dog den. Sensing the sharp odor of buffalo in his nostrils, he lifted his hooked staff to signal the hunters to halt.

"Why are we stopping?" Plenty Coups said.

Sees Plenty held up his hand to feel the wind. "Buffalo are grazing beyond the crown of this plateau," he said, pointing his staff toward the south. Their scent rides the wind."

Without speaking, Plenty Coups signed for two warriors to dismount and follow him. While the hunting party waited, Plenty Coups and the two warriors crept up the incline and disappeared.

Lone Elk heeled his pony's flanks and rode up beside Sees Plenty. "White man," he snarled, "you are no better than a dog that sniffs for deer. You can't kill bison for your lodge."

The muscles of Sees Plenty's jaws rippled, but he didn't reply. Lone Elk laughed. "Willow Calf will starve if she waits for you to bring her meat. She will have no hides to make robes from. You are a *bate*, a squaw with the genitals of a man. Why don't you wear squaw clothes, live in your own tipi, and let a man have Willow Calf?"

Rage soared up from Sees Plenty's belly until it slammed into his head like a sledgehammer. He swung his hooked staff around like a drum major's baton and slammed it across Lone Elk's chest. The force of the blow sent him tumbling to the ground. Sees Plenty leaped from his pony to face his tormentor. Several Foxes jumped from their ponies to intercede. Having a successful hunt depended on not stampeding the wily buffalo grazing in the valley beyond. Any battle between Sees Plenty and Lone Elk had to wait until the hunt was over.

Sees Plenty lunged against the hands that were restraining him. "Ye have the tongue of a snake. When the women come to butcher our kill, ye will face the tomahawk of Sees Plenty. Then we will see who is a *bate*."

* * *

When the hunter's cries and rifle reports ceased, bison carcasses were scattered across the valley for nearly a mile. Now there would be plenty of meat and hides for the coming season of snow and bitter cold in the Yellowstone Valley.

Vultures swarmed over the valley while the women went about skinning and butchering the kill. The feathered scavengers rode the wind for hours until pony-drawn travois, loaded with meat and hides, began to abandon the field of carnage. Piles of offal became blackened mounds of flapping wings while the smelly birds fought over coils of intestines.

Plenty Coups was standing in front of their tipi as Willow Calf and Sees Plenty arrived with their butchered buffalo lashed down on two travois. "Our people are grateful. You have found many bison for us my brother," Plenty Coups said, grasping Sees Plenty by the shoulders.

"*Acba-Dadea* showed me where to find the bison. We must give the Great Spirit our thanks."

"Spoken like a true medicine man. Tonight we dance."

Sees Plenty patted the tomahawk hanging from his waistband. "First, I must meet Lone Elk."

"Lone Elk is not here."

"Where can I find him?"

"I don't know, he hasn't returned to his lodge."

"Please," Willow Calf pleaded, stepping closer to Plenty Coups. "A dark spirit lurks inside Lone Elk."

Plenty Coups didn't speak; instead, his hands signed, *The eyes of Plenty Coups belong to Sees Plenty.*

Lone Elk didn't return during the ensuing weeks. Sees Plenty smoked kinnikinnick and prayed to *Acba-Dadea* every morning as the first rays of the sun cracked the undulating horizon. And then the remainder of each day was filled with learning the tenets of the Sun Dance from Medicine Hawk and Spotted Eagle. Their teachings were taking root and had begun to spawn changes within him that were transforming his mind into that of a Crow shaman. He reasoned no longer like a Scotch missionary; instead, he heeded only the beliefs of the Sun Dance religion. Willow Calf watched the transformation with concern. His humble and gentle nature had been replaced with arrogance and harshness. His concern for Joshua had turned into rejection and rage against him. And seeing the scalp of Lone Elk twisting in the wind atop his hooked staff had become an obsession.

Not until the day arrived for the villagers to begin their journey back to the valley of the Yellowstone did Sees Plenty set aside his obsession. Every tipi in the village had been taken down and lashed onto travois except for Medicine Hawk's. Sees Plenty and Willow Calf found him collapsed on the floor when they went to help disassemble his tipi. He tried to speak, but could only mumble incoherent words. Sees Plenty knelt beside him and held his ear close to the old Indian's lips, trying to understand him. Willow Calf straightened his legs, which had twisted beneath him when he had fallen. "Can ye sit up?" Sees Plenty asked, slipping his hands beneath Medicine Hawk's shoulders.

Medicine Hawk tried to arise, but his right leg and arm were useless. "Nay, ye cannot. Don't try anymore."

"What is wrong?" Willow Calf said, kneeling beside Sees Plenty.

"Paralysis."

"Why?"

"It is called apoplexy of the brain."

"What is to be done?"

"I will pray to *Acba-Dadea*."

"I will bring my father; he will pray also."

"Aye, and bring my pipe, kinnikinnick and pouch of sweet cedar."

Far into the night, the sounds of Sees Plenty and Spotted Eagle chanting their prayers arose from within Medicine Hawk's tipi. All of the villagers maintained a silent vigil around the lodge while the Great Spirit was asked to spare their beloved friend and medicine man.

The first rays of the morning sun set the plains aglow with orange, yellow and white hues being reflected by crystals of a September frost. Silence weighed heavily upon the village. All prayers had ceased and Medicine Hawk's death song sung by Sees Plenty had ended. Only subdued moaning and weeping sounded from within the lodge of Sees Plenty's father, mentor and friend. "Now Medicine Hawk walks in the hereafter," Sees Plenty called to the waiting mourners as he stepped from the tipi.

Chapter 26

In the dim twilight, Colin Condiff stared through the window of the Union Pacific coach at the endless stretch of rolling Nebraska prairie. The landscape was harsh, monotonous, and sparsely settled. The train infrequently passed by clapboard and "soddie" prairie houses, sheds, and more seldom, windmills whirling atop wooden derricks on farms scattered along the railroad. Green fields of corn and wheat surrounded these simple farm dwellings. A few of the homesteaders had a smattering of cattle that were grazing where millions of buffalo wandered less than a decade before.

Smoke from the locomotive rolled over the train and spilled across the prairie. Its acrid odor, seeping into the coach, fouled the air and stung the eyes of every passenger.

Colin wiped his eyes with a handkerchief and turned his attention to a man seated across the isle. He had overheard the fellow ask the conductor what time the train would reach Ogallala. When the conductor replied, "9:10 P. M.," the fellow seemed relieved.

The stranger was younger than Colin, probably no more than twenty-five. His once black hat had faded into a slate-colored hue from many days spent under a western sun. While trying to read a newspaper, his fingers toyed through his scraggly beard and mustache that were black as the inside of a tar bucket.

In the dim light of a coach lantern, the fellow was reading the *Omaha Register*. The headline across the front page in bold type caught Colin's eye. Gold! Gold!! Gold!!! Gold!!!!

Colin leaned over the arm of his chair and tried to read the article below the headline. The fellow glanced at Colin with piercing gray eyes. "You want t'read, buy a paper from the conductor."

"Sorry I disturbed ye," Colin replied, his words burred heavily with a Scottish accent.

The young man lowered the paper and grinned. "That's

okay. I'm Will Parker and who might you be?"

"Colin Condiff."

Will folded the paper and handed it to Colin. "You're welcome to it, I'm done readin'."

"I thank ye. Where are y'headed, Will?"

"Back home. Me an' Pa got a ranch in Star Valley. That's west o' the Salt Mountains. Where you headed?"

"Salt Lake."

Will's eyes darted toward Colin. Colin felt a bit uneasy as Will looked him over like a buyer getting ready to haggle the price of a horse. Colin responded by brushing aside a cowlick of sandy-red hair, and then stroked his beard of a darker, almost auburn hue, which was a nervous mannerism whenever he was ill at ease.

"That's Brigham's town," Will finally said, continuing to eye Colin.

"Aye, I know, I'm hopin' to get an interview with him."

"You a newspaper man?"

"Aye, I am."

Will wagged his head. "He won't talk to ya, unless you be one o' the Saints."

"Aye, so I've been told."

Colin started to unfold the *Omaha Register*, but hesitated, recalling the events that had led him to undertake this journey. It began when his editor at the *Chicago Times*, Mike Caldwell, called Colin into his office to tell him about a new assignment. He wanted Colin to do a series of articles on the Mormon movement. The assignment would carry him to New York, Ohio, Missouri and Illinois. All during the trip, he studied the *Book of Mormon*. At first he was quite skeptical of the writings, but then he began to view them differently. He was moved by the terrible persecution Joseph Smith and his followers endured as they sought a place to live and practice their religion. Finally, on the day that he stood in the Carthage, Illinois jail where Joseph Smith and his brother Hyrum were gunned down by a mob at five o'clock on the evening of June 27, 1844, Colin was moved to the depths of his soul. He knelt inside the barred cell and accepted the written account of

Mormon that had been revealed to Joseph Smith. The following morning, Colin wired a request to Mike Caldwell. He asked to continue his research by retracing the Mormon exodus to the Salt Lake Valley, and there he would compile his final article for the *Times* after an interview with Brigham Young. Caldwell accepted the request, and Colin headed for Council Bluffs, Iowa to begin his journey.

While pondering the change that had altered his life, his eyes fell on the headline once more. The article was credited to a Salt Lake newspaper.

Word has reached this city that gold has been discovered on South Pass near the Sweetwater River. A number of Saints have abandoned their farms and homes, against the pleading of sounder minds, to dig for gold on South Pass. The rush began last summer after Judge W. A. Carter, the sutler at Fort Bridger, reportedly received gold nuggets in trade for supplies from D. A. Marcom who operates a train of freight wagons between Fort Laramie and Salt Lake City. Marcom claimed that a man met him at the Oregon Trail on South Pass and proceeded to trade the nuggets for a rifle, ammunition, tools, coffee and whiskey. When asked who the man was, he said, "Didn't give his name, but from his appearance I reckon him to be a deserter or a cashiered soldier."

Colin folded the paper and stuffed it into his pocket. He pulled out his gold watch, a gift from his uncle Angus Leslie the morning Colin departed Turriff for Edinburgh to enroll at Elgin Academy. He pressed down on the stem, the cover flipped open and the watch's tiny music box began to play a Scottish ballad. He could see in the dim lantern light that it was two minutes until 8:00 P.M. "We should arrive at Ogallala in a little over an hour," he said to Will, shoving the watch back into his vest pocket.

Will, dozing for the moment, opened his eyes and glanced at Colin. "You gettin' off there, too?"

"Aye, I am."

"That's still a long ways from Brigham's town."

"Aye, but I'm goin' to take the same route the Saints followed."

Will nodded. "Reckon that's what ya need t'do, bein' you're writin' what they went through."

"Aye, I do."

"You'll be travelin' Immigrant Trail then."

"All the way."

"Y'goin' t'walk pullin' a Mormon cart?" Will asked, and chuckled at his own humor.

"Do ye want to walk with me?"

"Nope, but I'll ride along with ya if y'decide to buy yourself a horse."

"I'd consider it an honor to ride with ye."

"Better be careful with that watch. There's them that would slit your throat to take it off you."

* * *

Two days later, after buying two horses, two pack mules, two saddles, and provisions, Colin and Will were ready to ride out of Ogallala. The walnut stocks of two new model sixty-six "Yellow Boy" Winchester carbines jutted from their saddle scabbards. Besides his rifle, Will carried a double-barreled derringer in a shoulder holster beneath his parka and a walnut-handled .44 Hoard revolver strapped low on his hip. He had convinced Colin to at least arm himself with a carbine, because nobody in their right mind would ride this country unarmed.

Two men dressed in leather chaps, vests, and curl-brimmed Stetsons pulled low over cutting eyes stepped off the board sidewalk in front of the hotel. They walked down the street toward Will and Colin who were doing a final check of the packsaddles on their mules. "There's trouble in them boots," Will said, staring at their tied-down holsters. "Stick close t'yer rifle."

Minding Will's suggestion, Colin stood next to his horse within reach of his carbine.

One of the men chomped his cud of tobacco and spat. "Howdy, you boys got quite a load there."

Will stepped away from his pack mule. "Right smart."

The pair continued to walk toward Will. One fondled his holster and gave a toothy grin around a cigar jutting from the corner of his mouth. "Where you fellers from?"

Will glanced at Colin and nodded. Colin wondered what the nod meant. There was no way he could pull his carbine from the scabbard before being gunned down. Now he wished he'd taken Will's advice and armed himself with a six-shooter too.

"Star Valley," Will replied and patted his own holster.

The pair stopped walking. The tobacco chewer spat again and pointed at Will. "That's goddamn-awful Mormon country. The hotel clerk said you was a pair o' them sonsabitches."

Will said nothing, just stared at the foul-mouthed accuser.

"Well, are ya?"

"Who's askin'?" Will said, his hand ready to slap leather.

"Just say we don't want no sonsabitchin' Mormons stinkin' up our air."

Colin gawked at the confrontation taking place in the center of the street and wondered how he could have gotten himself into such a predicament. There was no doubt in his mind; he was going to be killed. He glanced at his pack mule, at Will, and then at the pair of gunmen. No way could Will shoot both of them before being shot down. Then a quick bullet would find Colin and that would be the end of it.

He decided their only hope would be an unexpected diversion. Without a second thought, he sent the toe of his boot accelerating into the pack mule's flank. He had never heard a mule scream before, but this one did as she bolted toward the pair of gunmen. The tobacco chewer filled his hand with his six-shooter and had barely cleared leather when Will's Hoard bellowed. The gunman spun around like a toy top when the big lead slug found its mark. The other fellow stepped aside as the bucking mule charged at him. The next shot from Will's Hoard bored into the second gunman's chest, sending him to his knees. The stricken man grasped his chest, and with eyes turning into emptiness, he fell face down into a mud puddle in the middle of the street. Men came running out of stores and saloons into the street. Within moments a din of angry voices surged from the mob. One taunter yelled, "Hang 'em, they're murderin'

Mormons."

"We'd better mount up and get out o' here," Will said, sliding the big Hoard back into his holster. "Back me up with your Winchester while I catch that mule."

Colin cranked a round into the chamber of his carbine. "Better let her go, that mob is gettin' mean."

"Okay," Will said, stepping into his stirrup, "let's ride."

They followed the Oregon Trail, which parallels the North Platte River, toward Fort Laramie. Colin spent most of the day looking back, fully expecting to be pursued by the mob. There were few trees along the trail, but each one they passed evoked images of himself and Will twisting in the wind beneath one of their arcing limbs.

Colin pondered the man he was riding beside. Neither Will nor he had confessed to the other any of their religious beliefs. It hadn't seemed important until the showdown in Ogallala. No matter whether Will were a Mormon or not, Colin wondered why he hadn't just denied being one and let the matter drop. They could have ridden out of Ogallala without being haunted by the threat of swift retaliation from the Mormon-haters.

After riding steadily for nearly thirty miles, they came to a section of the trail that descended down a steep grade. They dismounted and led their mounts and pack mule down the precipitous incline toward a sheltered basin. The steep roadbed bore stark evidence of the magnitude of hardships experienced by pioneers during two decades of the great westward migration. Deep ruts had been carved into the hillside as thousands of heavily laden wagons were winched down the hazardous slope with windlasses. When they reached level ground in the basin, dozens of graves lined both sides of the trail. Once black letters on a sign that had been faded by more than a decade of hot summer suns gave the place its name, *Ash Hollow*. Colin slipped off his woolen cap and gazed across the scattering of grave markers that wind and time had not destroyed. He squatted down to read a weathered sandstone marker. "What a sad place."

"A lot o' folks came a long ways to sleep the long sleep

in this godfersaken place," Will said and then then pointed at several trees. "That ought'a be a good spot t'camp."

"Aye," Colin said and pulled a journal from his pocket. "I'll be along after I make some notes."

Thus began Colin's journal. Each evening after making camp, he would pencil entries to use in writing his articles for the *Chicago Times*.

While Colin was busy with his journal, Will watered their horses and the pack mule at the river. The small grove of trees afforded a good campsite; however, anyone seeking to do them harm could be upon them without much warning. So there was to be no campfire, and supper would be dried apples and water; a combination that soon bloated their bellies and added misery to their sleepless night.

The night chill rolled up from the river and settled into Ash Hollow. Colin and Will wrapped themselves in blankets and settled down for the long night ahead. The inky sky was filled with stars, but the moon was only a sliver as it slowly inched its way toward the western horizon. Coyotes in the distance filled the night with their yelping and howling chants.

Colin's ponderous mood was broken by Will's abrupt question. "You one o' the Saints?"

"I intend to be baptized when I get to Salt Lake."

"Y'got a taste o' bein' one today. It ain't an easy life."

"I suppose not. How about you?"

"Yeah, brother, I am. Better get some sleep now. I'll keep an eye for a couple o' hours, and then it'll be your turn."

* * *

Four days into their ride, an approaching line of towering clouds whose pinnacles were flattened like giant anvils suddenly obscured the bright afternoon sunshine. Will tugged at the brim of his hat as a spinning whirlwind blasted them with grit. Tumbleweeds, reeling and bouncing before the gale, rolled across the hills and plains like bounding hares. Jagged streaks of fiery lightning zipped and cracked below the cloud's sooty base. The horses turned skittish and began to snort and whinny after a sudden discharge of lightning slammed into a solitary tree only a few hundred yards away. Colin looked skyward just as a wall of hail poured like a waterfall out of the cloud toward the ground. He pointed upward and yelled a warning to Will. "Lookout! Hail!"

Will tried to rein down his gelding, but the terrified horse refused to obey. He waved for Colin to follow as he pointed toward a log dwelling, stable and corral close to a towering bluff south of the river. The pack mule balked and began to buck. "I'm turnin' her loose," Will yelled, untying the mule's halter rope from his saddle.

Hailstones the size of peach pits began to pelt them by the time they reached the corral. The storm's fury descended with a torrent of hail, rain and wind moments after they found safety inside the stable.

Colin slipping off his horse. "What about the mule?"

Will stepped out of his stirrup and plopped down in a pile of old hay. "We'll look for 'im after the storm passes."

Colin looked around the stable. It apparently hadn't been used for some time. There were only a few dry horse droppings scattered inside a half dozen stalls.

"This place has been abandoned for quite a while," Will said, chewing on a straw. "It was a pony express station for several months before they shut it down in sixty-one."

Colin sat down and pulled out his journal. "That is interesting," he said and began to pencil an entry.

Will looked around the stable as Colin's scratching pencil awakened memories. "Yeah," he said, lying back in the hay. "Several of the Saints built it back in forty-seven. My Pa was one of 'em."

Colin stopped writing and looked at Will. "Your father?"

"Yeah, it was a rest stop for Saints headin' for Salt Lake."

It took a half-hour for the raging storm to subside and allow the sun to break through. They rode out of the corral intent upon finding their rebellious pack mule. Every bit of their supplies were strapped on the mule's pack saddle and they were still forty miles short of Fort Laramie.

They followed the mule's trail for several miles until her

tracks disappeared into a sea of tracks made by barefoot ponies. "Damned Injuns," Will said, pointing at the muddy tracks. "They stole our mule."

Colin chuckled. "Well, at least we'll not be eatin' dried apples tonight."

* * *

The following afternoon, saddle weary and hungry, they rode into the quadrangle of Fort Laramie. Corporal Hart asked them to have a seat while he informed Colonel Maynadier of their arrival.

While waiting, Colin listened to the busy sounds coming from the quadrangle. Clipped orders being called to troopers during mounted drill exercises were echoing across the parade grounds. Dozens of hoofs, pounding the already hardened soil, filled the air with dust that billowed and tumbled as a brisk southerly wind swept through the fort. Several women, dressed in calico skirts, walked along the boardwalk in front of the Colonel's office. Their stern voices, too far away to be understood, bespoke of their unhappiness with someone or something.

A corporal finally appeared in the doorway of Maynadier's office and motioned for them to enter.

Colonel Maynadier stepped from behind his desk, buttoning the final brass button of his tunic. He accepted their outstretched hands as they introduced themselves.

"I'm Colonel Maynadier," he said, picking up a cigar humidor. "Cigar? Mister Condiff—Mister Parker?"

"Nay, I don't use them," Colin replied.

"Do you mind if I smoke?" Maynadier said after Will refused the offer.

"Nay, please do," Colin said.

Maynadier gestured toward two ladder-backed chairs. "Please sit down and tell me what I can do for you,"

"I am a writer for the *Chicago Times*," Colin said. "I would appreciate learning the history of Fort Laramie."

The Colonel nodded, his eyes reflecting an inquisitive expression. "Your accent is Scottish is it not?"

"Aye, it is, why do y'ask?"

"We don't meet many Scots out here. However, our former surgeon spoke with a heavy brogue just like you."

"And what might be his name?"

"Leslie... Major Joshua Leslie."

"Joshua? He's my cousin. Where might I find him?"

"I'm sorry, Major Leslie has been killed by the Lakota."

"Killed? By Indians?"

"I'm afraid so... and I fear that his brother, the Reverend Joel Leslie, has suffered the same fate."

Colin slumped and buried his face in his hands. "Why? Why? Why?"

Chapter 27

Two days after being told that Joshua and Joel had been killed by the Indians, Colin and Will resumed their westward journey along the Oregon Trail. They rode into South Pass City, a hodgepodge of log huts on Willow Creek, four days later. They found it to be a bustling boomtown that had risen shortly after gold was discovered in 1868. Their innkeeper told them that the first man to discover gold on South Pass was Henry Watts who lived close to Miners Delight. He also told them that Watts was a little bonkers and would shoot at any strangers approaching his mine. Being certain that his editor would want an article covering the South Pass gold rush, Colin decided to interview Watts before they traveled on toward the Salt Lake Valley.

They reined their ponies eastward out of South Pass City at dawn the next day. They traversed eight miles of windswept bald ridges, deep wooded ravines, meandering creeks, and precipitous slopes bristling with outcroppings of quartz and black slate. It was harsh country, once the domain of Indians, elk and deer, now covered with hundreds of shanty dwellings. Most were log huts built wherever immigrant gold-seekers chose to start their diggings.

After watering their ponies at a trough in Atlantic City, which was about half the distance to Miners Delight, they rode east down a primitive trail. They reached Miners Delight nestled in a valley between two rocky inclines at about eight o'clock. Colin tied his pony to the hitching post and went into Delaney's store to get directions to Watts' place.

Delaney told him to look over the horses tied in front of Maudie's saloon and whorehouse on their way out of town. If one happened to be a roan mare, Watts would be inside; and, if not, he would be at his place on Beaver Creek. Maudie's hitching rail tethered a bevy of miners' ponies, but none of them was a roan.

A couple of miles farther found them riding along Beaver Creek toward a log hut standing in an aspen grove below a stone-faced bluff. Following Delaney's advice, Colin waved a white scarf over his head while he and Will stepped out of their stirrups and walked toward the cabin.

"Mister Watts!" Colin called, and waited for a reply.

"Get away," a voice boomed from the mine entrance as a man stepped out holding a Winchester at the ready.

"I'm a newspaper writer," Colin yelled. "I'm doin' an article on the gold rush here on South Pass."

"Get away; go talk to someone else."

"Might need t'do as he says," Will whispered. "Friendly ain't in his voice."

"Not yet," Colin whispered. He then called to Watts, "I've been told that ye were the first t'find gold up here."

The man straightened his hunched torso at Colin's words. "Aye, that I am."

"Y'speak like a highlander, Mister Watts."

Watts starting to walk toward them. "Aye."

"What county might ye be from?"

"Aberdeenshire."

"Ah, so am I, near Turriff on the river Deveron."

The man stopped and stared at Colin. "Is that ye... Colie?" he said, lowering his rifle.

Colin peered at the seedy miner attired in frayed buckskins and whose features were almost obscured by a gray mask of matted whiskers and unshorn locks. "Aye... I'm Colin Condiff. Is that ye—cousin Joshua?"

"Aye—I'm Joshua."

"Colonel Maynadier at Fort Laramie claimed the Indians killed both ye and Joel."

"Nay, come have a wee sip," Joshua said, motioning toward his cabin. "Then I'll tell ye what happened."

Colin and Will spent the day in Joshua's cabin listening to a story told by a man Colin didn't know anymore. He had become a scruffy character whose demeanor was completely changed from the polished physician that left Scotland only eight years before. Now he reeked of whiskey and the stench of going unwashed for months. All through the day, he drank an enormous quantity of whiskey, which thickened his speech and dulled his once quick wit. He would slump into a drunken stupor, snore for a few minutes, and then awaken to take another swig from his jug before continuing his story. Before dozing into a drunken stupor, he began to sob as he told them about his encounter with Jim Bridger in the mountains. The memory of Joel being tortured and blinded by his captors, and then escaping with the help of a medicine man to live with the Crow was overwhelming. *Why had he failed to rescue Joel?* So much time had been wasted on his greed for gold.

As the shadows of evening spilled into the ravine, Joshua had finished telling Colin and Will everything that had happened since he and Joel left Scotland. Colin sat watching his drunken cousin who was slumped over the table with an arm wrapped around his jug. A pall of sadness blanketed Colin as he listened to snoring mixed with babbling words. *How could any man have forsaken his brother for this squalid existence,* Colin thought, wagging his head in disgust.

Joshua aroused as Colin picked up the jug and emptied it on the earthen floor. "What're ye doin'?" Joshua shouted, grabbing for the jug.

"After ye sober up, we're goin' to find Joel."

* * *

The shrieks of geese winging southward echoed across glen and mountain, and foretold the coming of winter. Far behind lay the broken dreams of South Pass, the mine, the graves of Lucy and her baby, and the follies of a greedy man. Before the three horsemen, towered the Teton Mountains, resplendent in their hazy blue canopies crowned with summits of white. And beyond them, the fields of steaming plumes rising above geysers discovered by John Colter in 1808. Then they would follow the Yellowstone River along its course gouged through canyons between towering ocher walls punctuated with conifers deformed by prevailing winds. And finally, they would reach the Yellowstone Valley and the village of Chief Big Belly's Mountain Crow.

Joshua pondered his awakening conscience, which was no longer numbed by booze and obsessions. He felt alive for the first time in months, the tentacles of alcohol having been broken.

Over and over, he muttered to himself, "Am I my brother's keeper? Aye, and I, like Cain, must pay the price for my sins."

Colin and Will had become joined together by circumstances, and their individual commitments to the religious tenets revealed by the prophet Joseph Smith. Like the brother that he had become, Will took on Colin's need to find Joel and return him to civilization.

On the fourteenth day following their departure from Miners Delight, the trio reined their ponies and two pack mules along the Yellowstone River between Blackmore and Cowen peaks. Before them, the Yellowstone Valley with its expanding meadows came into view. A quickening wind stung their faces with pellets of sleet that were falling from a low overcast. The stirring aroma of wood smoke carried by the wind bespoke of cooking fires, the Crow village, and their reunion with Joel. Colin turned in his saddle and called to Joshua. "It can't be far now; we'll soon find Joel."

Joshua pulled the collar of his parka away from his mouth and yelled against the wind. "Aye, I hope the Crow will be friendly."

"They are," Will called, trying to pull his balky pack mule to a faster pace. "We'll have hot food and warm beds tonight."

A black and white dog scampering after a cottontail rabbit was the first indication of a nearby settlement. Then two young Crow warriors astride skewbald pintos, leading a pony with a slain buck deer tied to his back, appeared. They had just crossed the river when they spotted Joshua, Colin and Will. They reined their ponies into a grove of willows and cottonwoods and waited. "They're Crow," Will said, and nudged his pony's flanks. "Come on, let's go talk to 'em."

The Crow sat their ponies, eyeing Will who was in the lead. Their ponies turned skittish when they caught the scent of the pack mules. After settling their ponies, one of the Crows held up his hand as a sign of peace. "Hau," he called, lowering his hand.

"Hau," Will said, signing peace. "We are looking for the Crow village."

"We are Crow."

Joshua started to speak, but stopped when Will raised his hand. "Will you take us to your chief?" Will said.

"You come with us," the spokesman said, signing for them to follow.

A kaleidoscope of emotions somersaulted through Joshua's mind as they neared the village of tipis. Joy, dread, fear, guilt, regret, relief and anticipation, all of them gyrated like wispy ghosts within his mind. He listened to voices from the past, especially his mother's on the day he and Joel left for America. "Ye have no family in that far away land," she had said as they waited for the train to London. "I pray ye'll care for one another." He had been quick to answer with assuring words as he looped an arm around Joel's shoulders. "Aye, moms, ye needn't waste your time prayin' for that, I'll be lookin' after Joel."

"And I'll do the same for Joshua," Joel had added, leaning down to kiss their mom.

* * *

Sees Plenty sat facing the firepit, deep in thought and seldom speaking. The sudden death of Medicine Hawk had caused him to slip back into the shadow lands from which his old friend had rescued him many moons before. How he missed him, his kind and gentle spirit, and the essence of life that bubbled from him every day. No longer would he be awakened to smoke and pray each morning by the nudge of the old man's hand against his shoulder. Never again would the rhythmic chants tumble like rolling waters from those aged lips as they prayed to *Acba-Dadea*. As these memories rolled by like tumbleweeds bounding before the wind, he sensed the need to return once again to Medicine Hawk's burial scaffold.

He and Willow Calf had brought Medicine Hawk back to the valley of the Yellowstone where they and Plenty Coups built a burial scaffold next to the river. It was a quiet place, the one where Medicine Hawk and he had spent many hours during their teaching sessions. Each time he and Willow Calf returned, he gained renewed strength to walk the path that Medicine Hawk had encouraged him to follow. But without the old chief's wisdom and guidance, the arduous climb loomed like a switchback that ascends into clouds obscuring the summit of a mountain.

"Is it not a fine autumn day, a good time to visit Medicine Hawk?" he said to Willow Calf.

"Yes, soon we will walk to the river," she said without looking up from sewing beadwork onto a parfleche. "I have almost finished."

Sees Plenty listened to the wind whispering through the willows and cottonwoods and felt the reassuring touch of Willow Calf's hand leading him toward the scaffold. The wings of a bald eagle swished overhead and then grew silent as it glided toward Medicine Hawk's scaffold. Willow Calf looked skyward at the graceful bird and whispered, "A great spotted eagle visits Medicine Hawk."

"Ah, we must hurry," Sees Plenty said, "the Medicine Father brings a message from Medicine Hawk."

The eagle alighted atop one of the corner-poles of the scaffold above the deerskin-wrapped body of Medicine Hawk. It perched motionless until Sees Plenty and Willow Calf reached the clearing where the bier stood. "We must be careful or we will frighten the eagle," Willow Calf cautioned.

"Nay, the eagle will not fly away before he speaks with us."

After taking only a few more steps, Sees Plenty abruptly stopped. "Aye, I hear you Grandfather," he said, raising his arms.

Willow Calf had heard nothing but the wind in the trees. She looked at Sees Plenty whose face was lifted up toward the eagle. "What did you hear?"

"Shush," he whispered to her, and then called to the eagle, "Sees Plenty listens to you, Grandfather."

The eagle perched motionless while they stood near the bier. Willow Calf heard nothing but was certain Sees Plenty could hear the Medicine Father speaking to him through the eagle. Not until the eagle spread its wings and took flight did she speak. "What did the eagle say?"

Sees Plenty's blind eyes gazed upward as if he could

follow the eagle winging toward the snow-crowned peaks of the Absaroka Mountains. "Grandfather said that Plenty Coups would soon be chief of the children of Old Man Coyote. The old ways, the bison, and the dwelling in tipis, all will be no more with the coming of the white tribes. But the Medicine Fathers will preserve the children of Old Man Coyote through the sons of Sees Plenty and Willow Calf."

As he embraced her, Willow Calf said, "Yes, already the heart of our son lives in my womb."

"He will be a great shaman of our people," Sees Plenty said, pulling her closer. "You have made my heart sing today."

She started to speak, but a commotion caused by barking dogs and loud voices coming from the village caused Willow Calf to hesitate.

"What is happening?" he asked.

She peered through the trees at the great circle of tipis. "There are three white men riding toward the village."

"Mountain men?"

"One wears the buckskins, but the others do not."

Chapter 28

Chief Big Belly stepped from his lodge to meet Colin, Will and Joshua. Will had cautioned Colin and Joshua to let him do the talking since he knew the Crow and had met Big Belly and Spotted Eagle once at Fort Bridger. "Hau," Will said, signing peace.

"Hau," Big Belly said, "welcome to village of the Bird People."

Remembering that Big Belly savored Cuban cigars, Will pulled one from his pocket and handed it to the chief whose eyes spoke gratitude for the fine gift of tobacco. "I smoke, you smoke," Big Belly said, sniffing the cheroot's bouquet.

He wasn't a smoker, but not wishing to offend the chief, Will bit the tip from another cigar. He swiped a match to life across the saddle horn and leaned down to light the chief's stogie. Big Belly blew smoke to the four winds before speaking to Will again. "Who these fellow?" he said, pointing first at Colin and then Joshua.

"These are my friends, Colin Condiff and Joshua Leslie."

Big Belly raised his eyebrows when Will introduced Joshua. He walked up to Joshua sitting his pony and stared at the man's scrubby appearance. "Your name Leslie, man with hairy face?"

Joshua stepped out of his stirrup. "Aye, that's my name."

Big Belly eyeing Joshua's blue eyes and broad forehead. "You mountain man, man with hairy face Leslie?"

"Nay, I dig for gold."

Big Belly smiled and wagged his head. "Yellow metal make white man crazy. You crazy?"

"Aye, I suppose that I am a little bit crazy."

Big Belly laughed, loud and rumbling, within his huge chest. "Well, hairy face Leslie a little bit crazy, come, we smoke and talk big."

Colin slipped from his pony and stepped up to Big Belly. Anger at Joshua for delaying to ask about Joel sharpened his tongue. "We're lookin' for Joshua's brother Joel, might he be livin' with ye?"

Big Belly's expression hardened. "Joel Leslie is no more, he is Sees Plenty, a Crow medicine man."

"He's dead?" Colin asked.

"Joel Leslie ride away, come back Sees Plenty."

Joshua looked past Big Belly at Sees Plenty and Willow Calf as they walked from the river toward the village. "That's Joel," he said, stepping around Big Belly. He hurried to meet them, but stopped and stared at Joel when within a few paces of him. "My god, Joel, what have those heathens done t'ye?"

Joel said nothing. Willow Calf stared at Joshua and perceived the resemblance in spite of his heavy beard. "Joshua?"

"Aye."

"We were told that you had been killed."

"Nay, I'm alive as ye can see."

Joel stepped closer to Joshua and began to speak. "Where have ye been? It's been two years."

"I tried, but...."

"Tried? Did ye not know the Lakota captured me?"

"Aye."

"That they took away my sight and crippled my speech?"

"Aye."

"That Medicine Hawk brought me to the Crow?"

"Aye."

"Why did the man called Hook want to kill you?"

Joshua stood judged and found wanting before his brother. He opened his mouth to speak but no words came. Joel patiently waited for answers, but none were spoken. Joshua's tongue lay paralyzed in his mouth, muted by the truth. How could he explain something that was an enigma to him, also?

"Have ye been struck dumb?"

Joshua began to stammer, "I—uh—I'm sorry... brother."

"Ye ceased to be my brother two years ago. Go back to

wherever ye have been. I'm now a Crow medicine man."

"Nay, Joel, don't turn your back on God and family because of me."

"*Acba-Dadea* is my *God* and these people are my *family*."

Joel's words slashed through the tie that had bound them together since birth. Like a pall, loneliness fell across Joshua. Tears dimmed his vision as he tried to swallow the lump of sadness lodged in his throat. "My god, Joel, ye have lost your reason."

Joel didn't answer; instead, he and Willow Calf walked away. "I will not fail ye now," Joshua swore while watching them enter their tipi. "I'll take ye away from here tonight."

* * *

Bird Face LaRoche crept through the willows toward the campfire of Joshua, Colin and Will.

Following their supper of venison, which Chief Big Belly had brought to them, Joshua was telling the others about his decision to abduct Joel.

LaRoche slipped through the evening shadows like a fox hunting rodents until he was close enough to overhear their conversation. He squatted behind the trunk of an aspen and listened.

"How can we get Joel out of his lodge without his wife alarming the entire village?" Colin said.

"If she leaves their tipi after dark," Will responded, "we can hold her until we get Joel."

"What do we do if she doesn't come out?"

"Take both of them. We can turn her loose later."

"I'd rather not take her," Joshua said, barely above a whisper.

Colin assured Joshua with a pat on the shoulder. "We may not have any choice."

"Aye, I suppose not."

LaRoche smiled, he had heard enough for him to approach the camp. "Halloo, mon ami Joshua Leslie," he called and waited for a reply.

Joshua peered into the evening shadows. "Is that ye

Bird Face?"

LaRoche stood up and walked into the flickering light of the firepit. "Oui, mon ami, it is LaRoche. Can I share your coffee?"

"Ye're no friend of mine, LaRoche."

LaRoche walked into the light of the fire. "Oh, you wrong me. I have brought you good news."

Joshua stood up to face the scheming runt. "Good news, ye say?"

"Oui, for some of your coffee, I will tell you what it is."

After Joshua introduced LaRoche to Colin and Will, LaRoche poured himself a cup of coffee and sat down to sip and tell them his deal. Between sips, he proposed a plan that seemed to fit their problem. His friend, Lone Elk, who had deserted his father's Crow village, had managed an alliance between himself and Chief Red Cloud. Lone Elk had assured Red Cloud that many Crow warriors hated the bluecoats, but Chief Big Belly was a *bate* who wouldn't fight. However, many Crow warriors would follow Lone Elk into battle against the bluecoats. Red Cloud then agreed to grant hunting rights on all Lakota lands to Lone Elk and his warriors if they would lay siege to Fort C. F. Smith. Lone Elk had now returned to recruit his warriors and to take Willow Calf away from the white demon, Sees Plenty. LaRoche then voiced his proposition to Joshua.

"You can see that I am a very small man," LaRoche said, standing up tall as he could.

"Aye," Joshua said, "ye are a wee one."

"Will it not be easy for me to crawl into the tipi where Willow Calf sleeps?"

"Aye," Joshua said, nodding.

While I gag her to keep her from screaming, you can abduct your brother."

"Yeah," Will said, "we get Joel and your Lone Elk gets his squaw."

"Oui, is this not a good plan, mon ami Joshua?"

"Aye, but we need another mount for Joel. We've too far to travel with two riding one pony."

"Oh, that is so true, mon ami. That is why I have

brought extra ponies. I will give you one for your brother."

Joshua glanced at Colin and Will who nodded their approval of LaRoche's plan. He stood up and offered his hand while saying, "I accept."

"You have made a very good decision," LaRoche crooned, reaching for Joshua's hand. "When the smoke from the village fires cease to rise from the tipis, I will meet you beyond your brother's lodge."

* * *

Willow Calf lay in Sees Plenty's arms, watching embers in the firepit fading from red to gray. She had tried to speak with him about Joshua, but he had turned away refusing to talk about him. She felt his increasing anger and vindictive attitude toward his estranged brother. Their reunion had been filled with seething emotions that had surfaced like steam from one of Colter's geysers. Maybe tomorrow, Sees Plenty would have quieted his rage and would talk with Joshua once again. She hoped this would be true. Sleep finally came to her as she listened to the regular lub-dub sounds emitting from Sees Plenty's heart.

The stifling clasp of LaRoche's hand across her nose and mouth abruptly awakened Willow Calf. A scream convulsed her belly, but died in her throat. Sees Plenty reached for Willow Calf, but other hands gagged him, bound his wrists and dragged him out of the lodge.

* * *

Sunset reddened the western sky, spawned long shadows across the plains and ended another day on the highlands west of the Wind River Mountains. The Crow encampment in the valley of the Yellowstone lay far behind Joel and his abductors. Their ponies and pack mules had carried them up and across mountain passes, around steaming geysers, past the alpine Tetons, through Jackson Hole and down the Snake River. After riding through Hoback Canyon, they had hurried on until they reached the Green River where it spills from mountain slopes onto the high plains.

For nearly a week, they had pushed their mounts to the limit of their endurance trying to outdistance the Crow warriors that were certain to be pursuing them. Joel remained mute, refusing to speak with Joshua or the others. Joel's anger toward Joshua and his concern for Willow Calf filled every waking moment. He whispered vows of vengeance to himself and prayed to *Acba-Dadea* for the moment when he could escape from his tormentors.

While Will stood guard on the incline above their campsite, Colin rekindled their fire and Joshua left to stalk several deer watering at the river. Colin poured two cups of coffee and sat down beside Joel. Without speaking, Joel took a cup and began to sip from it. Colin watched his blind cousin who sat on the ground cross-legged and thought how much Joel had changed. Not his scarred eyes and impaired speech, but his demeanor had undergone a transformation. He seemed to have taken on the characteristics of the Indian that he claimed to have become. As he sipped coffee, Colin pondered how to get through to him. Maybe Joel would respond to a different approach. Colin decided to try. "Sees Plenty, your wife, what is her name?"

Joel remained silent as he sipped more coffee, then before sipping again, he spoke. "Willow Calf."

"Ah, a pretty name for a pretty lass," Colin said.

"Aye, she is, isn't she?"

"I know ye must be worried about her."

"What *has* happened to her, Colin?"

"Ye know a man by the name of LaRoche?"

Joel gripped his fists until their knuckles blanched. "I thought it was that runt. What has he done with her?"

"He intended to take her to the camp of Lone Elk."

Joel leaped to his feet, raised his arms skyward and cried, "A-h-h-h-e-e-e!"

"What is wrong?" Will yelled, running down the slope toward camp.

"It is nothing!" Colin called, waving Will to go back.

From that moment on, Joel refused to speak again. He sat facing the fire, silent as a Buddha guarding a Pagoda.

The following morning at first light, they broke camp and headed southeast toward South Pass. The sun stayed hidden behind a low overcast that had rolled across the mountains during the night. A quickening wind was blowing from the north, cold and laden with sleet and flakes of snow. As usual, Joshua frequently turned to scan the terrain behind them, always anticipating the sight of Crow warriors astride their spotted pintos in close pursuit. The country had always been open, high and devoid of Indians, but as he looked back this time, a sizable party of warriors was less than a mile behind and coming on fast.

"Look!" Joshua cried, pointing at the dust cloud rising above the galloping ponies.

Will scanned the plains, hoping to sight high ground, rocky outcroppings, anyplace where they could stand off the charging Crow. There were none, only sagebrush and bluestem that covered the monotonous rolling plain. He reined his pony to a halt, leaped to the ground and yanked his Winchester from the saddle scabbard. "Dismount!" he yelled and shot his pony dead.

One by one, they shot their ponies and pack mules after leading them into a circle. And then they waited for the coming onslaught, crouching behind their fort of dead ponies and mules.

The Crow stopped just beyond rifle range. "That's Big Belly," Will said, pointing at the chief astride his Paloose stud.

The Crow seemed to be reluctant to charge, probably because their medicine man, Sees Plenty, could be injured or killed in a shooting fight. "What do ye think they'll do now?" Joshua asked Will.

"Hard t'say," he said, eyeing the prancing Crow ponies. "They may wait 'til it's dark before trying to come at us."

"Well," Joshua said, peering at the heavy overcast, the blowing snow, and then the pools of horse blood that were beginning to freeze. "They'll not be waitin' until dark, not with this blizzard that's settin' in."

"I'm thinkin' you're right," Colin said. "There isn't anything but sage to build a fire with."

"Reckon they got the same opinion," Will said, pointing at a lone Crow walking his pony toward them carrying a white cloth tied to his lance.

"Aye," Joshua said, "Colin stay close to Joel while I walk out to meet the red savage."

"Keep alert," Will said. "He might try to trade you for their medicine man."

Joshua nodded, stepped across a dead pony and walked out to meet the Crow warrior. He walked about a hundred yards and stopped to await the Crow. He was well within range of Will and Colin's Winchesters if the warrior tried to capture him. The Crow finally dismounted and led his pony to meet Joshua. He held up his hand to sign peace and said, "Hau."

"Hello," Joshua said, holding up his hand also. "What do ye have to say?"

"I am Plenty Coups, a brother of Sees Plenty."

"Oh, a brother ye say?"

"We have come for Sees Plenty, and we will not leave without him."

"Can't let ye have him. He's a sick man."

"No, you are the one that is sick, Joshua Leslie."

"That may be, but ye'll have to kill me and my friends before ye'll get Joel."

"Then we will kill you," Plenty Coups said, glaring at Joshua. "We have many rifles. You only have three."

"So be it," Joshua said and started back toward their fort of dead horses.

"Joshua Leslie," Plenty Coups called, "tell Sees Plenty that Willow Calf is safe and waits for him in their tipi. The scalps of Lone Elk and the Lakota breed LaRoche hang above his lodge."

With those parting words, Plenty Coups wheeled his pony about and galloped back to join the other warriors.

Joshua crawled back behind their horseflesh barrier and reached for his Winchester. He cranked a round into the chamber and cradled the barrel across the pony's carcass. "They intend to kill us all," Joshua said. He then spoke directly to Joel. "That was Plenty Coups. He said your wife is safe and waitin' for ye in your tipi. Ye'll most likely be goin' back by mornin' after your cousin Colin, his friend Will, and I lose our scalps to your heathen friends."

"There's no need for anyone to die," Joel said. "I intend to return to my wife and my people whether ye live or not. I beg ye to let me walk out to join Plenty Coups."

Joshua glared down the barrel of his rifle trying to shut out the words of a mad man. "Nay, Joel, ye are insane. I'll not fail ye this time."

The standoff continued while the Crow apparently decided on how and when to attack. By mid-afternoon, the blowing snow was becoming more intense. The mounted Crow could hardly be seen through the streaming flakes. "Better get ready," Will said, "they ain't goin' to wait out this storm."

The sound of hooves crunching through the snow caused everyone to crouch lower. They waited for the onslaught, but something was amiss. The sounds weren't coming from where the Crow were last seen through the heavy snowfall. "They're behind us," Will yelled, and wheeled around to face the expected attack.

As the blurred images of horses appeared like an apparition, Joshua could see that their riders were not Crow. Then they heard the clanking of sabers against stirrups as the snow encrusted horsemen approached. They were cavalry troopers. "Thank god," Colin yelled and stood up to wave at the troop.

The troopers' commanding officer halted the column, stepped out of his stirrup, handed his reins to a trooper and walked to meet Joshua. "What are you men doing out here in this blizzard?" he asked, shielding his eyes from the wind and snow.

"We're besieged by hostile Crow," Joshua replied, and then pointed at their dead horses and pack mules. We had to kill and make a shield of our animals."

"I'm Major Stedman, commanding officer of Fort Fred Steele," the trooper said. "Are you certain they are Crow?"

"Aye, I am."

"Are any of your people injured?"

"Nay, we haven't been fired on as yet."

The officer stepped closer to Joshua and peered at his bearded face. "What's your name, sir?"

Joshua stared back at the officer, hoping that he had not been recognized. "Watts, Henry Watts," he said, trying to hide his identity from Stedman.

"Mister Watts, the Crow have always been a peaceable tribe. Just why have they attacked you?"

Joshua glanced back at Joel and wagged his head. "That man dressed like an Indian is my brother."

"Your brother?"

"Aye, he's been a Crow prisoner for the last two years."

"A prisoner of the Crow? I find that hard to believe," Stedman said, stepping across a dead mule to confront Joel.

Joel remained seated as the major squatted in front of him. "Your brother tells me that you have been a prisoner of the Crow. Is that true?"

Joel signed with his hands as he replied, "He is not my brother. I am Sees Plenty, a Crow shaman."

Stedman leaned closer to search Joel's features. He wagged his head as he looked into eyes whose milky corneas were exposed between burn-scarred lids. "Who blinded you?"

"Lakota."

"When did that happen?"

"Three summers and two winters ago."

"You were captured and tortured by the Lakota?"

"Aye."

"How did you wind up with the Crow?"

"Medicine Hawk, my father, rescued me."

Stedman brushed snow from Joels beard. "Your father is an Indian, a Crow? You do not look like an Indian."

Joshua squatted down beside the major. "He is my twin brother, a Presbyterian missionary. He has lost his wits and suffers from delusions of grandeur. We are trying to rescue him, but the Crow are determined to take him back to their encampment on the Yellowstone."

Stedman glanced at Joshua and nodded. He patted Joel on the shoulder and then stood up. He motioned for Joshua to follow him back to where his troopers were waiting. After Joshua explained how Joel had been rescued by Medicine Hawk from the encampment of the Lakota following his capture and torture by the Lakota, Major Stedman called to one of his troopers. "Sergeant Hart!"

"Yes, sir," Hart replied, dismounting.

Joshua eyed the sergeant, and immediately recognized him. He was Colonel Maynadier's former orderly, a corporal when serving at Fort Laramie in 1866.

"I joined the Fort Laramie garrison in September of 66," Stedman said to Joshua. "I now recall the incident to which you have spoken. Sergeant Hart, do you recognize this gentleman?"

Hart stepped up to study Joshua's features. "Yes, sir."

"Is he the garrison surgeon who deserted Fort Laramie?"

"Yes, sir. He is Major Leslie."

For a moment Major Stedman and Joshua stood motionless, staring into each others eyes. Then Stedman wagged his head and said, "I regret that we have met, Major Leslie. I'm certain that you know that I must place you under arrest."

"Aye, I know that, but I'd like to make a request before ye do."

"What is it?"

"I wish to speak with my brother."

"Very well, Major Leslie, go speak to your brother."

Joshua walked back to the circle of dead ponies and mules where Colin, Will, and Joel waited. "What did he say?" Colin asked, searching Joshua's eyes for an answer.

"I'm under arrest for desertion."

"He recognized ye?"

"Aye, now ye and Will go meet Major Stedman while I speak with Joel."

Joshua sat down in the snow beside Joel and placed an arm around his brother. Joel remained unyielding and silent. Joshua cleared the lump out of his throat and began to speak, subdued, and in earnest. "Before I tell ye what is happening here at this time, I want to tell ye something. I deserted Fort Laramie to come find ye soon as we got word ye were missing and presumed to be dead. I nearly died in the mountains after Jim Bridger befriended me. Jack Hooker and his squaw saved my life, but that is where I lost my wits. Ye see, I got gold fever while I was recovering from pneumonia and frostbite in their cabin. Hooker was a murdering wife beater, so I had to save Lucy from him. I took her to South Pass where we fell in love."

Joshua could feel the tenseness building within his brother as he continued to tell Joel his story. "Lucy and I lost our son. He came too soon and just couldn't make it. Then Hooker murdered her and I killed him. I didn't care anymore after that happened; not about myself, nor you, nor anything. I buried myself in a whiskey jug. Then Colin rescued me. That's when we came to get ya. But I'm sorry we did now—for what's happening here with the Army. I'm under arrest for desertion and I'll have to return to Fort Laramie and stand court-martial."

Joel remained mute, sitting rigid as a totem. Joshua now knew that all of his efforts had gone for naught. Joel had ceased to exist. The Scotsman that once was his brother, a Presbyterian missionary, had become a Crow shaman, a holy and mysterious man. Joshua's guilt for failing to meet his brother's needs welled up within him like a bitter brew. While pondering what he could do to make amends, to reach out one more time to the stranger sitting beside him, Joshua arrived at what he must do. He bid Joel goodbye in Gaelic, their mother tongue, stood up and went to make one last plea to Major Stedman.

Major Stedman agreed to let Joshua take Joel out to meet Big Belly, Plenty Coups, and their warriors. As they began to walk away from the soldiers, Joel began to chant his prayer to *Acba-Dadea*. His sacred language spilled across his tongue and rose above the winds howling out of the north. In the distance, the Crows began to sing and yelp their welcome to Sees Plenty. Within moments, Indian ponies with their jubilant riders were prancing around Joshua and Sees Plenty. One of the warriors led a piebald pony to meet him. After he crawled onto the little horse, Sees Plenty reined him around to face Joshua. He raised his hand and called out his farewell in the Absaroke language.

Joshua nodded as Sees Plenty and the other Crow warriors wheeled their ponies around and broke into a gallop toward the northwest. Joshua watched the party of horsemen until they faded into the curtain of blowing snow. "Only God knows whether I've failed ye again."

9 780097 228080